Deadly Deception

ANNE FARELL

Simon & Schuster
New York   London   Toronto   Sydney   Tokyo   Singapore

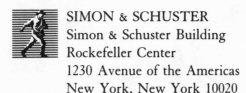
SIMON & SCHUSTER
Simon & Schuster Building
Rockefeller Center
1230 Avenue of the Americas
New York, New York 10020

SIMON & SCHUSTER and colophon are registered trademarks of Simon & Schuster Inc.

Designed by Irving Perkins Associates
Manufactured in the United States of America

10 9 8 7 6 5 4 3 2 1

Library of Congress Cataloging-in-Publication Data
Farell, Anne.
    Deadly deception/Anne Farell.
        p.   cm.
    I. Title.
    PS3556.A713D4   1992
813'.54—dc20   92–12837
                                                    CIP

ISBN 0-671-75339-8

Deadly Deception

I

Fifth Avenue in the low East Eighties overlooking Central Park was rarefied real estate belonging to the very, very rich who knew that no address in Manhattan, not Sutton Place or Beekman Place or Sniffen Court or Amster Yard, could quite equal theirs for programmed attitude response. From nanny to cab driver to produce deliverer to air-conditioner repairman, prices were raised along with eyebrows when an address like 1014 Fifth Avenue was given. But death could penetrate even this exalted atmosphere, as Beth Methany knew too well.

On this mid-April afternoon, the trees across the street in the park were filling out with green from their pale winter scrawniness, and the sun brightened most of the eight enormous rooms of the apartment. Except where Beth was working; the shades and drapes in this room had been drawn against the light, a more appropriate mood for her task than the natural joy she always experienced with sunshine. She was cleaning out her father's closets and drawers, packing and labeling them for various charitable organizations.

It was almost two months since his sudden death at age sixty-four, and only now could Beth bring herself to this painful chore. There were still moments when she would shake her head with disbelief. One minute he had been in his office dictating to his secretary; the next, this same woman was charging into Beth's office, her face as ashen as day-old snow. A massive heart attack. It seemed like only days, perhaps just hours, that Beth had come to accept the reality that he was gone. And the reality that at thirty-two, she was now in charge of it all, president of the Methany Corporation.

The bleat of the telephone made her flinch, and she let it ring three times before remembering that she had given Miranda, their housekeeper, the weekend off so that she alone could pack up her father's possessions.

"Hello?" she said, picking up the bedside extension.

"Beth, hi, it's me, Ben."

"Oh, Ben, hi. How are you?"

"I'm fine. The important question is how are you?"

Beth smiled. She had been dating Councilman Ben Wyler off and on for over a year, their relationship one of mutual affection without commitment. Divorced for four years, she knew better than to promise anybody what she could not give, and the corporation got most, and the best, of her. Ben had gone through a messy divorce himself a few years ago, with his wife getting a large chunk of his salary and a healthy bite of his considerable inheritance as well. At forty, Ben couldn't promise much more than affection either, his job as councilman just a stepping-stone in an ambitious political career, so ambitious that he was running for mayor in the fall.

"I'm doing okay," she said now. "I'm finally able to pack up his things."

"Want some company?"

"No, I don't think so, but thanks anyway. This is something I have to do myself, by myself."

There was a pause on his end, then: "You know, Beth, you've put your father on a pedestal he doesn't deserve. I don't mean to speak ill of the dead, but—"

"Then don't."

"What?"

"Stop, Ben, before you get started. We've been over this before and I'm really not in any mood to hear it again. You didn't know my father."

"That's true," came Ben's slow response, "but I knew the businessman and I have to believe that the two couldn't have been that different. No person could be that much of a Jekyll and Hyde."

"Ben, did you call to criticize my father or to find out if I'm holding up all right? If it's the latter, you're making it harder than it has to be."

"Sorry, it's just that, oh never mind. Anyway, I thought I'd see you at the Literacy Benefit last night. I missed you."

"I haven't been in much of a mood for going out, at least not in a crowd."

"Then we're still on for dinner Wednesday?"

"Sure, if you keep my father out of the conversation," she said lightly.

"Beth, we do have to talk about the Bronx project one of these days. It's not going away."

"Nor should it. Ben, why are you fighting me on this? What my father envisioned for the Bronx could eradicate that war zone for all time," she said, referring to a massive project David Methany had been working on at the time of his death to create a city-within-a-city in the Bronx, razing the burnt-out blight that existed there and stretching the borders of Manhattan further north.

"I'm fighting you on it," Ben said with exasperation, "because it's a typical Methany project that serves no purpose except to fill his coffers. Beth, the people—what about the people?"

"What about them?" she replied with equal tightness. "You know we'll compensate them, we always do."

Ben Wyler's laugh reeked of scorn. "Sure, and where can they go on the money they'll get for their slums? Come on, Beth, be real. This is a typical Methany maneuver—get rid of the old, poor residents to make room for the wealthy. I expected better of you."

"Then you expected wrong. I don't know why you're being so short-sighted. You and your precious Citizens Action Coalition. Methany City North will benefit everybody, rich and poor. There'll be new housing, new businesses, less crime. What's wrong with that? Tell me what's wrong with that, Ben, and then maybe I'll understand. But from where I'm sitting, I see only good."

"You're sitting behind the cash till," Ben snapped back, then sighed. "This is ridiculous, isn't it? I don't even know why we like each other when we can't stand what the other represents."

Beth laughed gently. "Maybe that's why we like each other."

"I suppose. But Beth, I'm going to fight you on this, that's fair warning."

"And I'll fight back, you know that."

"So, are we still on for Wednesday night?"

Beth laughed again. "Sure. What's a little professional difference between lovers?"

"If you need anything—"

"I'll be fine, thanks. See you Wednesday."

Beth's smile faded as she hung up the phone. For as long as she could remember, her father had had his detractors and critics, people who faulted David on his avarice—tearing down landmarks, ousting longtime residents to make room for real estate that catered strictly to the wealthy. But like his admirers, Beth knew better. She had spent summers during high school and college in his offices, working in every department from legal to accounting, property development to architectural planning, and she knew that in the tristate area of New York, New Jersey, and Connecticut, a David Methany building meant the finest

construction, the fewest problems with unions, the most vision-
ary of designs. Although he was primarily known for luxury
cooperative apartments in Manhattan, cluster houses and individual homes in the suburbs, David's few hotels in the resort
areas of Newport, Saratoga Springs, and Virginia Beach, and
his suburban office parks reflected the same attention to construction and detail. Obviously something, or someone, had to
occasionally suffer to make room for the new. In the case of
Methany City North, it would be the people who were living
in slums. How compensating them for practically uninhabitable
apartments could be bad was beyond her comprehension.

She got up from the bed and looked around the large expanse
of his bedroom. On Monday, people from the various charities
would come by to pick up the cartons. The coldness of the large
bedroom with its dark, heavy furniture and lack of human
reminders struck Beth like death itself. She could not imagine
living in these eight rooms without her father. When Beth's
mother had died twelve years ago, the apartment had never
seemed robbed of its personality, its life; David more than com-
pensated for what Isabel Methany took away in death. But
without him, Beth had an unpleasant vision of herself as a ten-
year-old again, wandering for the first time through the immense
halls of the Museum of Natural History, feeling dwarfed and
insignificant by the size and strength and power of the towering
dinosaurs. The apartment absent of David Methany would become one of those dinosaurs; she knew she would have to sell
it.

She supposed she should next tackle her father's at-home
office, but she didn't have the heart. There were too many
reminders of his strength and his legacy in that room for her
to deal with today. It was one thing to pack away tuxedos and
socks and dress studs, quite another to face the place where he
thought and dreamed and created. That would simply have to
wait until tomorrow.

2

There it was in exact detail, down to the Doric entry columns: Methany Place, a towering multiuse building in the Lincoln Center area of Manhattan that had elevated David Methany from a canny real estate developer to a man of architectural taste and business brilliance.

Beth stood in the doorway to her father's at-home office the next morning, staring at the scale model enclosed in Plexiglas that rested on a pedestal custom-measured to hold it. She had once asked David why he didn't keep the model in the office, which seemed the appropriate place for it, and he had laughingly told her that he needed it here for inspiration when he had to pay household bills.

What a triumph Methany Place had been for her father, she thought, going to sit behind the desk. Five floors of prime retail space that had attracted international stars of couture; an Italian restaurant that only two years ago had finally opened a branch on Rodeo Drive in Beverly Hills after seven years of constant importuning. From the beginning, nine years ago, Methany Place had been an overwhelming success. It drew tourists to the West Side, profiting shop owners, restaurateurs, and everyone associated with Lincoln Center. David had made special arrangements with both Albany and New York City: if he would provide reduced rents at long-term leases for several organizations affiliated with Lincoln Center, he would get a tax abatement until the year 2050 and have his air rights extended beyond the current legal limit. After the first five floors of retail space and the next three of Lincoln Center offices, he built an additional forty-eight floors of luxury cooperative apartments that were sold within the first eighteen months of availability.

But even then, Beth recalled, there had been people like Ben Wyler criticizing her father for displacing old, long-term residents who had no place to go with the meager compensation he gave them. The money his renovation brought into the area was ignored. The fact that he provided jobs for hundreds of workers was equally dismissed. The indisputable truth that Methany Place, like all his projects, was always completed on time and problem-free—no shoddy foundations, no union disputes, no shortfall on materials—was attributed not to careful attention to detail but to David's special arrangements with politicians and union bosses, and to less than savory strong-arm tactics.

She knew it was nothing more than professional jealousy, but she was tired of it, especially when so much good came from one of David's projects. Ben Wyler and his coalition would grandstand against Methany City North for a while, gain some press that would help his political plans, and then construction would proceed because it should, because it was a good project. Yes, the corporation would profit, as would many individuals. She knew she would have a fight on her hands, but she had total confidence that she would succeed.

She lifted the beige suede–framed photograph of herself and her father that he had kept on his desk. It had been taken when she had graduated from Barnard and the two had gone to Bermuda for a much-needed vacation. Isabel had died a few months earlier, and the week in the sun, resting, playing tennis, dreaming their dreams for Beth's place in the Methany Corporation, had been idyllic. Happiness glowed from their faces.

She rarely came into this room that she always had considered her father's sanctuary, as he had rarely entered the pottery studio he had made for her when she got divorced and moved back home, the apartment large enough for both father and daughter to have their privacy. The studio, converted from a former maid's room, contained a potter's wheel and all the other equipment she needed for her often-ignored and beloved hobby, with the exception of a firing kiln; the room was too small to tolerate that level of heat.

"I miss you, Daddy," she whispered to the photograph. "I miss you so much." Gently, she traced a finger over his thick, wiry salt-and-pepper hair, down to the square chin and firm jaw, over to the strong Roman nose. Then she kissed the smiling mouth before clutching the framed photograph to her heart.

Few people had ever seen David Methany look like this, carefree, his brown eyes warm, empty of calculation. Beth supposed her mother once had, when they had first been married, but certainly not by the time Beth was an aware human being. By then there had been only flat resignation in the eyes of both parents. Perhaps some of the many women David had had over the years could attest to a loving nature, as she could. And although she herself had witnessed the violent Methany temper directed at employees who fell short of their mark, or at opponents who stood in his way, or even at her mother when her artifice and pretense became particularly intolerable to him, Beth believed the true man to be the one in the photograph.

Who else would have had the patience and understanding to let her marry the wrong man, one who paid only lip service to her ambitions? Who else would have driven, himself, not their chauffeur, four hundred miles so she wouldn't miss an important college interview, even though he knew she would decide on Barnard to stay close to him? Whatever his detractors had to say against David Methany, whatever faults her mother criticized, Beth had known someone warm and giving and tender. It was to the memory of that person that she would make her presidency of the corporation one of which he would have been proud.

With a deep sigh of determination, she forced herself to the task at hand: cleaning out his desk. The drawers were almost empty—a Mark Cross telephone book, two Mont Blanc pens, some stamps, a few sheets of his letterhead stationery and matching envelopes, a desktop checkbook ledger. The second drawer was locked, but a key mixed in with some loose paper clips and rubber bands in the top drawer opened it. Typical of her father, Beth thought. Nobody would consider the obvious. The second drawer was actually an impressively neat file cabinet with alphabetized dividers. Most of the files seemed to contain papers and receipts pertinent to the current tax filing year, but the folder marked J. was thicker, and there was nothing in it that pertained to taxes.

Beth thumbed through the pile of letters and postcards, noting that the postmarks went back twelve years, some of them from shortly before her mother died. They were from all over the United States, Mexico, Canada, even a few from Europe. There must have been about forty pieces and they were all signed with the initial J. Some of them had words like Affectionately, Yours, Always, and then the initial. The messages, typewritten, even the postcards, were basically innocuous. A few of the earlier ones referred to a Lilly Jane person Beth had never heard her father mention. There were lines like "I know about Lilly Jane" or "Too bad Lilly Jane can't be with me here in Montreal, such a charming city." And "Lilly Jane will be remembered." With these exceptions, the postcards and letters had either a line or two about the place from which they had been sent, or nothing but the closing, also typewritten, and the initial, handwritten, as if the sender knew to detect identity from one handwritten initial would be difficult if not impossible. Curious. And discreet to the extreme.

Obviously, J. was a woman with whom her father had had a longstanding and important affair, important enough for him to keep her mail in a locked file drawer, and of a duration to precede her mother's death. She wondered idly which of the many women who had attended David's funeral was J.? She would have to ask a few people if they knew about her; certainly Fred Lincoln, their family attorney for the past thirty-five years, would know. Her father always said that what Fred didn't know about him wasn't worth knowing.

It was odd, Beth thought, that her father had never mentioned J. to her, never suggested that they meet. That hurt, more than a little. There was nothing Beth had not shared with her father, no personal relationship that had meant more than the one she had with him. He had always told her that he felt exactly the same toward her. Then why hadn't he ever spoken to her of J.?

Beth was neither surprised nor disappointed that there had been someone in her father's life while her mother had been alive. Ever since she had been old enough to understand, she had known that her father had not been faithful to her mother.

Beth gave as little thought to her mother dead as she had when she was alive. Isabel Methany had been held in extremely low regard by her only child, who viewed the woman as impossibly frivolous and self-absorbed. Parties and luncheons and shopping, shopping, shopping—these were the constructs of Isabel's life. Beth could not remember one time when her mother had asked a single question of either herself or David about the business. All she ever seemed to care about were the fruits of his labor, and that kind of selfishness Beth could neither understand nor tolerate.

Once, when she was in junior high school, she had asked her

father why he didn't divorce Isabel, and he had explained that he and her mother had made a sort of peace between themselves that would make the cost and the scandal of a divorce unnecessary. Besides, there was Beth to consider. Isabel would get custody, he told her, and that would destroy him.

After Isabel died, there had been speculation about when he would remarry and whom, but it had never happened. Beth had heard the gossip claiming that David was too greedy to risk his wealth in a possible divorce, prenuptial agreement or not. Too smart, his admirers would counter. Why marry the bareback rider when the whole circus was in town? And David's choice of women was, indeed, an unnumbered population. Beth knew the real reason why her father had not remarried, and that was because he had no love left after Beth and his work were given their share. He had told her this, no, she recalled, he had almost asked her permission that it was all right by her if he did not marry again. He had wanted her to understand him, understand how unfair it would be to another woman who, like Isabel, could not share his passion for his work. And Beth did understand, never more so than after her own divorce. It was only then that she felt a certain sympathy for what her mother's life had been like. And although she enjoyed the real estate business, she did not need an analyst to tell her that she had chosen it because it was adored by the man she adored, and thus would keep her close to him.

Beth gathered the correspondence together, debating whether to return it to the file, bring it to her room, or perhaps to the office. She decided on the desk drawer; she would ask some people about J. and if there was no satisfactory explanation, she would throw out the stuff. Obviously, J. had been someone special to her father, but not special enough, else why hadn't he introduced her to his daughter? No, Beth thought, definitely not special enough.

3

"Fred, I hope I haven't gotten you at a bad time? . . . I'm holding up all right, I suppose . . . No, no, I'm in the office . . . No, really, I want to be here . . . working is good for me . . . Listen, Fred, I was going through some of Dad's things yesterday and I came across correspondence from a woman with the initial J. Actually, I don't know it's a woman, but I think it is. Fred, I was wondering if you know who this J. person might be? Dad knew him or her for a long time, since before Mother died, so I figured you would know . . . Oh, from everywhere, Philadelphia, New York, Europe . . . No, just the initial J., although sometimes the closing was kind of affectionate. I guess that's what made me think it was a woman . . . You don't? Are you sure? I can't imagine Dad having secrets from *you* . . . Okay, well, thank you, Fred . . . Yes, dinner soon. Thanks again . . . 'Bye."

It was the next morning and Beth was in her office at Methany Place. She had not moved into her father's office and had no intention of doing so. Either she would divide the large corner space into two offices or she would turn it into another conference room. No one but her father belonged in that office as it was.

She came in this morning at her usual time of eight o'clock, preparing for a meeting with several Japanese bankers later in the day, but she had been watching the clock until nine-thirty when Fred Lincoln usually arrived at his Wall Street offices. Although she had spent yesterday finishing up packing her father's things, the mysterious correspondence hadn't been far from her mind. Fred Lincoln had proven useless. There was one more possibility.

She pressed the intercom that connected her to her secretary. "Karen, please ask Gene Cavelli to come in, and I'm going to need the personnel breakdown on those three guys from Sakuto Bank before our two o'clock meeting. Given how the Japanese don't like to deal with females in business, any edge those files can give me might help ... Thanks."

Not five minutes later a man closer to seven feet than six and stringbean-skinny strode into Beth's office. A Mount Rushmore demeanor belied one of the most generous-hearted and good-natured people Beth knew. Gene Cavelli had been with the Methany Corporation since he graduated from law school more than twenty-five years ago, and he had been like a second father to her. He had handled all the funeral arrangements and had contacted the charities for David's things. He was an invaluable friend and a brilliant corporate lawyer whose specialty was contract law. Although Gene was the chief corporate counsel, Beth thought it was not unlikely that he might know about the elusive J.

"Good morning," he said, taking a chair in front of her desk. "I assume this is about your meeting with the Sakuto fellows?"

"No, I'm all set on that. They had spoken to Dad in the range of twelve million. We'll see if they're still good for that with David Methany's daughter."

"You want me to sit in on it?"

"No, I don't think so, but thanks. Let the chauvinistic Japanese see that a Methany is a Methany regardless of gender," she grinned. "We need their twelve million if we have any hope of completing that condo in Rye on time. I think their infatuation with golf courses and the seashore should override any reluctance to do business with me."

She paused, and her face was completely serious as she asked:

"Gene, did you ever hear my father talk about someone whose first name began with the initial J?"

The fifty-year-old lawyer frowned, and ran a forefinger, long and bony like his entire frame, across his lips.

"Can you give me a little more to go on?" he said.

"Not really," she admitted, and then told him about the file of correspondence she had found.

"I'm assuming it's a female because of how some of the letters were signed, and I'm also assuming it's a woman my father was romantically involved with, but I could be wrong, of course."

"I'm sorry, Beth, but this isn't ringing any bells with me," Cavelli told her.

"What about a Lilly Jane?"

"Who?"

"Lilly Jane. She was mentioned in a couple of the letters. Do you know who she might be?" She had to remember to ask Fred Lincoln that question when next she spoke to him; she had completely forgotten about her.

Cavelli leaned forward in his chair. "Mentioned how?"

"I don't remember," Beth said, watching him carefully. "Casually, like Lilly Jane would have enjoyed some place, that kind of thing. Do you know her?"

The lawyer sat back, his mind churning with remnants of a long-forgotten rumor about a society lady named Lilly Jane and a scandalous affair with a very young and married David Methany.

"No, I don't," he finally said.

"But you do know something, Gene, I can see it in your face," Beth insisted.

"I don't know who J. is, Beth, nor do I know anyone named Lilly Jane. What I do know is that about thirty years ago, longer, I think, there was a society woman named Lilly Jane something or other. She must have been a friend of your father's and this J. person."

"But that was thirty years ago. The correspondence is only twelve years old. It doesn't make any sense."

"All I know is that when I started here, people were still talking about Lilly Jane . . . Litwin, that was her name. She had been married to the New York City D.A., I think, I don't remember. She had committed suicide at a young age and she had been pregnant at the time, not by her husband. It created quite a stir because rumor had it that your father was seeing her, so it became part of the Methany mystique passed on to all newcomers here. More than that I can't tell you, because I don't know. And I agree, a scandal from thirty years ago wouldn't seem to have any connection with correspondence that started twelve years ago. The only reasonable explanation must be what I said—a mutual friend who suddenly reappeared after a long time. Fred Lincoln might be more helpful, although David only told people, his lawyers included, what he felt they needed to know to do their jobs."

Beth studied him a moment, her brown eyes turning almost black with concentration. Fred Lincoln had used the exact same words, and they reflected the high value her father had placed on his personal privacy, an attitude she had inherited. If Gene Cavelli knew anything more about J. or Lilly Jane, it was not knowledge he had learned from David. J. would remain a mystery, Beth realized. Whoever she was died when David Methany had.

4

It was only when the woman took him fully in her mouth and the hot moistness seemed to devour him that David Methany's attention to the New York City skyline was diverted. Until that moment when he could no longer ignore the insistent pressure for release, the woman's lips and tongue and fingernails had been nothing more than an amusing diversion on this weekday afternoon. David Methany had remarkable powers of concentration and could keep his mind on the rehabilitation project he was working on for a block of tenements in the East Seventies while his body heated and swelled. It gave him a certain amount of pleasure to know that other men did not have this same ability to divide their passions, especially not when the mouth and lips and tongue and fingernails belonged to one of the most exquisite women in New York City.

She was kneeling between his legs as he sat in his leather desk chair, and now her hands snaked around until she was pressing his buttocks up, sinking him into her.

Three fast, hard thrusts, a gravel-voiced "Aah," and it was over.

As his heartbeat returned to normal, he placed his hands on the woman's shoulders and gently pushed her off him. While she was still on her knees, her chest heaving, he swiveled his chair away from her and began to scan some papers on his desk.

"Thank you, Lilly Jane, that was lovely."

"You prick," the woman named Lilly Jane said as she straightened, walked around to the front of the desk, and sat down in a chair.

"Don't be crude."

"Excuse me, but I think it rather goes with the actions." She rummaged in her Christian Dior bag for the antique Cartier compact, and deftly reapplied her lipstick and patted down her wavy blond hair, sprayed into a perfect flip that had not moved during the earlier activity.

"For a fancy society babe such as yourself, Lilly Jane Litwin, you have a genuinely foul mouth," David said, smiling at her.

"You don't need pedigree to give a good blow job, darling," she said, and stood up. "Will you and Isabel be at the party tonight?"

David Methany's moment of social exchange was over. Ignoring the question, he lifted the receiver of his telephone and pressed the buzzer to his secretary. "Get Art Dennison in here, now," he snapped. "Then get my wife on the phone." He looked up and his brows raised. "You still here?"

"David—"

"Lilly Jane, please leave. I'm very busy, I didn't invite you here this afternoon, and I'd like you to go, now. Don't overstay your welcome, okay?"

Lilly Jane Litwin was not used to being spoken to this way. Then again, she thought as she walked to the door, she was not used to going to the office of a man who was not her husband in the middle of the afternoon and getting on her knees for him. But David Methany was not an ordinary man. Unfortunately, he was more aware of that fact than anyone else.

Lilly Jane had her hand on the doorknob and was about to speak when the intercom buzzed and David was back on the phone. "Hello, Isabel. I'll be a little late tonight, so if you want to go on to the party without me, I'll meet you there... All right, but don't start in on me when I get home. If you want me to go with you, then be prepared to arrive a little late."

Lilly Jane's jaw was clenched as she opened the door, almost bumping into the man David had summoned. The man's smile was dirty with innuendo. She supposed he recognized her from her practically daily appearances in the society columns. Or, knowing David, she thought with disgust, he was probably bragging to everyone that he had been bedding Lilly Jane Litwin for the past three weeks. Poor Isabel, married to a man whose most voracious appetite was for power. At least she could not say that about her dear Harry. But it was exactly that cocky masculinity of David's that drew her to him, making her an adulteress for the first time in her ten years of marriage.

She closed the door to David's office, ignoring the secretary as she walked past her, down the hallway to the elevator. Once outside on Madison Avenue and Forty-fourth Street, she took a deep breath, as if to clear her soul of its moral pollution. He was a bastard, no doubt about it. He was beneath her in every way. He was nothing more than a hustling real estate salesman, shrewd and clever enough to have made himself a millionaire by the age of twenty-five, a mere five years ago. But for all the money and self-importance, he was still a hustling real estate operator from Long Island for whom breeding meant category of dog.

She turned the corner, glancing around desultorily for a tax-icab before continuing to walk east toward her apartment on Park Avenue in the Sixties. The walk would do her good, give her time to think, clear her head. Who was she kidding? she asked herself. She wasn't muddled about David Methany; she knew just what she was doing and why. He was a selfish, arrogant, not very nice man—and she couldn't get enough of him.

She simply could not help herself. That's what her friend Emily Corbin said about food, and with David Methany, Lilly Jane finally understood the helplessness, the weakness, the ineffability of the attraction to something bad for oneself. He had less money than a lot of other men she could have, and whatever success he had achieved had not blunted his brashness, because he saw no reason to change, polish being a sign of weakness he felt was better suited to fey antiques dealers. That was his tremendous power, why she was drawn to him in spite of herself and her complete awareness that he was not worth a hundred Harrys; hell, he wasn't worth even *one* Harry. Emily always said how ashamed she was of her craving for sweets; how she knew, was totally *aware,* that whipped cream and chocolate and ice cream had as lethal an effect on her as rotgut whiskey on an alcoholic, but *she couldn't help herself.* That's how Lilly Jane was with David Methany. She knew he was not in her league yet she accepted his cavalier treatment, understanding too well that her appeal for him was not her looks or her sexual prowess, but the fact that she was Lilly Jane Litwin, darling of New York society, born and bred to the manner for which he had little use and less respect.

She accepted because, like her friend Emily, she couldn't help herself. His extraordinary disregard for everything she was became a magnet for her. He had the power to make her forget herself, and as great as was her shame for craving his brand of masculinity, even deeper was her need for it. Because he was not a gentleman and made no pretense of being one; because he had no moral strictures and no rules of polite behavior in or out of the bedroom. David Methany exuded a confidence that was an awesome aphrodisiac to Lilly Jane, a powerful potion that smelled bad and tasted bad, and that she knew was a poison to her well-being—and that she could neither resist nor get enough of. She was addicted to his kind of masculinity much as Emily Corbin was to rich food. Lilly Jane never felt particularly good about herself *after* she was with David, as Emily never felt good after she had gorged on a banana split, but the fantasy of anticipation and the pleasure of the act itself were remarkably effective blinders to "after."

If it was the masculine side of David Methany that had been serviced ten minutes ago, now it was the power side of him that was being exercised, all thoughts of Lilly Jane and her ministrations forgotten as he told Art Dennison what was on his mind.

"Get that prick off my case, Art. I don't give a fuck that his dumbfuck window installers aren't getting two coffee breaks a day. I want that apartment building finished and I want it finished on time. Do you understand me?" David roared, using the profanity that was as cathartic for him as a workout in a gym was for other men.

"David, it'll be done on time, don't worry. You're getting yourself all worked up over nothing, a minor problem, that's all it is. Trust me."

"Cut the crap. If I wanted to be pacified, I could go suck on Lilly Jane Litwin's tit. I pay you to make sure there is no trouble with the unions. How minor a fucking problem is it when the window installers are threatening a work stoppage because they're not getting two fucking coffee breaks a day? I pay you a helluva good salary to make sure there are no problems, so maybe it's time I found someone who'll do exactly that."

Art Dennison flushed a hot red and felt a wave of nausea course through him. He wanted desperately to sit down, but David Methany had not indicated that was permissible. The man was impossible to work for—mean, insulting, foul-mouthed. He made whores out of all his employees because he paid them so well. What made it tolerable, aside from the money, was the indisputable fact that the man was a real estate genius. He was tearing down a row of tenements from First Avenue to the East River to make room for a thirty-story luxury high-rise, one of the first to go that far east. He was redefining the silk-stocking district, clearing the way for a new future in Manhattan housing. But the unions made demands and they were used to getting those demands met. David made his arrangements with the union bosses at the planning stage of a development to avoid problems later, but this project on East Seventy-fifth Street had gotten enough bad publicity about the destruction of potential historic landmarks that the unions thought they could flex their muscles now, during the construction. Art had no idea how to do it, but he knew he had to get those window installers back in line.

"I'll take care of it," he assured David.

"Damn right you will," David shot back. "You're going to tell that fucking union boss that I'll pay his men triple overtime instead of the second coffee break. That'll shut him up—money always does."

"But the cost—"

"Don't talk to me about the fucking cost," David cut him off impatiently. "I said tell him we'll pay triple overtime. I didn't say I'd actually do it."

David's laugh was ragged with derision, his dark brown eyes sparking contempt. "Art, instead of standing there holding your dick in your hands, get the fuck out of my face and do what I told you!"

"There's something else," the young executive said, ignoring the dismissal. "The elevator installers are still threatening their work stoppage because of pressure to finish at a pace they claim undermines their safety. I mentioned this to you last week and—"

"Yeah, I know all about it." David's smile was thin and mean and metal-cold. "I'll deal with Alex Tannen myself, which is what I told you I would do. Now go take care of the window installers before I really lose my temper." David picked up the telephone and started to dial before Art could say anything further. What he wanted to tell him was that he had already spoken to Alex Tannen, the head of the elevator installers' union, and the man refused to push his crew unless they were guaranteed a deadline bonus. Well, let David find out for himself, he thought, as he left the office. There were some people the bastard could not control. . . .

"Alex, how are you? Good, good . . . Look, I don't want to waste your time, but I understand we've got ourselves a little problem . . . Right, right, I've got a problem." As the man on the other end of the telephone explained why his men were entitled to a special safety bonus, no emotion registered on David's face. One hand held the phone, the other doodled idly on a piece of paper. He seemed the image of attentive concentration. In truth, he was not listening to a word the other man was saying. He had what he needed in front of him on the desk. And what that file contained made it unnecessary to pay attention to Alex Tannen.

"I appreciate what you're saying," David finally spoke, his voice calm. "But to tell you the truth, I think you're underestimating the seriousness of your problems. And yes, I do mean *your* problems." He opened the file in front of him. "It seems you have a certain debt to some difficult types down in the Bahamas . . . Whoa there, let me finish, Alex, please." His voice remained even; he was smoothly giving the waiter his order for lunch.

"You are overdrawn at First Manhattan where you have a joint checking account with your wife. You are overdrawn at Empire State Savings and Loan where you have a joint savings account with her. You have borrowed against your union fund.

In fact, you have depleted your individual union account, and I see here, now wait a minute, where is it, oh yeah, here it is ... What was that, Alex? Yes, I have complete financial statements on you, including one from Merit Savings and Loan, which handles all your union's accounts, both individual and group. From what I can tell, there have been ten withdrawals to the tune of $120,000 in the last four months. Now I know that you're the only one with the authority to transfer funds from the general account to an individual account. And funny thing, Alex, this $120,000? It all seems to have landed in your individual account, then was withdrawn within three days and redeposited into a new account you've opened in *your name only*—at First Bank of New York. Tell me, Alex, I'm curious. What are you going to say the next time one of your men needs money for an operation? Are you going to tell him there isn't enough in the union's funds because you've been skimming off the top to pay your gambling debts? I'd like to know how you're going to handle this, Alex, because I think your men who you tell me work so hard and under such difficult conditions are entitled to the truth. Don't you?"

David waited easily through the silence at the other end. He closed the folder and began to doodle again, but now that metallic hardness appeared in his eyes, and the pressure on the pencil made the circles and squares angular and dark.

"You fucking piece of shit," he hissed after sufficient time had elapsed. "You're a fucking thief and you're going to tell your men to get the elevators done without one extra dime from me or else you're finished. You get that, prickhead? Finished." At no time did David raise his voice as he had with Art Dennison. With real threat, as he was using against Alex Tannen, he had a far more potent weapon: damaging information.

More silence, then: "Yes, Alex, I agree the building's going to be a beauty and I'm glad you appreciate the need to get it

done on time ... I have absolute confidence you'll handle your
men ... Don't be so hard on them, Alex, they're not lazy, just
a little bit greedy." David was grinning tightly as he hung up
on the other man's babbling assurances that all would be taken
care of as David wished.

The real estate mogul got up and stood by his window, never
failing to be entranced by the skyline. Someday, the entire city
would be marked by Methany projects. Already he had changed
the area near Bloomingdale's on Third Avenue in the East Sixties
by building a luxury residential hotel with prices as steep as the
height of the building. And there was the office building on
Sixth Avenue and Fifty-first Street, done on speculation three
years ago because he had believed so strongly that major corporations wanted to be housed luxuriously. He had been proved
right; the thirty floors leased within nine months of completion.

He sat back down, wallowing in self-satisfaction. He was
ridiculously young to be so successful, but what was even more
gratifying than the money and the power was the enormous
pleasure he got each and every day from what he did. Ever since
he had been a teenager working summers for his father's aluminum-siding company, he had felt an affinity for the world of
real estate. He loved everything about it, the planning stages,
the slow, steady construction of the building, watching the foun-
dation being laid, each floor put in place. And as he studied and
learned, in college but with far more worthwhile training on
the job, he found he had a natural nose for business. He understood wheeling and dealing, cajoling and hanging tough, and
every single part of it thrilled him more than a dozen Lilly Jane
Litwins.

For a moment, the smile faded from his handsome face, and
the brown eyes turned soft. He wished Isabel understood him
better, appreciated how much his work meant to him. But she
did not. She liked spending his money, and socializing with

people he had little use for; she had no interest in what he did, only in what it gave her. David never considered divorcing Isabel. There was no reason to pay the alimony that she would demand; no reason to give up the protection she unknowingly supplied when other women became difficult. And he wanted to have a child one day; unlike other women, Isabel would no doubt leave the rearing of the child to him, which is exactly how he wanted it.

Still, there were times when the pride he felt knowing the city was changing because of him was not enough. When the triumph he experienced exercising his power over an Alex Tannen was not enough. When getting a rich society beauty like Lilly Jane Litwin on her knees in his office was not enough. No, there were lonely times and empty times that not even the most exciting blueprints for a new Methany project could fill.

5

Harry Litwin surveyed the men sitting at the scratched and dulled mahogany conference table that had been part of the U.S. District Court Building almost as long as the grime on the windows. As the youngest U.S. attorney ever to have been appointed in Manhattan, at thirty-six Harry had held the job for the past two years, and this afternoon he was having his weekly review of the information gathered to date, preparatory to prosecuting the biggest case of his career.

He was not yet ready to bring formal charges; he still needed more irrefutable facts and documentation to verify the rumors he had heard for years about David Methany's business practices—practices that included bribery, money laundering, extortion, even physical threats. This was the kind of case that could take Harry from the District Court Building to Gracie Mansion, and he was not about to make one false step in proving that Methany's so-called Midas touch was in reality as heavy-handed as Goliath's club.

He opened his folder and nodded to his group of handpicked assistant D.A.s. "All right, gentlemen, anything new this week?"

"We've got him on more extortion and physical threats," one young attorney said. "Two private investigators he used have promised to testify in exchange for us not revoking their licenses." The young man smiled. "These guys know of at least four different occasions when Methany went after two rival contractors who were coming in with lower bids. Nothing as obvious as broken bones, but there were suspicious fires and an equally strange break-in at one guy's home."

"We need proof that Methany was behind this," Harry said.

"Nothing in writing," the lawyer admitted. "Just the word of the P.I.s against Methany's."

Harry frowned. "Not good enough."

"I've got the same thing," another of the D.A.s spoke up. "Methany basically blackmailed the leader of the local glazier's union with some old police record. The guy couldn't risk it coming out, so he shaved the price off his quote to Methany and made up the difference to his men out of his own pocket. I've convinced him to testify, but again, it's his word against Methany's, and the guy does have a record."

Harry shook his head, clearly not pleased. "There isn't a judge, let alone a jury, who would decide against David Methany without solid proof. Dig deeper. Get stuff that's in writing," he insisted. He turned to another of his men. "What about the money laundering, Lewis? Anything on that?"

"We're up to four cartons of records," the D.A. confirmed. "His nice middle-class father has more bank accounts in the Bahamas than grains of sand on the beach. Amazing how lucrative the aluminum-siding business has become, and how many new corporations he's had to create to handle the business." His grin was smug as he patted the folder before him.

"Good, that's more like it," Harry said. "Remember, I have no intention of bringing charges against David Methany and his battery of lawyers unless we are 100 percent positive we can get convictions. Paper trails, taped conversations—this is what we've got to have. We haven't worked hard all these months to get our case thrown out of court because of insufficient evidence. Get those private eyes and that union leader to check and recheck their records, their bank accounts, anything. There's got to be some paper on what they did that will tie the action back to Methany."

"Time's on our side," the attorney named Lewis said. "The buildup in the press has been great. All the rumors and innuendo are bringing people forth with their own Methany story to tell."

"Dismissable as jealous competitors or disgruntled suppliers," Harry countered. "I've told you before—stories about Methany have been around for longer than I've been in office. The only reason we stand a chance of actually prosecuting the bastard is because maybe, just maybe, he finally went too far wanting to tear down that nursing home over on Riverside Drive. It took public outcry in the press to convince the powers-that-be to fork over sufficient funds for an investigation that should have begun with my predecessor. And what a pile of shit we're finding."

His men laughed appreciatively, but Harry knew there was nothing amusing about what they had been unearthing. It was one thing for David Methany not to be a nice fellow, but what he and his group had discovered was that not being nice was the least of David Methany's offenses. It went beyond mere greed or even the desire to be without equal in his field. David Methany was talented enough to have achieved success without gangster methods, but Harry was beginning to understand that David enjoyed twisting arms, enjoyed the power of the threat, enjoyed getting away with less than honest business practices. There was more than a touch of the crook to David Methany, and that is what motivated the D.A. in his prosecution.

Proof, that's what he needed. The IRS was looking into David's tax returns, but Harry would prefer to have the kind of proof that came from a victim—it would go over better in court. Besides, he knew David was too clever to make any kind of mistake with his taxes.

"All right, men, let's keep at it," he said now, standing up. "Brad," he added, looking at one of his group, "don't forget that business with the Indians who did the high-floor work on that office tower over on Sixth."

"I've been checking into that, Harry, but I can't get any of them to admit they worked at night with only the light from their hard hats—at twenty-five floors above the ground. These guys need the work and they're afraid of Methany."

"Well, keep trying," Harry said, then left the conference room for his own office.

Amazing, he thought, that David Methany could have such power as to intimidate a construction crew foreman to get his men to work at night without proper safety measures. And probably without compensatory pay, either. It was no doubt a case of work under these conditions or go hungry. The guy was damned lucky. No accidents reported. That, of course, was the key: *reported*. Lord knew what would come out if people actually had the guts to talk.

There were other cases pending aside from David Methany, but none that so occupied Harry's thoughts. Maybe because he did not have occasion to socialize with other criminals, as he did with David and his wife, Isabel. Not that they came close to Lilly Jane's exalted background, but Isabel tried hard, and David's money opened doors mere breeding could not keep closed.

Harry ran a hand through his blond hair, embarrassed. If Lilly Jane could hear him, she would laugh and call him a pretentious snob, and rightly so. His own background was nothing if not pure-blood middle-class—just ask Lilly Jane's parents who, he was convinced, would have preferred him to come from dirt poverty instead of the mediocrity of the bourgeoisie. Harry had always believed that it was her parents' disapproval as well as his earnestness and drive, so unlike boys of her class who could afford to be frivolous, that had appealed to Lilly Jane. They had met on the beach at East Hampton, bathing suits being a great equalizer. By the time they had their clothes on, it was too late.

Ah, Lilly Jane, and a smile warmed his blue eyes and brought a dusting of color to his pale cheeks. If ever there was a couple that did not belong together, he thought not for the first time in their almost ten years of marriage, it was them—yet he adored her and, he liked to believe, she was more than passingly fond of him. In that way that opposites have, they were good for each other, his predictablity and steadfastness anchoring her enthusiasms; his good-natured indulgence of her desires forestalling a need for her to seek satisfaction elsewhere.

And what did Lilly Jane give him? Yes, she was silly at times, and yes, her wealthy and well-connected family certainly had not hindered his career. But what Harry loved about Lilly Jane was that in addition to being quite beautiful, even with her thirty-first birthday looming, he believed her to be equally lovely inside, a deeply, sincerely, good-hearted human being. She gave generously of her time and her money to a variety of charities, but that was easy for her. What Harry saw as unusual was her ability to listen and not judge; to have so much in her favor and never to feel superior or exercise her privileges to another's disadvantage. It would utterly devastate him, he occasionally thought, if she were ever to awaken one morning and decide she wanted someone else. He might, if he ever found out, tolerate a passing dalliance, but to lose her completely . . . he could not conceive of going on without her.

Harry knew that in bed there were no surprises between them, and for that he blamed himself. But he had never considered sex more than an appetite, certainly not an arena for showmanship or even abiding pleasure. The fact that his appetite had gotten him in trouble twice before he was nineteen was testimony to his stupidity, nothing else, and a vasectomy quickly protected him against himself. Fortunately, Lilly Jane had not

cared about motherhood, avowing that this way she did not have
to share Harry—little knowing that his career would absorb his
time and attention far more than could any child.

At thirty-six, though, Harry was beginning to wonder if perhaps a child would not be a good thing for him and Lilly Jane.
She probably wouldn't want to ruin her gorgeous figure, but it
seemed that they had so much it was only right to share with
another, some little baby with Lilly Jane's looks and his brains.
He grinned broadly. Now that would be something. One of
these days he would discuss the possibility with her because, of
course, it would mean a reversal of the operation. Yes, a baby
was definitely something to consider. After this business with
David Methany was done, and he was well on his way to Gracie
Mansion.

While her husband was determining how solid a case he had
against David Methany, Lilly Jane Litwin was deciding what
to wear to her assignation later that afternoon with her lover,
the same David Methany.

Before marriage, there had been only two men with whom
she had had sex, and since, her idea of seduction always stopped
short of the bedroom. Getting a man to want her was more an
act to confirm her desirability than any genuine physical longing.
Except with David.

On more than one occasion recently, she had found herself
wondering whether she was falling in love with him. The times
between their being together were becoming more and more
intolerable to her. And instead of enjoying the slight danger of
the situation when she and Harry were at the same social event
as David and his wife, Lilly Jane would squirm with longing
and atypical jealousy.

She did not want to love David Methany. She loved Harry,

she truly did. He might not thrill her, but he loved her without judgment and he was an innately kind and good human being. What they had together would last when they were old and not so pretty any longer. What she was experiencing with David was lust, and there was nothing decent or long-lasting about it. She knew that, and yet . . . and yet. . . .

She took the topper from her crystal bottle of Bal à Versailles and touched it to the crevice between her breasts. In less than forty-five minutes, she would be meeting him at their favorite trysting place, the Rowland Court Hotel, a small and discreet establishment in the East Sixties off Madison Avenue that catered to illicit lovers of a certain pedigree, and movie stars. Forty-five minutes . . . it seemed like forever to her hungry senses.

6

Isabel Methany sat at the round, glass-topped table for two in what had become her breakfast nook, a small pantry off the kitchen that the architects had enlarged by taking over an adjoining maid's room. The breakfast nook afforded an unobstructed view of Park Avenue that she adored, although she dreamed of the day when David would be successful enough that they could afford Fifth Avenue. Rooms overlooking Central Park would be a dream come true, as if she did not already feel like Cinderella married to her prince.

She did not need to read the newspaper again, however, to know that she was not married to a prince, Charming or otherwise. Today's articles were even more damning than usual, and Isabel had a feeling that Harry Litwin was getting close to actually bringing charges against her husband for a variety of offenses that made her cringe with disgust and fear.

She was not really surprised, though, that David was guilty of improprieties. Married to him for only four years, since she was twenty-two, she was not sure if he had been faithful to her for even one of those four years, and she had no illusions about what the rest of their married life together would be like.

That was just fine with her. She would have children by him someday, and she would lead a very good, carefree, social, monied life as his wife. How many other young girls from Long Island without a college education and equipped to be a wife and not much more had it as good as she did? She was ballast for David, a reminder of their roots, since his family and hers lived minutes from each other. She and David had met at a local Chinese restaurant one Sunday evening when they had each been out with their families, and David's father, who had put up the siding on her family's house, came over to say hello. It was all Kismet, Isabel believed, and so she would tolerate nasty headlines and sexual dalliances. She knew that David was truly a very decent young man with a brilliant mind for business. In time, he would settle down and be a perfect husband, too.

"Good morning, darling," she greeted David as he entered the breakfast area. "I didn't hear you come in."

"Good morning, Isabel," he said, taking a seat. "I see you're reading those rags again. I thought I told you I didn't want them in the house anymore."

"Oh darling, they're so foolish, what does it matter?"

David's smile was small. "You don't believe what they say?"

"About you being dishonest?" She reached over and touched his hand. "Don't be ridiculous."

"You should," he said softly, removing his hand to lift his goblet of freshly squeezed grapefruit juice.

"Don't joke, David," she remonstrated.

"My dear Isabel, I am not joking, believe me. What our good district attorney is hoping to charge me with are all so-called crimes I've actually committed." His laugh was puffy with confidence. "Of course, getting proof will be something else entirely."

Isabel did not know whether her husband was teasing her or not. Often that was the case. He would say something that struck her as not being particularly nice, but then he would say he was only teasing, so she never quite knew. She began to laugh. "You *are* joking."

All humor left David's face, and his brown eyes grew as hard and cold as the glass top on the table. "As you wish, Isabel."

She could feel her stomach shrivel with a sensation that had become all too familiar over the past four years. It was not exactly fear, no, not that. And it wasn't quite dread, either. But it was tension, absolutely it was the kind of tension that came from being constantly kept off-balance. When they had first begun to date, she had found David's unpredictability sexy and exciting, but in marriage, it left her feeling not unlike the odd girl in gym class, never chosen for the team not because she wasn't good enough but because she "didn't get it"—*it* being the unwritten rules of teammanship, not the rules of the game. That's how her husband made her feel—left out, confused, not quite "with it," slightly stupid. There was an inside joke going on, and he refused to let her share it.

"David, please don't shut me out," she said now.

" 'David, please don't shut me out,' " he mimicked, and she breathed deeply and looked away from the meanness in his face. She loved him, she *did,* she told herself. This was a stage, nothing more than a phase that his success and money were taking him through, a flexing of his power muscles. When he got used to it all, he would soften, become kind to her again.

"Isabel," he said, pouring himself coffee, "I'm sorry—"

"That's all right, darling, I know you're under a lot of pressure."

"You didn't let me finish. What I was going to say is that I'm sorry you have such faith in me."

"David!"

"It really would be much better if you believed the press, Isabel. Understand what I am, what you married. It would make things so much easier."

Isabel took another deep breath and got up from the table. She was a voluptuously built woman whose shortness would make her plump, permanently, with one pregnancy. She had warm brown eyes and a slightly too wide nose and a generous mouth with almost pouty lips; her hair she had professionally straightened and lightened. At twenty-six, Isabel was pretty with nothing that signaled a lasting appeal. She was not special, and if she were smart about anything, it was knowing this about herself. And so she studied fashion magazines and studied the women with whom she lunched and the women at the functions she and David attended, determined, with the help of her husband's money and the social opportunities it provided, to acquire *style*. This desire allowed her to be grateful to her husband, and tolerant. In turn, she was making herself adjust to the tension.

"David, I'd like to ask you a question," she abruptly declared, clenching her hands into little fists at her sides. She shouldn't do this, she knew that, but suddenly she decided she wanted the truth, wanted it out in the open so she could face, and deal with, her future without pretense.

"Yes," he stated tiredly, "I will be home in time for dinner at the Lamberts. Black tie, right?"

"Yes, but that's not the question."

"Oh?" He stopped buttering his toast and looked over at her expectantly.

"David, do you love me?" she blurted.

His hand with the butter knife remained poised in midair, and he continued to look at her with a startled expression on his face. "Isabel . . ."

"Please answer me, David," she said with uncharacteristic force.

David sat back and stared at his wife of four years. "Yes, I believe I do," he finally said. "Not in the way you might want me to, though, I'm afraid."

"What do you mean?" Isabel asked with a breathless expectancy in her voice.

"I'm glad you're my wife, Isabel," he explained. "I love the fact that you're so forgettable."

"What did you say?" she barely whispered.

"You don't intrude on my life," David went on conversationally, either unaware or uncaring of the effect his words were having on the woman he had chosen to share his most intimate life. "That's very good, you see, very good. Another woman might be more exciting to me or more demanding, but you . . ." He smiled at her as if she were a horse he had bought at auction who had turned out better than he had anticipated. "You're quite satisfactory, Isabel, and there's nothing I love more than being satisfied in my expectations. In fact, despite the incomprehensible pleasure you get wasting your time with those silly rich women you seem to admire, I think you are the perfect companion for me and will make an excellent mother for my future children. So yes, Isabel, I do love you, in my fashion."

If Isabel Methany née Decortis had thought more of herself she would not, as her husband so abruptly put it, admire the silly rich women whose approval she sought, and then she would also have been the type of woman who did not need to ask her husband if he loved her. In fact, if Isabel Methany née Decortis thought more of herself, she would have packed up her bags, left the apartment, and sued her husband for every cent he had.

But Isabel had absolutely no self-confidence, none. She could never hide this, and so David was able to use it to his advantage whenever he wished. Were it not for him, Isabel was convinced she would have ended up with a dentist, or worse, an insurance agent. She knew her strongest asset was her youth. The fact, therefore, that David Methany had chosen her because she did not thrill him too much might not be flattering, but it would, in the long run, serve her well. Without him, she would be totally insignificant. With him, she was insignificant only to him. It was a fine distinction, but an important one. And perhaps, in time, she might be able to change how he felt about her; become so stylish and chic and sophisticated that he would desire and love her. She wanted that very much because, in truth, she loved her husband the way a woman is supposed to love a man, and she wanted that feeling reciprocated. She was not yet ready to see her marriage as one of conditional clauses.

"Am I supposed to be pleased by what you've said?" she dared ask.

David shrugged disinterestedly. "Don't romanticize what we have, Isabel. You serve a very practical purpose for me and you do it well—better," he said thoughtfully, "than most women could. We can stay together a long time, a long, relatively *happy* time, if you can accept what we are and not desire more."

"I see," she mumbled, edging away from the table.

"I hope you do. There is one thing, though," he added, giving her a glance of assessment.

"And that is?" she prompted, dreading his next words.

He sighed. "I wish—no, that would be a foolish waste of energy. It's just that sometimes it would be nice if you took more interest in what I do for a living. I think we could be perfect together if you cared about how I earned a livelihood instead of how much I earned at it."

"I see," she repeated, and at that precise moment, Isabel did see—that her only weapon against the callous disregard of her husband would be a similar attitude toward his work. If she could hurt him at all, she realized at that moment, it was through a lack of proper awe and respect for what he did. Isabel was wise enough, even at that young age, to understand that there was really little she could do to wound her husband; he was far too mighty for the likes of her. But even a small pinprick would measure some satisfaction, and she vowed that for as long as they were together, she would not ask one question about his work, not express one word of praise, doubt, confusion, criticism, *nothing*. It would be as if all that mattered was how much he brought her, not unlike the fact that what mattered to him was how easily he could forget her.

"I gather from the rather pale cast to your skin and the enormity of your eyes that you are stunned by what I've said," David stated. "I'm sorry, but you were the one who opened this conversation."

"That's true, David," she conceded. "Had I known the cruelty within you, however, I would not—"

"I'm not being cruel, Isabel," he stopped her. "Just honest. The fact is that the truth is not always pleasant, but cruel? No, I don't have any desire to hurt you."

"Are you saying, then, that this is a marriage of convenience?"

"Isn't every marriage ultimately that?" he rejoined quickly.

"I suppose I had thought, or at least had wished to believe, that there was some feeling between us, that's all," she admitted.

"There is feeling, Isabel. If it's not quite as idealized as you might like, I'm sorry, but there is feeling, probably much more in its way than what exists between most of the couples we know."

"It will take a certain amount of adjustment, I'm sure you'll understand, to accustom myself to your—what did you call it— oh, yes, *honest* approach to marriage and our relationship."

"Don't be acerbic, Isabel, you do it so poorly." He began to eat again, bored now. "If you were really honest," he went on as if talking to himself, testing his philosophy before making an oration, "you'd admit that love has very little to do with your feelings for me. I give you a great deal that is valuable, so valuable, in fact, that the lack of love is hardly felt at all." He put down his toast and looked at her stonily. "Isn't that right? Darling?"

Moisture came into Isabel's eyes. She must not cry, she told herself. She must not let him see how deeply he had wounded her.

Never again, she silently vowed, would she let him know how much she loved him. The only quality David had any respect for was strength. By asking about his feelings for her, she had given him access to her weakness: a belief in his love for her, a belief that she mattered to him not as an asset but as a necessity. More than a romantic, she was a fool. Now she understood how thoroughly she had deluded herself. In courtship, David had been ardent, attentive. She had loved how he called her every day, celebrated the anniversary of their first date every month for the seven months until they got married. How thoughtful, how romantic, how loving. In marriage, when he began coming home late, when their dinner conversation consisted of her gossip and his indifference, when she would occasionally turn to him in bed and he would not respond— she did not stop loving him, telling herself that this was the normal, natural development of a marriage. Sometimes he could be sarcastic and even slightly mean to her, but she still loved him, still loved the clever, energetic, ambitious man she had married who now was too busy, merely too busy, to continue to be ardent and attentive and thoughtful and loving.

Pretense—what they had together was nothing but pretense. The courtship had been a masterful charade, the marriage a cunningly deliberate arrangement. She was suitable: to his needs, his plans, his self-image. She wondered sadly if there were some way to gain confidence from suitability.

David Methany, the man she had married with wild passion in her veins and love in her heart, was a figment of her needy imagination. David Methany, the man who was her husband, was a stranger.

David Methany had not wanted to hurt his wife, but it was important that she understand the parameters of their relationship so as not to harbor any false illusions that could someday prove injurious to both of them.

It was nothing more than a matter of approach, he told himself. His was realistic, practical, less burdened by emotional baggage than most. As a result, there should be less hurt, but that certainly had not been the case this morning, he considered ruefully. Usually, it was a matter of Isabel looking good, comporting herself well as the wife of a powerful businessman. She was a proper companion for him, asking nothing in return save a blank check. This morning's conversation had been a bizarre aberration, something characteristic of a more traditional union wherein the man shares his business activities with his wife and she voices her pride and interest. Even admitting to a desire for Isabel to express a curiosity about his work had been strange. He enjoyed her disinterest since it left him free to act without explanation. And he welcomed her lack of emotional demands. As such, he deemed theirs a good marriage, requiring nothing important of each other. He sincerely hoped that she would come to understand how much he valued her, appreciate it for what it was, and accept it without false expectations for anything more storybook.

At first, that was what had appealed to him about Lilly Jane Litwin—no false expectations. That and the irrefutable fact that she was married to the man who was so open about his desire to "get" David Methany. Lilly Jane had been a delicious flirtation and then had turned out to be a wonderful sexual partner, but lately she had seemed a little too clingy, too familiar . . . like her coming to his office, uninvited. With him, nothing could breed contempt quicker than assumption of familiarity in a woman and detectable greed in a man. In fact, he had been ready to call it off with Lilly Jane after the fifth or sixth time they had been together—the novelty had certainly worn off as had the sense of triumph—but then Harry Litwin had stepped up his attack against him, and suddenly, sex with Harry Litwin's wife had become smart, not just pleasurable, and certainly worth his time for a while longer.

Poor Harry Litwin, David mused complacently. He should have married someone safe and controllable and insecure, like Isabel Decortis. Women rich and beautiful and privileged and spoiled could get a guy into all kinds of trouble.

7

"Don't laugh. Please, David, please don't laugh."

"But my darling Lilly Jane, what else do you expect me to do—cry? Strut around proudly? Of course I have to laugh because you being pregnant by me is enormously funny."

"David, don't—"

"Shut up, you sow!"

In the bedroom of Suite 23 at the Rowland Court Hotel, Lilly Jane cringed at the ugly words, the gravelly harshness of David's voice; even more, she winced at the sight of him, eyes almost black with rage, skin flushed, the tendons in his neck and the top of his hands fat like ropes. She had not expected him to be pleased, but neither had she anticipated such cruelty.

She should never have told him. It would have been simple to call one of her friends and get the name of a reliable doctor who, for a princely sum, would perform the illegal abortion. Yet she had hesitated and hesitated until now, a good two months into the pregnancy, it was almost too late. She had waited because in her foolish sexual obsession, she had imbued this child with the ability to restore some of the magic missing recently between her and David. And, if she were to be totally honest, there was a part of her that had been fantasizing about mutual divorces, new marriages. Even though she still loved her husband, lately she could barely tolerate his touch without the counterpoint of David's passion. She supposed, if she were to continue to be honest with herself, that it was not that she loved David so much, but that she was unable to want a life without him. For the past several weeks he had become casual about seeing her, and even when they were together, he had seemed removed, distant, almost bored. Not thinking clearly, she had mistakenly convinced herself that a child would enable David to accept his vulnerabilities, acknowledge how much she meant to him. But she meant nothing to him, *nothing;* and the man who did cherish her would soon be destroyed.

Harry. She had to tell him and soon. He would be sick over it. He might go on with the marriage, but his trust in her, his loyalty, his unquestioning love—all would be gone. And she needed him now, perhaps for the first time in their entire marriage. She needed him because she wanted this baby, a fact so unexpected that she did not know whether to laugh or cry over it. For years she had accepted Harry's vasectomy with seeming equanimity, yet the moment she knew she was pregnant, she realized her self-delusion.

Self-delusion had become a comfortable cloak to wear, she thought miserably. Certainly she was also guilty of it regarding David. Even though in her heart she knew better—because silly though she might appear, she was not stupid—she had nevertheless convinced herself that behind his facade of arrogance and self-absorption had to be a layer of decency that made him worth loving. If he were not truly kind and warm and loving, needing only the right woman to bring out these qualities, then her self-abasement was for nought. To be with one out of desire was understandable; to claim goodness for the devil was unforgivable. She still wanted David sexually, and a fragment of her refused to believe that more noble emotions were not also involved, and that these other feelings were deserved, not created as a camouflage for her shame.

Suddenly, David halted in front of her. She had to strain backward to look up into his smoldering eyes.

"Is it mine?"

"Of course! I haven't been with any—"

"Get rid of it."

She shook her head. "No, absolutely not."

"Get rid of it, Lilly Jane."

Tears misted her vision as she reached for his hand. He backed away from her, retreating to the dressing table chair. "David, please, just think about this, that's all I'm asking. Don't make any decision immediately. This could be wonderful for us, really." To what depths would she sink for this man and the sick power she allowed him to have over her? she wondered, nauseated by her whine. The contempt on his face mirrored her own.

"What were you thinking of, Lilly Jane? Just tell me that."

His voice was surprisingly soft and the gentleness in it gave her hope. She smiled tentatively and shrugged. "It was an accident, so obviously I wasn't thinking. But now? I don't know, maybe we could get married."

"You're the wife of the man determined to forge his career at my expense." David shook his head, incredulous. "No, somehow I don't see him letting you go for me."

"That's business, David. I'm sure we could work it all out."

"What about Isabel?" If Lilly Jane had any idea of the effort it was costing David Methany to sit in that small boudoir chair and maintain the evenness in his voice, the blandness in his eyes, she would have scurried from the room with the haste of a lion being pursued by a hyena. But David was good, very good at deception.

Lilly Jane again shrugged. "She doesn't matter to you, so why pretend otherwise? You'd have to pay her off, that's all. It's not like with Harry and me. I love him, in my way."

"Then why leave him? I don't understand."

"Because I want you, David," she whispered, holding his eyes. "I didn't expect this to happen. I thought it was sex, nothing lasting, nothing fine, but it's more than that for me, David. I don't know if it's love, but it's more than sex for me and it's more than I feel for my husband."

"Because you don't have me," David told her.

"That's not true. I know you think I'm spoiled, that I only want what I can't get, but that's not true with you. I wish it were, because you make it awfully difficult to care for you sometimes. Like today," she said on another tentative laugh.

David said nothing, just kept staring at her. Then, abruptly, he got to his feet and walked out into the living room area of the suite.

"David?" Lilly Jane called after him.

"I'll be back in a minute, just want to fix a drink."

Which was only part of the truth. David needed time alone to let the anger seep out of him and to make some sort of sense of this other emotion running through him, an emotion he imagined others might call regret, but that was so foreign to him that all he could label it was confusion.

He had laughed at her out of shock. He had been angry because he had been caught by surprise. And what he was experiencing now was peculiar because he was realizing that he wanted a baby, and forcing Lilly Jane to kill one fathered by him hurt him deeply—but so it had to be. He did not want to marry her, and he could not afford for there to be some little Methany bastard running around, a potential threat, a potential blackmailer. No, this particular baby could not exist, and this particular affair had to come to an end. If what he was feeling really was regret, then it was not only for the loss of the baby but for the end to the relationship with Lilly Jane; she had not yet exhausted her usefulness to him.

"I thought you were getting a drink," Lilly Jane said when he returned to the bedroom.

David glanced down at his empty hand. "I changed my mind."

He sat next to her on the bed and took one of her hands, ice-cold, in his. "Lilly Jane, this won't work. I'm sorry, but it really won't."

"No, I suppose it won't," she wearily agreed.

"You have to get rid of it. Unless you intend for Harry to raise it as his own."

"You know he could never do that."

"That's right, Harry had a vasectomy, I forgot." David got up and walked over to the window that looked out on a land-scaped garden, a touch of London in Manhattan. "What were you thinking, Lilly Jane?" he muttered. "Whatever were you thinking?"

"I told you, I—"

"I know, I know," he stopped her, turning around. "You have no choice."

"I'm not getting rid of this baby, David. I'm not."

"What about your husband?"

"I don't know, I'll think of something."

"If you don't, I will." He had spoken softly, but there was unmistakable menace in his tone.

"What in the world are you talking about?"

"You, you silly woman. You've given me the best weapon against your husband and his relentless campaign to get me—you."

"I don't understand," Lilly Jane murmured, getting to her feet, her face ashen with dread as she approached him.

He was smiling with complacency as he placed his hands on her shoulders. Whatever odd emotions he had experienced moments before were neatly dispatched into the realm of the impractical; returned in full force was the clever, cunning businessman who knew how to take advantage of an opportunity.

"I'm talking about this baby and how your husband would react if he knew that *I* was its father."

"You wouldn't be so vicious," she breathed, stepping out of his grasp.

"Vicious!" he repeated. "No. Selfish, perhaps, but vicious? No, I don't think so. You've handed over to me control of a situation that had been becoming somewhat unmanageable. You're pregnant by me. Your husband is preparing a criminal indictment against me. That's an opportunity I can't walk away from. But don't take it personally, darling. It's business, that's all."

"You really are a bastard," she gasped, stunned.

"Which I believe is one of the things that turns you on," he shot back.

"I won't do it. I absolutely refuse to get rid of this child."

"Then I'll tell Harry all about us."

"He'd never believe you."

"No?" David laughed with confidence. "I think there are a few intimate details about you that I could share with him as irrefutable proof."

"You'll destroy me," she managed, her voice thick.

"No, you're destroying yourself," he insisted. "Just get rid of this baby and everything will be fine."

She looked at him a moment and then smiled thinly. "How do I know you still wouldn't tell Harry about us?"

"I could have done that already if I had wanted to," he reminded her. "And frankly, you have no guarantee that I won't. Getting your husband to drop the case against me would be a terrific way for you to ensure my silence, of course."

"I couldn't do that."

"Oh, you could, Lilly Jane. And you will, or else there's no telling what I might say or when, or, most importantly, to whom."

"So this is something you will always have over me, is that it?"

"Now you understand the impossibility of having a little bastard by me. The danger is not dissimilar."

She stared at him—at the thick, almost raven black hair and the dark brown eyes so intelligent and alive, at the chiseled jaw and Roman nose, at the thin, wide, mobile mouth—and she felt her stomach roil with self-disgust. Despite all that had transpired this afternoon, despite finally acknowledging what kind of man he was, she wanted him and she knew that she would not leave this hotel room today without having him.

She walked over to the bed and began to remove the jacket of her suit. There were no words now, just the soft rustle of silk and nylon. When she was in her slip and panties, she turned around; he was still by the window, fully clothed, just watching her.

"No sense wasting a good bed," she said with forced flippancy.

"Lilly Jane, about the baby . . . ?"

"It's made my breasts fuller, want to see?" And she eased down the straps of her slip to reveal how her breasts overflowed the bra.

"Lilly Jane—"

"I heard everything you had to say, David, and I understand."

"Does that mean you'll get rid of it?"

"It means that you made it perfectly clear what would happen if I didn't. Now, would you please fuck me?"

He studied her, weighing her words, and because he was now aroused and because he could not conceive of her daring to go against him, he decided that she had acquiesced to his wishes. So he got undressed and did what she had asked him to do. But even as he was pumping with more vigor and urgency than he had shown in quite a while, bringing Lilly Jane to that excruciating point of pleasure she had come to need so badly, she maintained enough of herself to know, without a doubt, that she would never get rid of David Methany's child, consequences be damned.

8

TWO-AND-A-HALF MONTHS LATER

"Lilly Jane, honey, don't get angry at me, but I think you've been indulging in a few too many desserts. You've put on a little weight, not that I mind, of course. You're more beautiful than ever, but I know how you watch your figure and I thought I should point this out to you."

"Thank you, Harry. I was planning to start a diet tomorrow."

FOUR MONTHS LATER

"It's David Methany, Mr. Litwin," came his secretary's voice over the intercom. "Do you wish to speak with him?"

Harry Litwin's lean, serious face spared itself a rare grin. He knew he had the crook reeling. In exchange for immunity from prosecution for his own offenses, Alex Tannen would testify against Methany. The teamster's testimony as well as new documents linking David with a known enforcer whose fists were registered lethal weapons would put Methany out of business for many years.

"Oh, I'll speak to him, Mary," Harry said to his secretary, the smile in his voice obvious.

"David, how are you?" he began, enjoying the hypocrisy, as

he could not when he found himself in a social situation with his target. Then, with their wives at their sides, Harry always felt somewhat guilty, as if he were attacking a personal friend. Only when he was in his office, with the testimony against David piled in front of him, did he know without doubt or hesitation that he had to prosecute this man who was as devious and dishonest as the most masterful Mafia kingpin, and more dangerous—because most of the time he could use money as a threat instead of menace.

"... Good, I'm glad to hear it. No. I mean it. I wouldn't want you to get sick on me just as I'm about to bring the case to a grand jury ..." Harry laughed. "What do you mean there won't be a case? David, I appreciate your power, believe me, but there's nothing that can stop me from going ahead with this. My staff has compiled some pretty airtight evidence that ... What did you say about Lilly Jane?" And then there was only silence for tick after tock after tick after tock of the mahogany-cased Seth Thomas clock on his desk.

It could have been three minutes later or ten minutes or a lifetime. Harry Litwin certainly found time the least of his concerns. But at some point during that conversation he agreed to drop the investigation against David Methany and destroy all evidence extant.

FIVE MONTHS LATER

If the scene were not so pathetic, it would be almost humorous, Harry thought, like something out of a bad period farce. There they were, the two of them, on the occasion of his wife's thirty-first birthday, and instead of a party with friends, they sat in cold, uneasy silence in the antique-filled dining room of their luxurious apartment, alone except for their maid who served them dinner, and the seven-month fetus growing in his wife's belly. A baby fathered by the man who was supposed to make his career and who had managed to completely destroy it.

"Harry, we have to talk."

He looked across the eight-foot expanse of table at his wife of ten years and wondered if he had fooled himself into believing she was a truly good person—and had been hiding a perverse and devious nature the entire time. It hardly mattered now, of course. He had to continue to live with her for a while. In addition to dropping the case against Methany, to leave Lilly Jane would stamp *true* to the rumors circulating among their set that David was the father of the baby she was carrying. Only she and his doctor knew about the vasectomy—unless, of course! She must have told Methany about it. That's when he knew the strength of his weapon. Oh, Lilly Jane, you foolish woman, how could you? With these exceptions, though, the baby was thought to be his, and he accepted the congratulations of his staff and colleagues as if he, too, believed the fiction. At the appropriate time, when no baby came home from the hospital with them, he would create some unfortunate tale. The pity it would engender might help bury the rumors as well as the confusion and curiosity about why he had dropped the Methany investigation.

"We can't go on like this," she began again. "We're like strangers, and it's killing me, Harry."

A sharp crackle of laughter pierced the wallpapered room and he noted with pleasure that his wife shivered with fright at the sudden intrusive sound. "I'm afraid that how you feel about anything these days matters little to me," he said, distressed by this newly discovered capacity of his to hurt another. "You certainly didn't give any consideration to my feelings when you slept with that man." He studied her pale face for a moment. "He was the only one, wasn't he, Lilly Jane?" In his voice was the old Harry, gentle and caring and just slightly, sweetly unsure of himself. He heard it in his ears and knew he must guard against it; the old Harry must be put to rest.

"Harry, I swear to you he was the only one. I told you that. I love *you.* I always have."

He shook his head. "Yet you are pregnant by another man."

"How many times do I have to explain this to you? I couldn't help myself. I don't know what came over me. If I could have stopped, I would have, but I couldn't. Oh, Harry, haven't you ever felt passionate, truly passionate about anything?" she cried.

He put down his utensils, placed his hands on either side of his dinner plate, and stared at her a moment or two, wondering how they had lived together so long and she could still ask him a question like that. Were husbands and wives forever doomed to remain strangers to each other?

"I was truly passionate about you, Lilly Jane," he finally spoke, "and I'm surprised and saddened that you never felt or understood that. I apologize deeply for not being the type of man who could properly express what I felt. I realize now that if I had been, you wouldn't have needed the likes of David Methany." He smiled sadly, no longer seeing her. "You know, it's funny. I was passionate about him, too, about the case I was gathering against him." He looked at her sharply again. "That's what makes this whole thing such a damn shame. A double whammy as they say."

"Oh, Harry, I'm so very sorry."

"I know you are, Lilly Jane, but there's one thing that still confuses me. You knew I would have to find out, so why didn't you get an abortion? All of what has happened could easily have been avoided if you had only had an abortion."

"Even though they're illegal?"

He briefly shut his eyes at her weak attempt at humor.

"I'm sorry," she quickly said. "I never considered an abortion, Harry. I thought that somehow you would understand or something. I don't know what I was thinking, I just knew I couldn't get rid of this baby. I explained that to you already, why do we have to go over it again?"

"You should have told me yourself instead of allowing me to find out from *him*. Do you have any idea what you have done to me, to my career? I'm a laughingstock, Lilly Jane. I don't even think the worst corporation would hire me as a counsel, let alone any reputable firm."

"I know, I know, you've said as much enumerable times. I see no point in going into it yet again."

"I see a point, because I still don't understand. Explain to me why you let it go on so long that it ruined a marriage and a career?"

"I've said time and again, I don't know why except I couldn't kill this baby!" she shouted.

"But if you wanted a baby so badly why didn't you discuss it with me? I could have had the operation reversed any time."

She sighed. "I didn't know I wanted a baby until I realized I was pregnant. How many times do I have to repeat this?"

"Until I understand how your mind works."

"It's very simple, Harry. David Methany excited me. Oh, please, don't look at me as if I've stabbed you. It had nothing to do with us, with how I feel about you, it really didn't. I love you more than anything on earth. I know that's hard to believe under the circumstances, but it's true. With David I was caught up in some crazy spell, and at first the fact that I was carrying his baby became a sign to me, as if we belonged together. Of course he wanted me to get rid of it from the beginning and I should have listened to him, but I never thought he'd hurt *you,* because I never thought he was really capable of such treachery against *me.* I thought, I guess, that he cared for me. Now I realize that I was nothing but another body, and far more important than that, a way to get you. Oh, but Harry, please, don't let what I've done ruin what we've had together, what we can have again."

"I don't know what we can have anymore, Lilly Jane," he said in a thick whisper.

"If we keep the baby we'll have something to build with."

"No. We've talked about this before and I haven't changed my mind," he said without hesitation. "I know how much this baby means to you, but there is no way while I have a breath left in my body that I will raise it and care for it. You ask far too much when you ask me to raise the baby fathered by the man who has ruined me."

"But Harry, you can—"

"No, Lilly Jane, and not another word on the subject. You know my old law school friend, Edward Whittington. He's a good man, a fine lawyer, and completely trustworthy. He'll be in town from Chicago this week, and you can reassure yourself personally about your baby's adoptive parents. I'm sure he's found very good people."

"If you'd only—"

"Stop right now. If there is any remote possibility of you and me trying to have a life together without constant recriminations, that baby cannot be part of it."

SIX MONTHS LATER

David Methany sat at his desk, his chair swiveled to face the New York City skyline. For once, he derived no pleasure from the sight. What he had to do robbed him of all positive feeling.

He did not like to hurt people. Even when the cause was just, he did not like to hurt people. In the past, and he imagined that it would happen again in the future, he had had to hire certain rough types to turn a situation his way. There had been at least three occasions when he had used a certain well-muscled enforcer to convince different union heads that their demands were out of line. Only once had the man been forced to actually inflict pain; the other times the mere sight of him and knowledge of his reputation had been enough to make the difficult behave.

Then there had been the time when a particularly greedy former lover had wanted a payoff for her services. Her husband was on the zoning board for an area where David had been planning to build a new high-rise, and one vote in either direction could make a difference. He would not tolerate being placed in such a vulnerable position, and so an unfortunate horseback-riding accident in Central Park during which the former lover took a nasty spill frightened her sufficiently to get her to stop her extortionary attempts. She had been smart enough to realize that the girth straps had been tampered with, and she had no doubt by whom, or at least by whose instructions.

Once, two other builders who were bidding for the same job—a condo development in Stamford, Connecticut—came in with lower bids than he did. This was early in his career, and he had not built as wide a network of "aides" as he had now. He knew he could not lower his own bid because he was not as big as his competitors and did not have the same resources. He also knew that he had to get this job. It was a key project in a key location, and the commercial opportunities at street level could mean incredible lease revenues.

Oddly enough, it was his soon-to-be wife who provided him with the connection that would prove helpful so many times in his career. Isabel's father owned a restaurant in Sag Harbor and operated it during the summer season; the rest of the time he taught business classes at Southampton College, but from Memorial Day to Labor Day he hobnobbed with the rich and famous who had made his chef famous and his unpretentious café a place to be seen.

One evening David had been complaining to Isabel about the problem he was having with these two competitors when she told him about this customer of her father's who ate at the restaurant three nights a week—he only came out to the Hamptons during the week, never on the weekends when the rest of the world was there. The customer turned out to be a highly respected detective who had been with the Queens police force and then went to work as an investigator for the Nassau County district attorney. What information he couldn't get on someone wasn't available to be had. David had been singularly impressed by his fiancée's understanding of his needs and her acceptance of his methods. Vernon Marks had become probably the most valuable member of his entire staff. Thanks to him, David was able to get the kind of information on his two competitors that he got on Alex Tannen, information that forced them to remove themselves from the condo project. Harry Litwin, no doubt, would call this extortion, but David paid Marks a monthly retainer as his research associate, as innocent and legal a job as being his secretary.

This time, though, he could call on no one to help him. The job that lay ahead had to be done by him and him alone. He had had moments these past few weeks when he had thought there would be little danger in letting her go through with the pregnancy; after all, he had already achieved his major goal by getting Litwin to drop the case. But then common sense would take over, and he knew that Lilly Jane and the unborn child posed too great a risk. He could not leave anything to chance, certainly not the possibility that one day, drunk or depressed or for no reason except something to talk about, Lilly Jane could tell someone that David Methany had fathered a bastard by her. Or she could tell the child herself, and most dangerous of all, the child could use the information to hurt or weaken David. He couldn't allow that kind of exposure, especially if he had children with Isabel. Sad as it was, Lilly Jane and her unborn child had to be silenced, permanently. There could be no loose ends, nothing to put his future and the future of his legitimate children in jeopardy. And because David Methany was a careful man, this time he prepared to get his own hands dirty.

SIX-AND-A-HALF MONTHS LATER

Lilly Jane stood looking out the window of the suite at the Rowland Court Hotel. There was the lovely English garden, in full bloom now, a blaze of color and beauty hidden from the eyes of most New Yorkers.

This would be the last time she would ever see Suite 23 at the Rowland Court with David Methany. She was surprised to be here now, but when he called yesterday and suggested that they meet once more, for old times' sake, as a belated celebration for her birthday, and to part as friends, she had not hesitated to accept.

In a way, she was embarrassed for David to see her like this, eight-and-a-half months pregnant and ripe as a melon. Everything about her was full and heavy, but soon she would be giving up this child she was carrying, and her beauty and slenderness would return—only she didn't want that nearly as much as she wanted to keep the baby. Still, as her husband had sacrificed the most important case of his career, so she too would sacrifice what meant a lot to her.

She heard his key in the door, waited for him in the bedroom. She had not been out socially for several months, for Harry's sake. So when she slowly faced David now, she was not prepared for the deep shock to her system the sight of him caused. She had thought, had convinced herself to believe, that his actions against her husband had been an effective douse to her passion. She had been wrong.

She wanted him as she always had. She drank in the sight of the raven hair and square chin and chiseled cheekbones, did not mind the harshness in the thin, wide mouth or dark eyes. She admitted his uncompromising selfishness, despaired of what he had cost her and her husband. Yet she felt the blood rush to her head and heard the pounding of her heart and sensed the weakness in her thighs and the throbbing in her nipples. She was eight-and-a-half months pregnant and she was in a room alone with the man who had made her that way, the man who had made a fool of her husband; despite it all, she longed to be held and stroked and moistened by this man. Never before as at that moment did she loathe being a woman.

"David," she whispered, stepping toward him.

"You're looking radiant," he told her, meeting her in the middle of the room and grasping her hands in his. He leaned over and kissed her on the cheek.

"How chaste," she teased.

His smile was skimpy. "I've ordered room service, champagne and raspberries, your favorites."

"Sex with you was my favorite," she said, glancing down at her stomach.

"I've missed you."

"Have you really?" She wanted to believe, wanted there to be just a small measure of reciprocity to her feelings.

"You're a remarkably sensual and exciting woman, Lilly Jane. I can't wait for you to be back to the way I remember you."

"No, David, I don't think that's possible. I've got to stick by Harry. After what you did to him—"

"Me?" There was almost unbelievable shock in his voice. "I didn't do anything, Lilly Jane. I told you, I made it crystal-clear to you that day right here in this very room. I told you that if you didn't act, I would. Well, for whatever reason, you ignored me. You're responsible for what happened to Harry, not me."

"You're such an incredible bastard," she said, shaking her head, not really angry.

"Why didn't you get rid of it, Lilly Jane?" he asked gently.

She sat down on the edge of the bed. "I'm not really sure. I thought at first you would leave Isabel, as I told you. I wanted you to. Then I thought Harry would be happy about it. By the time I figured out that the only person who wanted the baby was me, it was too late to do anything but have it. Talk about your stupid broad," she said, laughing at herself.

"A poor decision," David agreed. "I wish it could have—" The knock on the door by the room service waiter interrupted whatever David was about to say, and he was grateful to avoid an additional platitude. He went out to the living room, returning moments later with a small bowl of raspberries topped with powdered sugar, and two flutes of champagne.

Lilly Jane placed the fruit on the bed and took her champagne while David settled himself next to her. He lifted his glass in a toast. "To your health, Lilly Jane."

"And to lovers, former and future," she responded, smiling as she clinked his glass. She drained the champagne. "I'm not supposed to be drinking, but this is a special occasion and this is a delicious champagne. More, please. In fact, why don't you bring in the bottle?"

"No. I like doing something for you," David said as he went back to the sitting room. Into her glass, he poured more Roederer Cristal as well as more of the liquid Valium from the vial in his jacket pocket. He let three, four, six drops of the colorless liquid into the bubbly wine, twisted his wrist gently around the flute stem so the Valium would mix in well.

David was not sure how much Valium it would take to kill her. He had come upon it as a solution to the Lilly Jane issue after a discussion with Isabel about a friend of hers who had started taking the liquid tranquilizer because she had developed an immunity to the pills. Ironic that it should be his wife who gave him the method for murder. Getting a prescription for it had been simple: his dentist was an old college chum whose entire practice was built on David's referrals. An explanation about Isabel's nerves and not wanting to go to her own doctor, a white-haired Park Avenue asshole, had convinced his old pal to write the prescription. David loved having people in his debt; it made business so much like pleasure.

By the third glass of champagne and the twentieth drop of liquid Valium, Lilly Jane was grimacing, holding her distended belly.

"David?"

"What is it, honey?"

"I don't feel too well, David. I think you better get me into a cab."

"Oh, Lilly Jane, so soon? We've just gotten here. We may never have another chance like this, darling."

"I know, David, but I really don't—" And then she bent over, holding her stomach and moaning. When she looked up, David was standing in the doorway between the bedroom and the sitting room, hands folded across his chest, impassively observing her pain.

"David—" she managed, eyes closing.

"I'm sorry, darling, I really am, but I told you to get rid of it. You wouldn't listen."

"What have you done? Oh, good lord, what have you done?"

"If it's any consolation, darling, you were one hell of a great lay." And with that, he turned his back on her as she began to tremble and shake, fighting to stay conscious. On the room-service tray, in plain view next to the almost empty bottle of champagne, he placed the amber vial of liquid Valium, it too almost empty. The shame of the illegitimate pregnancy, her husband's disgrace—good motivations for suicide.

He walked back to the doorway to check on her progress; he would not want to leave prematurely.

Confusion and pain made her eyes glassy, the blue unnaturally bright against the white. She reached out one hand to him. "David, please, help me," and then she closed her eyes, her head went back, and she slid off the edge of the bed onto the carpeted floor, her head lolling to one side, her swollen belly obscuring the rest of her.

"You have no one to blame but yourself," he said to her unconscious form. "Good-bye, you little fool."

And then David Methany, lover of the woman, father of the unborn child, murderer of both, calmly and confidently walked out of the hotel room and into his future.

9

Beth sat at her desk, eyes scanning the neatly arranged stacks of telephone message slips, correspondence needing her signature, two computer printouts of monies received during the past month, finally resting on a memo from George Bardy, her chief financial officer. The memo was a reminder that in sixty days the corporation had to make $6.5 million in bank loan payments—and the corporation did not have $6.5 million that was not tied up either in new construction or other, older bank debts.

Where in the world was she going to get the money when the flat real estate market was creating vacancies and tenants knew they could negotiate for the best possible terms? Everything else seemed to be against her as well, she thought, immobilized this morning, as she was too often lately, by the enormity of her responsibilities. She tried to imagine what her father would have done under similar circumstances, when financial pressures pushed aside creativity and leadership. Her father, she knew, would not have allowed the situation to get so out of control. It was now June and not only had she still not adapted to being president of the Methany Corporation, she was more aware than ever that her gender, youth, and inexperience all combined to make her easy prey for old enemies of her father whose grudge match would be against the daughter.

There was the lawsuit by the doormen's union, who claimed David Methany had made an unholy alliance with their recently dead union leader for a lower-than-standard hourly rate in exchange for assignment to a new luxury building of his, where the tenants' tips were practically guaranteed to be extravagant. This was really a nuisance suit, she knew, more a way of testing her mettle, because there was no way anyone, not even the mighty Methany, could guarantee anything as personal as tips, and there was no union leader dumb enough to believe he could. If the union leader made some arrangement with David, the payoff was personal, of that Beth was sure.

There was also another nuisance suit, this one from a former Methany bookkeeper, who claimed David had fired her because of her continuing obesity after giving birth to her fourth child. Since everyone Beth had spoken to had told her the woman had been overweight for the eight years and all four children she had had while working at Methany, Beth was not too concerned about the outcome of this case. The question would be more one of whether she should pay her something just to go away or fight for the principles involved. She would let Gene Cavelli guide her decision on this one.

And then there was Zev Milman's petty blackmail scheme. She had just about resolved how to handle it. Milman was a fifty-three-year-old, midlevel numbers-cruncher who managed the books for what had been David's latest diversion: backing Broadway plays. With his uncanny eye for knowing what people wanted, he had made another fortune or two as an angel for some big winners, but the past two years had not been quite as successful. Milman explained all this to Beth, with the dried lips and prison pallor of the born loser, the kind of overcooked-pasta coloring that led people to ignore and dismiss anything he had to say. But Beth couldn't do that, not when he went on to speak of tax shelters and loss carryovers, and a few other variations on one theme: the IRS. So by giving him a hike in pay to $43,000 after ten years' employment and a three-year-old Ford Taurus, Beth was sure the gnat would fly off her back. The last thing she needed right now were her father's personal tax problems.

The banks were the biggest headache. With the declining value of the dollar, Methany's foreign lenders were concerned about their investments. The domestic banks, having their own problems these days, were watching the corporation's fortunes closely. Beth knew that renegotiation of the loans at a higher interest rate would be impossible, yet the market was such that she didn't know what alternatives she had, short of default. The thought of banks being Methany partners instead of lenders made her cringe.

She did not know which issues to tackle first. She had her lawyers and her labor experts and her financial wizards, but ultimately, everything came to rest in this office, on her shoulders, as it once had with her father. And each of these problems was nothing compared to the matter of the tax abatement for Methany City North, the Bronx renewal project. If she lost the abatement, which Ben Wyler was making his mission and which would be voted on in three weeks, without a question she would have to renegotiate her loans at no doubt prime plus one, or see them called. The shortfall that would result in other Methany operations that needed the infusion of capital would be disastrous. Businessmen and competitors, New York's social set and the gossip columnists, all would comment wryly at how far the apple had fallen from the tree. They would not demean themselves by even mentioning her being a woman; no, it would simply be a matter of regret that her father's genius had been inherited by one so unworthy.

No matter what it took, Beth vowed, she would not let her father's name be sullied by her own ineptitude. She had to fight back. But too much depended on the tax abatement. With it, she could borrow from other banks to pay off the $6.5 million, and at a favorable rate of interest because the Methany magic would seem strong. With it, she could even float a bond. Without it, she didn't know what she would do.

For the first time that morning, she smiled, a slight, tight movement, but it felt good, hopeful. She had made today's lunch date with Ben Wyler over two weeks ago, just to touch base with each other since their schedules had not seemed to coincide. Perfect timing, she thought; just perfect.

It was a glorious afternoon, the kind of day New Yorkers loved to brag about to Southern Californians. No clouds, no humidity, not even any meanness in the air. Beth and Ben were at the Boathouse restaurant in Central Park, which was one of her favorites. The food was less than mediocre, but she loved the atmosphere. The restaurant and its dining patio abutted Central Park's lake where lovers young and old took out boats, able for a few hours to pretend that the lake was clean and the concrete canyons were sky-kissing mountains and their romance would last. Beth wished she, too, could escape reality for a few hours, but not today; today all sociability was weighted down by the burden of her business responsibilities.

As Ben chatted about certain mutual friends, a play he had recently seen with his mother and stepfather that he didn't recommend, Beth sat, impatiently polite. She wished that she could see Ben as she once had, a lovely, intelligent, ambitious man whose company she enjoyed. He was good-looking in a thin, almost ascetic way that disguised a powerful sexuality. It was that, and the fact that when he wasn't disparaging her father, she genuinely liked him, that drew her to him. But that had been before his determined stand against her father's dream loomed so successful. For months now, but with accelerated passion the past few weeks, he had been using the press to attack Methany City North as nothing but a rich man's scheme to get richer at the public's, the *poor* public's, expense. And the polls were showing his increasing popularity as a mayoral candidate, the result of this "public conscience" position. Beth knew that this was no political act with Ben but a sincere belief that the Methanys of the world did nothing good for anyone that wasn't going to be better for themselves. While she admired his rectitude as a strength in a would-be mayor, it was only serving to alienate her from him as a man, and especially as a lover. His rigid self-righteousness was blinding him to how much benefit could be reaped by so many from her father's vision. She *had* to convince him of this.

"We have to talk about Methany City North, Ben," she stated, unwilling to wait any longer.

"Beth, can't we just have a purely social conversation? We haven't seen each other in a while and—"

"Not today, I'm afraid. Too much is at stake. Ben, you've got to get off your soapbox against my father. You're hurting my chances of getting the tax abatement and—"

"Exactly my purpose."

She glared at him. "You're wrong, Ben, all wrong. Methany City North can do a world of good. Why won't you stop!"

"It's out of the question, don't waste your breath," he said, a cold hardness in his eyes, his voice.

"Why are you doing this to me?"

"This has nothing to do with you. Why do you refuse to understand that?"

"I can't turn off the personal and professional the way you can," she told him. "I'm asking you to please back off so the abatement can go through, and you're telling me you won't. Not that you can't but that you won't. To me, that's personal."

He shook his head. "You're wrong. What I don't like and

approve of are your father's methods for rehabilitation of an area like the South Bronx. That has nothing to do with how I feel about you."

"Don't you understand that when you attack him you attack me? Or did you think that what we shared in bed gave you some special license to go against my father with immunity from me?"

"What we've shared in bed has been good enough to warrant a special license, wouldn't you say?" he asked, grinning.

Reluctantly, she returned the smile. "I suppose," she conceded.

"Good, then that's that," Ben said. "Now eat up and let's spend the rest of the afternoon in bed, together, making wild passionate love that has nothing to do with real estate or tax abatements or elections or anything but plain, old-fashioned, healthy lust."

"I'm sorry, Ben, I really am," Beth said, shaking her head.

A pink flush of anger colored his cheeks. "Then why did you agree to have lunch with me today?" he asked.

"At first because I wanted to see you, *you,* a man I care about. But now it's because I need your help, the help of a councilman who can hurt me professionally. I can't afford to lose this abatement, Ben. Without it, I'm ruined."

His laugh was riddled with scorn. "Ruined, you, a Methany? Don't be absurd."

"I'm serious, Ben. Without that tax abatement, my father's project will never see the light of day, and a lot of other—"

"Without that abatement," he cut her off, "a lot of people won't have to find a new place to live. Without that abatement, you'll have to pay back some of your bank loans like any ordinary borrower or risk having your properties owned by the bank. And without that abatement," he was speaking softly, calmly, the arguments long ago thought out and valid to his ears, "you'll be forced to continue your overpriced luxury co-ops, gouging the Japanese, Germans, and South American drug dealers who don't need the cash and certainly don't want it in American dollars."

He leaned forward, his green-gray eyes alive with conviction. "No, Beth, with the tax abatement, part of what I hope will soon be my constituency will forfeit whatever poor hovel they call home and be left with nowhere, do you hear me, *nowhere* to go because your father so effectively destroyed the real estate market in this city. It's because of him that there's no decent rental market for the poor and middle classes. Those people in the Bronx don't want city housing; they want to pay what they can afford. Whatever you'll hand out won't be enough for them to go anywhere but homeless. I'm sorry, Beth, because I'm genuinely fond of you and I thought we had a good thing together, but this has become more than a political issue. I really hate what your father stood for and how he did his business. I'm going to fight Methany City North with all the ammunition I've got, because it's wrong and because the man behind it was a grade-A bastard."

Across the table, Beth sat mesmerized by the strength of this man's hatred toward her father. How little she had really known him. Made love with him several times a month; went to parties and ski weekends and even a vacation in Mexico together, and yet, she had never seen how deep his loathing for David ran. In the past, she had dismissed his negative remarks as the words of a bleeding-heart liberal politician testing out his rhetoric. She could not believe that he would be capable of making love to the daughter of a man he hated. There was something too dishonest, too shallow, about that, and yet, he had done exactly that. As a result, she foolishly had believed that she could convince him, because of their personal relationship, to back off. But the tax abatement issue was just the first way he was going after her father and all he represented. She knew she had no friend in Ben Wyler, perhaps never had.

"You're a coward, Ben. A weak political coward."

"Beth!"

"I don't remember hearing you talk like this to me or to the press when my father was alive. And running for office has nothing to do with it. If he were here now, you'd never have the balls to speak out against him this way, you'd find something else to use as a political platform. No, he's the perfect target because *he's* dead and *I'm* a woman and your lover so I can't fight back. Well, I'm sorry, Ben, but this Methany has been fucked by you for the very last time!"

Her heartbeat was a jackhammer and she could feel heat burning her cheeks, but she forced herself to calmly fold her cloth napkin over her untouched salad, and slowly, smoothly ease back her chair and stand.

"There's no reason for this," he immediately objected. "We should be able to—"

"You didn't really think I'd sit across a table from you after what you said, did you? My loyalty is to one man and one man only. And if I'm ever lucky enough to meet someone as kind and generous and supportive as my father was to me, then he can have my loyalty too. Sadly, you are not that man." She swung her purse strap over her shoulder. "You know, Ben, if you were as talented as you are small-minded and jealous, you might make a damned good politician. As it is, though, your pettiness and phoniness will probably get you elected, and then you can be no better than you have to be and as bad as you'll know how to be."

"Beth, I—"

She had already turned her back and started to walk away, so whatever remonstrance he was making fell into the Central Park lake with the rest of the muck.

When Beth returned to the office that afternoon, there was one meeting after another, and it was not until seven o'clock that she found herself alone with time to think of what had happened earlier at lunch. But she was so preoccupied with the assorted problems of the day that only when she came across an invitation to a private black-tie showing at the Whitney Museum did the loss of Ben really hit her. She knew she could always find someone to escort her to the various business functions that made up her social life, but with Ben, she had been able to have fun while performing her duties. Now, there would be no relief from the loneliness.

Loneliness. She leaned back in her desk chair and momentarily shut her eyes against the stark vision that word created in her mind, and worse, the shock she felt in using the word to describe herself. She well knew that it was a situation for which she was solely responsible. She alone had caused the dissolution of her marriage, never having time for her husband, never having interest in doing fun, frivolous, *young* things. For her, it was her father, the business, and occasionally, rarely, her pottery. The business made her happy; working for and with her father made her happy. Her husband had made her happy, too, but not happy enough, a difference he carefully pointed out to her the morning he left.

In the three years since the divorce and the year prior when they had been separated, Beth had not once felt that a social life based on business obligations was unusual or that not having a regular boyfriend left a void. Not even the lack of sex mattered much. What she experienced each day at the office was more exhilarating than any quick coupling. And then when she met Ben at a fund-raiser, she thought life could not get any better for her.

Now he was gone too. She was left with no one, not her father, not Ben, not even a close girlfriend to whom she could turn. And it was that, she realized, far more than not having Ben, that sharpened the sense of loneliness for her. The tidy, insular, and seemingly perfect world that had existed between her father and her had obviated the need for others, even for friendships. Beth was intelligent enough to be aware that this was neither right nor healthy; that to have so many needs and desires satisfied by one's father was somehow not "normal," and yet, she truly had never felt compelled to seek out the company of others. David had fulfilled so many of her human needs that she had been able to subjugate her female needs. The result was that now, for the first time in her thirty-two years, she felt unbearably alone.

With an effort, she straightened and went back to the stack of mail, telling herself that even without a boyfriend and no prospect for one, without a female confidante who might help her get out of herself, she still had a company to run and salaries to pay and problems to solve.

She sorted through the various correspondence until there were only two postcards left. One was an announcement from Bergdorf's about their fur storage; the other was a picture post-card of Queen Street in Toronto.

Frowning with curiosity, she turned over the glossy card. There was nothing on the other side.

Nothing.

Except the initial J.

And so it began again.

10

"Good evening, Miranda."

"Good evening, Miss Beth. You look exhausted."

Beth nodded wearily at the Nicaraguan housekeeper who had been with her parents since their marriage. She was more a member of her family than the legions of uncles and aunts and cousins who came out of the woodwork periodically, looking for a handout and claiming Isabel or David had been their "favorite."

"I am, Miranda. I'm absolutely pooped. I think I'll enjoy this rare night at home by just having a hot bath and going straight to bed."

"You are not going to bed without dinner. That's a sure way to get yourself sick and ugly. You'll be so skinny you'll pass through the air."

Beth laughed. "Okay, first a bath, then how about soup and a grilled-cheese sandwich?"

"How about chicken salad, a glass of wine, and fresh melon and berries for dessert? Plus some homemade brown bread."

"You didn't have me until the bread. You know I can't resist that."

"That's what I was counting on." Miranda turned to go into the kitchen, then stopped. "I'll bring everything to your room if you want."

"No, that's all right. I'll eat in the breakfast room, though, not at the dining table. It's too big and lonely for just one."

After a bath and changing into a favorite pair of sweatpants and a Columbia University T-shirt, a decrepit but beloved relic of her ex-husband's alma mater, Beth picked up the day's mail from the foyer table where Miranda always left it, and went in for dinner.

"If you don't need anything more, Miss Beth, I think I'll go on in to my room. Geraldo's on and I hate to miss him."

Beth smiled. "Of course, Miranda, go ahead. I'm just fine."

When Beth was alone, she did not immediately start eating, nor did she immediately sort through the day's mail. From the moment she had seen that picture postcard from Canada, an hour and a half ago, she had not been able to think of anything but J. Who was this person and why was she doing this? After all, it had been David who had known her, David with whom she had had a relationship. An uneasiness had come over Beth when she had held that card in her hands, an unexplainable yet unshakable feeling that the card, with its postmark of only four days ago, had been sent to deliberately unnerve her. But why? To what purpose?

She would wait until tomorrow and then speak to both Fred and Gene again about this. They had to know something, something that they were uncomfortable discussing with her. Well, she knew her father hadn't been faithful to her mother, if that's what was bothering them. She had to find out about J. and put a stop to this nonsense before it got out of hand.

As she went through her mail, however, she quickly realized that the situation had already progressed beyond her control. There in the pile of catalogues and bills and invitations was an envelope with a two-day-old New York postmark. There was no return address. In the envelope was a folded sheet of matching dove gray vellum. On it was typed:

Dear Beth,
The fun begins.
J.

The initial was handwritten. The loops were large, the stroke strong, emphatic, and disturbingly familiar.

Beth placed the letter facedown on the table, looking at it with distaste as if it were some arcane voodoo curse. Her stomach became a hard knot of nervousness, and she pushed away the plate of chicken salad that had suddenly become nauseating to her. This was unbelievable. What was happening? Who was J. and why, above all, *why* was *she* being haunted by this person? First the card, then the letter with its threat of more to come.

And it was a threat, of that Beth had no doubt. If there were anything innocent and friendly about the note, then J. would not have to hide herself. And why did she keep referring to the sender as a female? She had no knowledge of that, just conjecture. For all she knew, J. could be a man, some business associate of her father's, some displeased competitor who, not satisfied with David's death, was out to hurt his daughter. It was all too ridiculous; David's so-called enemies sought power and money, not frightening a thirty-two-year-old woman.

Think rationally, she told herself. Who in her past, who now, had a name beginning with the letter *J?* She thought and thought and came up totally empty. Not a first name, not a last name; no one. Besides, whoever this person was knew her father. That's what made the whole thing so odd and so scary. Her father had been dead four months now; if J. had not known that, correspondence would have been coming during that time, but there had been nothing for four months, until today. Not only that, but the message in the letter was clearly directed at Beth, not David. That meant that J. knew *her.* And what did she mean by "The fun begins"? It sounded so damn menacing.

She picked up the dove gray vellum sheet and read the note again, as if in the few words would be some clue, some revealing point of identification. Her eyes lingered on the inked J., a strong, heavy signature, the loops wide, the hand steady. There was something oddly, vaguely familiar about the signature that struck Beth almost as ridiculous and frightening as the letter itself. She did not know anyone with that initial. So why in the world did the signature look familiar?

There was no way she could wait until morning to discuss this with Fred and Gene; she had to speak with them now.

The next fifteen minutes brought no satisfaction. Neither attorney could enlighten her one whit. Gene repeated what history he knew about David and Lilly Jane Litwin, and Fred was as useful as a dead car battery. But the conversations had served her well, she realized. The uneasiness had given way to a slow, simmering anger. She was not angry because of this intrusion into her life, but because she had to wait for the next installment. It was the passivity that riled her, putting her in a position that was alien and unwanted: needing someone else to act first before she could take a step. Without a return address, without a single clue as to J.'s identity, Beth had no choice but to wait for the next message. Maybe that one would give her some idea of why and who.

The ribbon of anger restored her appetite as if she knew she had to keep up her strength for the mysterious J. But when she was finished eating, she again was alone, with the letter and the card that she had taken home with her, and the breakup with Ben and the abatement problem. She did not feel self-pity, because that was not in her nature, but it was as if a scratchy, heavy, smothering blanket of sadness had been wrapped around her. She needed to talk to someone; more, she needed to laugh with someone.

She got up from the table and went into the small pottery

studio that usually was a source of solace for her. She sat down at the potter's wheel, but the familiar delight she experienced by squeezing and kneading the cool, moist clay was missing tonight.

She cleaned up and headed for her bedroom, her mind active, her body exhausted. She was about to get under the comforter when the telephone rang, the sound jarring her sensitive nerves.

"Hello?" she said into the night table phone. She glanced at the enamel Tiffany clock: almost ten.

"Miss Methany?"

"Yes, this is Beth Methany. Who is this?"

"I'm sorry to be bothering you this late at night, but it's Alyson Gentry, Miss Methany, and I'm afraid I've got—"

"Please call me Beth. Is there some problem that couldn't have waited until morning?" Beth was curious. She had very little to do with Alyson Gentry and knew very little about her. She was a real estate lawyer who reported to Gene and who had been with the company about three or four years. She recalled her father and Gene once discussing her, favorably commenting on her total professionalism. They had seemed impressed with her ability to maintain a pleasant, cordial, collegial relationship with people at the office without anyone knowing a single personal fact about her except that she was about thirty-three or thirty-four and single, jogged every day, and ran regularly in marathons. Beth had never had a private conversation with her since she dealt exclusively with Gene, which made this telephone call so peculiar. Whatever the problem was, why hadn't he mentioned it when Beth phoned him earlier?

"I'm afraid there is a problem that couldn't wait," Alyson was saying now. "I called Gene about it, and he suggested I speak with you directly because I've been more on top of this situation."

So much for why Gene had said nothing, Beth thought; he might not even have known about the problem earlier. "And what exactly is this situation?" she asked.

"It's that building of ours over on Central Park West, Methany Palace, or so it'll be called someday." The attorney then refreshed Beth's memory about the former residential hotel that David had bought several years ago with the plan to gut and renovate it and turn it into an extremely high-scale luxury co-op, ripping down walls to make sprawling, costly apartments.

"Alyson, I still don't understand what couldn't have waited until tomorrow," Beth said. "This problem has been with us for a while. What's happened that's different?"

"The residents—most of whom, you'll remember, are young at sixty-five—are marching, with pickets, up and down Central Park West as if this were 1970 and they were antiwar revolutionaries. Every newspaper and television crew is out there," Alyson told her. "The publicity is nothing short of disastrous, especially—"

"Especially with Methany City North pending," Beth supplied for her, grimacing as the enormity of the situation hit her. Any negative publicity about ousting long-term and elderly residents who had no place else to go would just fuel Ben Wyler's fire against the tax abatement. Beth had to put a stop to this, and Alyson Gentry was right, it had to be done tonight.

"They've been so quiet lately," she mused out loud. "I wonder what started them going again?"

"Ben Wyler."

"What did you say?"

"I'm sorry, Beth, I know you and he—"

"Never mind about that," she cut her off abruptly. "Just tell me what's going on and how Ben's involved."

"He's leading them. He's at the head of the marchers carrying a placard that says 'Methany the Heartless Makes Us All Homeless.' It's really pretty awful."

"It's ridiculous is what it is," Beth snapped. "And you say the networks and newspapers are there?"

"That's why I called. I wouldn't have known anything about it myself, but I live right off Central Park West in the Seventies, and I was walking home when I saw the marchers, the TV crews, what have you. I'm sure the eleven o'clock news will cover this and I wanted to prepare you. They'll no doubt call you for a comment."

"Great, just what I need now. Look, Alyson, thanks for the advance warning. Let's discuss what we're going to do about this whole thing tomorrow. Right now, I better figure out what to say to the piranhas from the press." And although there was a thin humor in her voice, Beth felt only dread at the adverse publicity, and outrage at Ben, who had to have known about tonight when he was with her earlier, trying to seduce her back into his bed.

"Beth, I'm sorry about this."

"No, don't be. I'm grateful in a way. I knew Ben was determined to kill Methany City North. I didn't know he wanted to destroy all the other projects my father had planned, too. I guess love does not conquer all," she added on an acid laugh.

There was silence from Alyson, and Beth imagined the other woman shaking her head in commiseration. Then: "Good night, Beth. And good luck."

No sooner did Beth hang up than the phone rang—and rang for the next forty-five minutes. To television and newspaper reporters alike, she made the same comment: "For Councilman Ben Wyler to get elderly people out of their beds for the sake of politics is a tactic beneath contempt. The Methany Corporation has always believed in the people first, and while there have been disagreements in the past over the usage of this particular residence, neither the tenants nor this company have ever seen the necessity to go to the streets to fight a battle. Mr. Wyler is using these people for his own motives, motives that have nothing to do with keeping a roof over their heads. Perhaps I and others who believe in the generosity of what my father had planned for people currently residing in buildings he had earmarked for change would do better to march and bring our side to the media. That way we can have a regular circus instead of the sideshow Councilman Wyler has created. Thank you, no further comment."

She heard herself on television, accompanied by an old photograph, since she had refused to let anyone come to the apartment. The next morning she again heard herself on the news and read about herself in the morning papers. When she got to her office, there were six messages from Ben; before she had left the apartment, he had left two messages on the answering machine, and that did not count the three from the night before, after the telecasts. She knew she would have to speak to him at some point, but right now she was savoring every second of her triumph in his foolish little game of one-upmanship.

"Yes, Karen?" she said into her intercom. "Oh, all right, put him through. I might as well get this over with."

"Ben."

"Hello, Beth. Thanks for finally taking my call."

"You're too persistent to ignore for long."

"I think that's a left-handed compliment, but I'm not sure."

"Ben, get to the point, please, I'm busy. As I'm sure you must be, too—another rally to lead, perhaps? Or is that only for your evenings?"

"You know, this is a side of you I wasn't aware of. I kind of like it."

"Ben—"

"Okay, okay. I've been calling for a couple of reasons, Beth. The first was to congratulate you for handling an explosive situation so well that you've effectively silenced me—for a while, that is. You got the media looking at me as someone manipulating old people instead of trying to rescue them. Worthy of your father, Beth."

She was grinning now. "Well, thank you, Ben. Maybe you'll take heed now and lay off the tax abatement."

"Not a chance."

"You said there were a few reasons you've been calling," she prompted, instantly serious again.

"Right. Well, you're not going to like this, but one reason was to tell you that you're being unbelievably naive. That remark you made about not going to the streets. Beth, you did know, you *had* to have known, that when your father first bought the Feldon Manor Hotel and the tenants wouldn't move, there were several incidents of strange fires, elevators breaking down, other mishaps that were unusual in type and frequency."

"I know about that, but so what?"

"So what! Your father was behind them. They were his way of so-called 'encouraging' the people to get out."

"That's disgusting! How dare you? How *dare* you!"

"It's the truth, damn it!"

"You don't know that. You don't know one damn thing. If you did, you would have used it already. Ben, stop blowing smoke, it's beneath you. Admit when you're licked, you'll be a better man for it."

"You're right, Beth, I don't have the kind of proof I can take into court, but I don't need that because I'm not planning to sue anybody. I'm just going to stop your father's brand of highway robbery once and for all, and if you're a victim, well, I'm sorry—but in a way, you are already, just by being his daughter."

"You don't stop, do you? Good-bye, Ben. See you on television."

After she hung up, she sat considering his words, especially what he had said about the incidence of mishaps. For years she had heard rumors that her father would go to any length to get a contract or finish a project on time. She had frequently heard her parents arguing, her mother accusing David of an arrogance that led him to believe he was above ordinary constraints, he coming right back at her by waving a huge wad of cash and reminding her that she never complained how he got the money just as long as he got it. And she remembered once there had been a cover story on her father in the Sunday *Times*. She had been only about fourteen at the time, and so proud of how handsome her father looked that the article was all but forgotten, but her mother had spoken to her afterward about not believing everything you read, and how the article said some nasty things about how ruthless her father was that weren't true and she mustn't believe them.

Thinking back now, Beth realized that that must have been one of the few times Isabel had ever stood up for her husband. Then, as now, though, Beth gave little credence to whatever whispers and rumors were spread about her father. Jealousy was as much a part of success as instant credit and charity requests.

She pressed the intercom. "Ask Alyson Gentry to come in, please, Karen."

A few moments later the real estate lawyer was sitting across from Beth. She had been trying to recall what Alyson looked like, but her memory had come up empty. Now she remembered seeing the exceptionally attractive, well-groomed woman who wore Armani suits and a sleek, Sassoon-style haircut in a few meetings with Gene.

"I just wanted to say thank you for last night," she began, smiling. "I'm sorry you got stuck with this mess."

"Oh, no, it's great. Usually I'm preparing contracts or I'm in court arguing minor labor disputes for Gene. The Central Park West issue is the kind of thing that got me interested in working for the Methany Corporation in the first place."

"Oh?"

Alyson nodded. "The beauty of law, at least for me, is in its interpretation. Your father understood that instinctively. His way of reading the law was extraordinarily clever—he knew just how far he could go to get what he wanted. That's what I enjoy, too, though I haven't had much chance to do that."

Beth smiled appropriately, but the young lawyer's words, coming so soon after what Ben had said about David's methods, struck her as unusually disturbing. She supposed she could ask Alyson about those rumors, but she couldn't imagine that one so low on the totem pole would know anything about how David had operated. Besides, this woman worked for *her;* how would it seem if she had to ask her questions about her own father!

"I'll speak to Gene about this," Beth promised. "Get you some real problems to work on. Lord knows we have enough of them," she laughed.

"Well, I don't think the one with Feldon Manor is going away so quickly."

"Sure it will. Since it was Ben who sparked it, I see no reason why everything won't settle down as before."

"But don't you want to begin work on it? It must be costing a fortune in interest on loans just to stay in a holding pattern," Alyson remarked, brushing her hand through her cap of straight, golden brown hair.

"It is, but I've got enough on my plate right now that Methany Palace will just have to wait. I adored my father and have nothing but admiration for his visions, but sometimes he leaped before he looked, as with Methany Palace."

"Oh, I don't know," Alyson answered slowly, smiling. "It's a typical Methany project—great location and tremendous in- cipient publicity. It can't miss."

"Once I figure out how to get rid of the current tenants," Beth reminded her.

"I'm sure we'll think of something."

Beth's eyebrows went up at the pronoun. "I'm sure I will," she amended gently.

Alyson nodded in immediate understanding of the rebuke, then stood. Beth watched her with interest, appreciating that she had not apologized for her presumption. She was above average in height and slender, but what struck one immediately were her incredible cat eyes of a striking hazel color. They were eyes that blazed with intelligence, yet the unusual shape and color signaled female sensuality as clearly as a written invitation. It was an unusual and, Beth would guess, highly irresistible combination to the men in the company, who no doubt had tried to get closer only to have been politely rebuffed. Alyson Gentry did not strike Beth as a woman who would play in her own backyard.

As Alyson started toward the door, Beth observed that the young lawyer had the kind of looks and style she had always wished for herself. Although her face might be considered a little too angular, too strong for conventional standards of beauty, Beth admired the high cheekbones and squared-off chin, so reminiscent of her father's kind of face, hard planes and bones, a face that hid its softness from the world. And the way she carried herself in the Armani suit, on heels Beth would have tripped over ... well, she had Armanis in her closet, too, but since she was only five foot three, they hung better on the height of the closet rod than on her. She had definitely inherited her mother's height, her mother's slightly too-full bosom, and her naturally curly hair that finally had become fashionable instead of merely deadly.

"Thanks again for helping me out last night, Alyson," Beth now said. "I won't forget it."

When Beth was alone again, she looked down at her appointments for the day, and for the first time in a long while, did not feel paralyzed with indecision. She had handled Ben; she had handled the press. *She* had done this. And *she* would get to the bottom of the J. mystery, too. Whatever else she might be, she was first a Methany, and as her father's child, that meant being someone who would not let anyone or anything scare her.

In the sanctuary of her office, Alyson Gentry flipped open the file on Methany Palace, refamiliarizing herself with the history of the sixty-four tenants still remaining. Gene had turned over this headache to her almost three years ago, at the time of the most frequent and ugliest publicity, a hot potato that neither David nor Gene had wanted to touch, so it had been given to the junior member of the legal staff and the only female.

When she first took on the project, there had been almost one hundred longtime residents, but she had gotten a quick tutorship in Methany methods from the master himself, and after certain unexplained fires, break-ins, and equipment break-downs, twenty-five of the one hundred got the message and found new places to live. The others got themselves a lawyer who made a lot of noise in the press for a brief while. David got bored, and things quieted down. Since then, death had been a major cause of attrition, and Alyson had been moved on to other legal matters. The incident last night could not have come at a better time. She was restless with the simplicity of her work. There was no challenge, no artfulness to her legal preparations. Labor disputes and contract problems required book knowledge, not brains.

She did not want to see the publicity die down or the problem go away. No, Alyson needed to keep this one alive. The corporation could use it for the sake of the Bronx renewal project, and her career needed the boost. Alyson was proud of her drive, prouder of her patience. She had watched and learned from

David Methany, knowing that it was better to wait for the right opportunity then to fail by being anxious and premature. Methany Palace was the right opportunity. David had wanted it; he had had a vision of what it could be, and three years was long enough to wait. She would have her victory, and the company would get its tax abatement *and* a super-luxury co-op that would sell even in a flat market—because it would be so expensive, and more importantly, because it would be a Methany.

She picked up the telephone and pressed numbers she had memorized a while ago. One evening when Gene and David and the rest of the legal staff had stayed late to celebrate a particularly sweet victory, David had lifted his glass in a toast to a man who he said had been very helpful to him, on this recent matter and others in the past. Gene had asked him who he was, and all David had said was that he was a special friend. Alyson realized immediately that this special friend helped David out secretly, since not even Gene knew him; perhaps that was why this particular issue had resolved itself outside of court. Alyson had then dug and dug and learned enough that she wanted him as her special friend, too, should the need ever arise.

Three rings, and then a male voice picked up.

"Hello, Vernon Marks? This is..."

II

"It's so tragic about Lilly Jane Litwin."

"What is?"

"Why, her suicide, of course." Isabel Methany was trying to make conversation with her husband, who sat across from her at the breakfast table, the only place, lately, where they seemed to be together and then only because she had started to get up at the unearthly hour of five-thirty in order to be dressed and have coffee with him.

"Oh yes," he said, not looking up from reading *The Wall Street Journal.* "Tragic."

"Did you know she was eight-and-a-half months pregnant?"

"No. Really?"

"That's what makes it all so horrible. I can't imagine what could have been so wrong with her life that she couldn't have somehow worked things out. After all, she was young, beautiful, had a husband who adored her, money, position. Surely she could have gotten help from someone for whatever the problem was, but to take your own life and your baby's . . ." Isabel shivered and her face went white.

"Maybe it was all the negative publicity about Harry," David suggested, glancing up over the rim of the newspaper.

"You mean because of you?"

"Sure. By the time he finally realized he was whistling in the wind with his so-called white-collar crimes that I allegedly committed against the helpless and innocent, it was too late. He knew he risked terrible ridicule, but he didn't know how to stop what he had begun. He had sought the press, got it, and then came up empty-handed. After all, one of his strongest, mind you, strongest witnesses was a union leader known to have skimmed from his union's funds. He was trying to—"

"How did you know that?"

"What?"

"How did you know who the district attorney's witnesses were?"

"Isabel, those things get around, especially when you're the target of the investigation."

"No, I don't think this information about a union leader just 'got around' as you say." She spoke consideringly, forgetting or perhaps just shelving her vow not to give her husband what he sought, her interest in his work.

"I think you pulled what I am beginning to understand is a typical David Methany maneuver."

"And that is?"

"I think you made it your business to know what kind of case Harry had against you, find out just how reliable his witnesses were, how strong his paper evidence. I think you used someone to gain access to his files or had access yourself to someone on Harry's staff. You don't leave things to chance, David. *That* I've already learned."

David folded his paper and placed it on the side of the table by his plate of fresh melon. Then he sat back and looked at his wife, a smile spreading slowly across his face. "I'm impressed, Isabel, I truly am."

She shrugged, willing herself not to be seduced by his words, not to feel pleasure at his praise; she failed. "I'm interested in you, David," she told him. "In how your mind works."

"My mind works quite simply. If I am here and I want something that's there, I will do anything to get from here to there. Simple, really."

She nodded. "Yes, it is, and once one understands the phrase—'do anything'—it becomes simpler still."

David laughed, a sound of genuine delight. "That's right, my dear. Absolutely correct."

Isabel looked pensive. "Poor Harry Litwin. He never stood a chance against you, did he?"

"Not really." David's face suddenly turned serious again, and his eyes went flat, dark with intensity. He was not seeing his wife or the breakfast food or the paper by his plate; his vision was riveted on another scene, another person.

"David?"

"Sorry, I was thinking of Litwin and his foolish case. You know, if every businessman was investigated on the methods he used, not only wouldn't there be free enterprise, but everyone would want to work in the D.A.'s office," he laughed.

"So you think Harry Litwin dropped his case against you because he knew he couldn't win? That his evidence and witnesses were too weak?"

"Harry had no case against me, just a lot of publicity that he thought would help him realize his political ambitions. When push came to shove, and he knew he had to go to a grand jury to get an indictment against me because the gathering of the so-called evidence and the attached press coverage had been going on long enough, he saw that he had made a jackass of himself and his office. I think that's what did his lovely wife in. The shame of it all."

Isabel weighed his assessment, then: "No, I don't agree. I didn't know Lilly Jane all that well, but she never struck me as someone who would buckle under from a little negative publicity. Besides, it wasn't really a scandal, just a humiliating embarrassment, something that would pass when the next juicy

piece of dirt caught people's attention. Lilly Jane was sophisticated enough to know what others enjoyed talking about, and
it wasn't one's husband's professional mistakes, but sex."

David grinned. "Is that what you women talk about at your
endless lunches?"

She nodded. "Endlessly. So you see, Harry's foolishness with
you wouldn't have mattered that much to her."

"But the child wasn't Harry's, Isabel. You must have known
that, and that, my dear, is a scandal of the first order. Especially
for one with her exalted background."

"David, what in the world are you talking about? Of course
the child was Harry's, who else's would it have been?" She
watched then as David's entire face moved like a mobile in the
wind, first the pleasant side, now the contemptuous one. A
pursing of the thin lips, a lifting of the brows, a tilt of the head.
She looked away, embarrassed by how stupid he made her feel
without having said a word.

"I don't believe that," she finally said, not meeting her husband's eyes. "I don't believe Lilly Jane was ever unfaithful. She
was a flirt, not an adulteress."

Isabel sneaked a peek to see that David's expression of cy-
nicism had become more implacable, a Mount Rushmore of
incredulity. "Don't look at me like that, as if I'm some kind of
imbecile."

"Well, darling, either you're incredibly naive or you are an
imbecile. Lilly Jane Litwin may have been a flirt, as you say,
but her husband was incapable of getting her with child, to put
it delicately."

"Do you mean that—"

"I mean that Harry Litwin had a vasectomy when he was
much younger, in college, I think. There was no way he could
have made Lilly Jane pregnant, no way."

"How in heaven's name would you know such a thing?"

Isabel asked, now looking at her husband with a mixture of disgust and shock on her face.

He smiled slowly, a viper-like expression that chilled Isabel this warm morning. "Why, how in heaven's name would you think I know?" he asked in a ridiculing, sing-song imitation of her words. "Obviously, Lilly Jane told me."

"I'm sorry, but that's hardly obvious to me. Why would Lilly Jane tell *you* that—" And then Isabel swallowed and stopped, her stomach clenching as if to ward off a physical blow.

She did not doubt that David was unfaithful to her, often and with any variety of women, including those she socialized with and called "friend." The truth was that she could not imagine the likes of Lilly Jane Litwin with her husband. The refinement to which she had been bred he would never acquire, no matter the millions he achieved; she knew that because she recognized in herself the same lack, the same inability to totally mask the slightly rough edges that signaled one type of upbringing—hers and David's—versus another. And even though Harry Litwin came from a working-class family, an Ivy League education had smoothed out what needed smoothing; Lilly Jane had seen to the rest. For her and David, Isabel knew, there was nothing to be done; what money could buy would make the lack of elegance perhaps less noticeable, less laughable, but it could not hide it, only camouflage it with those who did not know better. With those who did, like Lilly Jane, the outsider could either be herself or imitate; Isabel chose to imitate. And it was because she chose to imitate one such as Lilly Jane Litwin that she could not conceive of her finding desirable the same type of man she enjoyed, a man like David Methany. Still, his drive, his self-confidence, could be heady enticements to one used to men being polite and careful.

She had to know; she had to. But would he tell her the truth? Yes, just to hurt her, if for no other reason.

"David, the child wasn't yours, was it? Just tell me that. Please," she implored in a heart-sick whisper, her eyes saucer-round and bright as new porcelain.

She watched, fingernails pressing into the soft flesh of her palms, and she waited for an answer. She watched and she waited, and moisture erupted on her upper lip, tingled in her scalp. She watched and she waited, and she could feel the dryness on her tongue, the back of her throat. Fear and dread. Dread and fear. This was her husband, the man she married, and he was deliberately letting the silence drag on, knowing and enjoying what it was doing to her. She should be wise to him, be able to withstand his manipulations by now, but he was too cunning, and she too insecure.

"Please, David," she repeated.

"No, Isabel," he at last relented. "I don't think I will give you an answer to that question." His tone was bored, as if, Isabel thought, he had grown tired of a game that had not interested him much anyway. "You see, if I tell you the child was mine, you'll be upset because, one, I had an affair, and two, because a baby's life, a Methany baby at that, was snuffed out. If I tell you the child was not mine, you'll be relieved and possibly erroneously so. I don't want you upset, because then you disturb the equilibrium of my life, and I don't want you to have any false illusions, so no, I don't think I'll tell you anything more."

Isabel's eyes glazed over with disbelief, and her breathing became shallow and rapid. He is not a monster, she told herself. *He is not.* Monstrous husbands swigged beer and slapped around their wives and wore sleeveless undershirts. Monstrous husbands grew fat and sloppy and sexually repugnant. The man across from her at the breakfast table was becoming more handsome and appealing with each new success, the wealth and power vitamins to his well-being. But this man was growing meaner as well—or was it only that he was allowing his true self to emerge more and more since he had the power and money to frighten other people into accepting him exactly as he was? Isabel knew that this was a man she should not like, a man capable of hurting her, his own wife, without apology or regret. What utterly amazed her had nothing to do with him, only with herself. She tolerated the emotional slapping and smacking, even invited it by trying to share with him as a wife would with a husband. She must not lapse into weakness again; she must remember for the future that David's idea of a wife was not as a companion, only a social convenience, an occasionally necessary appurtenance to make his life easier, used only when it suited him, like a telephone or maid service.

"Why do you do it, David?" she asked in a voice grown older and wearier than it had any right to be.

"Do what, my darling?" he said, picking up his newspaper again.

"Hurt me so viciously."

"You're wrong, Isabel. You do it to yourself," he insisted. "You ask me questions that have answers you aren't going to like. You know that yet you go ahead and ask them anyway. Just assume I have other interests and that I am intelligent enough never to let matters go so far that they can hurt me. Never, no matter who else may get hurt."

She heard the words, and she understood the meaning. Slowly, she nodded. "You are not a nice man, David Methany," she pronounced.

He laughed, another sound of true pleasure. "You're right, Isabel. I'm not, but I'm not a dull one either."

"No, that you're not," Isabel agreed, knowing that her own weaknesses created a need for this man that permitted her to ignore his failings and accept his punishments.

"What do you think will happen to Harry Litwin now?" she

asked conversationally, the gracious loser, the obedient geisha. She knew her place and it was not alongside her husband. "Does everyone know he wasn't the father?"

"If by everyone you mean your set of friends, I have no idea. I'm sure it wasn't the type of thing Harry and Lilly Jane went around announcing to people."

"Yet you knew," she mutterd under her breath; he heard.

"Yes, I knew," and he smiled.

"He'll be fine," Isabel said, shaking off a new wave of helplessness. "Besides, he had no right to make you his scapegoat," she stated with surprising ferocity. "With all the dreadful and really dangerous criminals out there, you'd think he'd have better things to do with his time and the taxpayers' money than go after someone like you who's trying to bring decent housing to this city."

David's bridge of thick eyebrows rose in surprise. "Why, thank you, Isabel. I had no idea you felt that way about my work."

"That's because you don't care how I feel about anything," she shot back.

David nodded, grinning. "That's true, but still . . ."

"Oh, David, please. For once let's just try to talk with each other instead of you attacking me until I retreat. You've already won one battle this morning," she admitted. "Anyway, the fact is indisputable that you've done a great deal of good for this city, and Harry Litwin was out of line in going after you."

"So you didn't believe what you were reading about me?"

"I didn't care. There's a difference."

David was silent a moment, appraising, and Isabel experienced an unusual sensation: she was actually pleasing and interesting her husband, she could tell. It was a heady feeling, as if she had just succeeded in getting the prom king to notice her over the true beauties at the dance.

"You're full of surprises this morning, darling. I knew the money was important to you, but I had no idea you could be so ruthless about it. I'm impressed."

"I am not ruthless," she protested staunchly. "I am simply being practical."

"Indeed you are, and I find it quite refreshing. This may be a match made in heaven after all, Isabel. You bring me a former police detective, and I give you Bonwit's, Best's, and Bergdorf's. Both of us are pleased, because we get what we want at little cost to the other. I'm delighted to discover that you are not only shallow, my dear wife, but amoral as well. Difficult to imagine, but we may learn to live with each other and actually like it."

"This is ridiculous, David, stop it right now!" Isabel flared. "Don't make fun of my loyalty to you. I genuinely believe in what you do, and I really do care about how you achieve your successes. I don't think you're capable of true criminality, so these minor little infractions," she waved her hand dismissively, shooing way a loose spot of bothersome lint, "mean nothing. You haven't physically hurt anyone, and everyone, *everyone* in business has a few tricks that are outside the law. I admire you for your ingenuity, David, and I think Harry Litwin was a fool to start up with you. If he's made a mess of his career he has no one to blame but himself. It's just a shame someone as lovely as Lilly Jane had to bear the consequences."

As she spoke, Isabel believed every word. She was not trying to please her husband, an effort she knew was hopeless if embarked on intentionally. No, she really thought that what David was doing helped many people, not just the rich. If he used certain questionable methods, he never actually hurt anybody. Besides, that was the risk of doing business with him. A competitor had to be aware that he was up against the toughest and the best, and also one of the smartest, when up against David. To work any way but his was to jeopardize far more than she did if she displeased him as his wife. All she could lose was her self-respect.

"Two suicides in the family," Isabel said one morning three weeks later. "What an awful, awful tragedy."

"Yes it is, but you said it yourself, darling," David reminded her. "You said Harry Litwin had no one to blame but himself. I guess he finally realized that, too, when he decided to put a gun to his head. Damn shame, though. He was a tough prosecutor."

"Well, may he rest in peace," Isabel said. "The last weeks of his life certainly didn't give him any."

"But he did it to himself, remember that."

"Yes, David, I'll remember," and she looked steadily at her husband, understanding clearly, fully, and not fearlessly that David's power as an adversary was such that he had pulled the trigger as surely as if his hand, not Harry Litwin's, had been wrapped around that gun.

Yes, to do business with David was to have far more at stake than one's self-respect.

12

The wheel of the 1989 Honda Prelude felt strange under her hands. It had been over a month since Beth had driven her car, and then only to visit the cemetery in Long Island where her parents were buried. She often thought it would be more economical simply to rent a car whenever she wanted one, but the extravagance of garaging her own car seemed worth the sense of freedom it gave her. She loved to drive, even the short distance to the Methany weekend home on Milton Point in Rye, New York, not even twenty-five miles from Manhattan. For most of Rye's residents, the town was their primary home and they commuted to work in New York, but for David, it had had everything a weekend retreat should have, plus proximity to the city.

Although it was already the third weekend in July, Beth had not been out to the house since shortly after David had died. Miranda oversaw the couple who came in weekly to check the pipes and keep everything in working order. She had called ahead, and no doubt Beth would find the refrigerator and cupboards stocked more for a week's stay than a weekend's.

That visit months ago, Beth now recalled, had been intended as a respite from her grief, but instead she had spent the time poring over family photograph albums, wallowing in her loss the way a reformed alcoholic would relish past benders. This time she was going as a respite from work, which had occupied every waking hour, seven days a week, for month after month after month. It was a combination of guilt and fear that drove her, feeling that if she dared to ignore the business even for a few hours, she would be disappointing her father and perhaps courting damage to all he had built. She seemed incapable of relaxing, not even with her pottery. There was the incident with Ben over Methany Palace, his threats against Methany City North, the money due the banks, and just to make everything more frustrating, there was the mysterious correspondence from J. She needed time away from anything to do with the Methany Corporation. She was only thirty-two years old, she reminded herself, taking a right off the Hutchinson River Parkway to connect with the Playland Parkway that would lead to Milton Point. She had a right to some fun, damn it!

But fun is only possible if you let yourself enjoy something, she thought, understanding all too well that unless she rid her mind of the worries crowding it, this weekend, though spent at the home she adored, would be no different than any other. Regardless of the temptation to think about work, she would make every effort to relax for the next two-and-a-half days. And she nodded earnestly, as if sealing a silent vow.

She exited Playland Parkway and made a right onto Forest Avenue, passing the circle that led to both the beach and the amusement park that was the legendary Playland. Buses of visitors were unloading even though it wasn't yet noon, but these groups from Staten Island and the Bronx, from Elizabeth, New Jersey, and Bedford-Stuyvesant in Brooklyn, had to cram a summer's worth of fresh air and pleasure into a few short hours. They would, Beth knew, stroll along the boardwalk and maybe fly a kite in the picnic area or take out a rowboat on the man-made lake; they would ride in the bumper cars and go on the ferris wheel, and frolic in the waters of Long Island Sound or in the Playland pool. All visitors, locals and others, had to reserve plenty of time for the food, a junk-food addict's fantasy of cotton candy and caramel apples and pizza and frankfurters and French fries, everything dripping with grease and a flavor as distinctive and memorable as the sting of salt water.

Beth loved Playland and remembered as if it were yesterday when her parents had taken her there for the first time. She had been eight years old, and there was nothing she hadn't squealed over with delight. To this day, she could recall how her first sight of the giant roller coaster had made her stomach knot with scary anticipation. The taste of cotton candy was unique, the music on the carousel, the gentle sweetness of children's laughter, and even though the years brought change and a new imbalance of visitors from white to black, for Beth, Playland tore down rank and privilege and became its name, a land of play for everyone for as many hours as they could afford to stay away from reality.

She could feel the tension drain from her as she made a left onto 42 Milton Point Drive. Midway up the gravel driveway to her house, she slowed and stopped, taking in the view of the house and beyond, soaking in the joy the vision always gave her, as it had since that first time more than twenty years ago. There was nothing spectacular about the sprawling white-shingled Colonial from the front. It was the rear of the house that made it extraordinary, with its veranda off the master bedroom upstairs, its huge flagstone patio and flagstone path leading down to their own private white sand beach. A few houses to the left gave way to the Milton Point Harbor, where leasing a berth in the marina could cost as much as the boat itself. All the homes along Milton Point Drive fronted on Long Island Sound, and each had patches of private beachfront, making this one of the most expensive and exclusive locations in all of New York State real estate. Some owners, not content with nature, also had swimming pools, and there were enough grass and clay tennis courts to make a country club owner envious. The Methanys had none of these extras, the view and their beach always enough. And for Beth, there was the special treasure of the pottery studio built out of an old boat shed. She had everything she needed there, including a kiln, and whether it was the completeness of the equipment or the fact that one wall of the shed had been replaced by glass overlooking the beach and water, Beth felt a serenity here and a sense of artistic creativity that she experienced nowhere else.

Thirty minutes later she was sitting on the patio with a glass of iced tea and her first moment of utter mindlessness in longer than she cared to estimate when the cellular phone on the wicker table beside her rang. She hated the damn thing, but knew it would be irresponsible not to be available to her staff at all times.

"Hello?"

"Beth, I'm sorry to bother you on the weekend, but—"

"Who is this?"

"Oh, sorry. It's Alyson. Alyson Gentry."

"Oh. Hello. I hope you'll understand when I say I'm beginning to dread your calls."

The other woman laughed slightly. "And with good reason, I'm afraid."

"Is it Methany Palace again?"

"It is, and this time Ben Wyler didn't have a damn thing to do with it."

"When I left the city this morning, there was nothing. What could have happened in—"

"What happened is a resident of the apartment building by the name of Lewis Wilkes, Jr. Ring a bell?"

"No, should it?"

"He was the one responsible for the first press backlash against your father's plans for the building years ago."

"I don't remember," Beth said, feeling oddly defensive and inferior, as if this other woman had been closer to her father than she. "I must have been involved in other matters," she added stiffly.

"Of course," Alyson quickly agreed. "The only reason I know about him is because I was part of the legal team investigating the steps we could take to get the residents out of there. It seems that Lewis Wilkes, Jr.—and how anyone seventy-seven can still be called a junior is beyond me—has connections as high as they go with the landmark commission for the city of New York. He's a retired attorney for the city's real estate board, and what he doesn't know about real estate isn't to be learned."

"And he went to the press two years ago complaining that my father would be destroying an important building and hurting lifelong tenants," Beth supplied, although it was a guess.

"Exactly," Alyson confirmed.

"Was he also the one who started the lies about my father's supposed strong-arm tactics for getting people to leave?" Beth asked. There was only silence as reply. "Alyson?"

"Yes, right, he was the one." Beth frowned at the peculiar remoteness in the lawyer's voice, the absurdly obvious obfuscation, but before she could question it, Alyson was speaking again.

"It seems that because of Wilkes's age and his impeccable reputation—which are two euphemisms for having connections—he has managed to get our eminent senior state senator to put a little pressure on the not-so-honorable Judge Wendell Carvey, a political beast if ever there was one, and Carvey has slapped a restraining order against Methany Corporation, legally stopping you from making any physical alterations to the building known as 422 Central Park West, Feldon Manor Hotel."

"What!"

"There's more. Wilkes has also managed to just about sew up landmark status for the building, and held a surprise press conference not thirty minutes ago to announce that. In effect, you're sitting with a multimillion-dollar lox that has neither bagel nor cream cheese to make it taste good."

"Oh, shit." Not the most professional reaction, Beth knew, but certainly the most honest. "What do you suggest?"

"I don't think we can wait to strategize on Monday," Alyson told her.

"No, I agree, but I'm not about to drive back into the city. I need this weekend away regardless of the problems facing me. Would you mind coming up here to the house? I know it's your weekend, too, but—" But I'm the boss and so you'll have to come to me, was left unspoken.

"Of course I don't mind. I can get a train in about thirty, forty minutes and be up there by—"

"No, call our car service, you deserve that at least. Do you want to spend the weekend?" Beth asked out of politeness, not desire.

"No, thanks anyway," Alyson said. "A few hours should be enough to give us a sense of how we want to handle this."

"Okay, then, I'll see you soon."

"What do you mean he got the mayor to agree to a special investigator to look into criminal charges against us?" Beth was repeating shrilly an hour and a half later, as she and Alyson sat in the living room, the Long Island Sound and the white beach as distant as if a Caribbean island.

"I'm afraid it's true, Beth, and we've got to do something to stop it and get that damn restraining order lifted."

"Alyson, this is a disaster," Beth told her. "I've got the banks breathing down my neck and that tax abatement—well, thank goodness the voting's been postponed, but still, what I don't need is a special investigator looking into how I conduct my business." She shut her eyes briefly against the enormity of her responsibilities. She loved the company, loved what she did, but sometimes, like now, when everything seemed stacked against her, it became too much, and not quite worth all the sacrifice. But it was her choice, hers, she reminded herself, and she wouldn't have it any other way.

"Not to mention that absurd landmark business," Alyson said. "The building is only sixty years old. Wilkes has more claim as an antique than Feldon Manor," she joked humorlessly.

Beth shook her head and poured them both more iced tea. "I can't believe this," she muttered. "I really can't believe any of it."

"Wilkes is an old man, a widower, kids off on their own. He has nothing to do with his time except call in old favors and cause trouble, probably reminds him he's still breathing."

"But why start up again now, after being quiet for two years?"

Alyson took her time replying. She got up from the comfort of the down-cushioned sofa and went to the French doors that led to the patio and the blue waters beyond. Her large eyes drank in the privilege of her environment, and then she turned around, absorbing the comfort and beauty of the room. With a small smile, she focused again on Beth.

"Sorry, but this is all so incredibly beautiful. I can almost forget why I'm here."

Beth nodded knowingly. "Thank you. The next time you come I hope it'll be under more pleasant circumstances so you can really enjoy it."

"I'll look forward to that." She ran her fingers through her cap of hair as if to recall herself to the moment. "Anyway, in answer to your question why Wilkes has started up again, it's because for the past year and a half or so he'd been living in Palm Beach with a woman who died four months ago. It seems Wilkes sold the condo that she had owned and came back up to New York where, it turns out, he was illegally subletting his own apartment until a month ago."

Beth immediately brightened. "That's it—we'll get him on the illegal sublet."

Alyson shook her head. "And be accused of heartless cruelty to the aged? I don't think so," she said, rejoining Beth on the sofa.

"You're right, of course," Beth conceded, then she studied Alyson a moment.

"What?"

"Oh, nothing. I was just thinking that you're a pretty impressive person," Beth told her, smiling. "For someone so young, you seem so tough, so . . . I don't know," she laughed gently, "so seasoned. Or maybe it's just that lawyer sharpness. Whatever, it's very impressive."

Alyson also laughed. "First of all, I'm thirty-four, hardly a child. And I'm about as tough as a toasted marshmallow. Oh, sure, there's a nice little crust on the outside for the world to see, but inside," she shook her head, "inside it's pure mush. That's part of good legal training, you know," she teased. "Moot court, wills, ethics, and pretense."

Beth's smile grew wider. "I'm glad to hear this. You were beginning to make me feel awfully ill-equipped for my job." And even though she said it lightly, there was a small part of her that meant it. Alyson Gentry *was* sharp; intelligence radiated from her like sunlight off bright new hubcaps. Beth never questioned her abilities or intelligence, but there was something about the lawyer that seemed to eclipse her own assets. Then again, Beth told herself, all Alyson Gentry had had to concentrate on was the law, while she had had to learn everything about the real estate business plus contend with David Methany himself, a demanding boss, teacher, and father.

Looking at Alyson, Beth saw a hard calculation come into her eyes. "You have a plan?" she said.

Alyson nodded. "You're not going to like it."

"I don't like anything you've had to say so far," Beth told her.

Alyson sat back and crossed her long legs, clad in white linen pants. Over them was a long white linen tunic and over that a black-and-white linen tablecloth-checked Armani jacket. She looked cool and elegant and impossibly competent to Beth, whose denim cutoffs and I LOVE ICE CREAM tank top seemed ridiculously adolescent instead of what she had always considered them: comfortable and appropriate for the beach. She self-consciously pushed away her hair which, in its natural curliness, bounced right back on her forehead.

"I could," Alyson began slowly, "spare you a great deal of anguish by just going ahead and doing what I think needs to be done."

"You could," Beth agreed, an edge shading her voice, "but then I would either fire you, at the worst, or severely reprimand you, at the least. I am, regardless of what others may think about the situation, the head of Methany Corporation, and nothing, not one damn thing, gets done without my knowing about it and without my approval." She paused, staring steadily at the other woman. It was that uniquely Beth look, not intense, not challenging, just implacably honest and unafraid. "I don't mean to sound neurotically controlling," she continued, more gently, "but things are difficult enough for me without there being any confusion as to how things get done. I'm sure you understand."

"I understand perfectly," Alyson said. "I was only suggesting that if certain, shall we say, not very nice methods are called into play to get our desired result, it might be better if you were ignorant, therefore innocent, of them."

"How not very nice?" Beth asked warily.

The lawyer said nothing as she went to her briefcase and extracted a folder containing several typewritten sheets of paper.

"What's that?"

"Profiles on the remaining tenants and their families, if extant, and a plan of harassment suitable for each. I had it prepared after the incident with Ben Wyler, just in case."

"Prepared how?"

"Beth," Alyson began, shaking her head, "please. I don't mean to be insubordinant, but I am a lawyer. Even corporate real estate lawyers have their so-called informers."

"Give me an idea of what kind of harassment," Beth said. "I know the stories about my father, and I don't want to perpetuate those myths. I don't want to—"

"They weren't myths."

Alyson had spoken softly, almost inaudibly, but as Beth looked into her face, into eyes as clear and guileless as a meadow pond, she knew she was looking at the truth. Now she understood the lawyer's hesitation on the phone earlier when Beth had made reference to her father's tactics. She understood, too, and appreciated, the lawyer's desire to keep her ignorant as a form of protection so that she would not be tainted by her father's reputation.

"I'm truly sorry," Alyson said.

Beth could not answer. She was seven, eight, eleven, and her kite had flown away, her bicycle lost air in its tires, her birthday cake did not have enough mocha; the world was not completely, totally to her specifications. She was not hurt or angry, not even shocked. She was disappointed, a far more lasting and corrosive damage that ate away at her innocence, not just her hopes.

"I suppose I knew about my father's questionable ways of doing business and just didn't want to deal with them as fact. Not very professional, I guess," she laughed dryly at herself, "but very filial." She took a deep breath and focused her attention on Alyson with all the self-possession she could muster, a batter warming up for the plate. "What are you proposing?"

"Do you really want the specifics?"

Beth considered the question. "No, I suppose the specifics don't really matter, do they?"

"It's more a matter of how far you want me to go."

"You personally?"

"Well, yes, me personally. I'll be the one who has to set things up with certain people, so yes, I'll be personally involved."

"I don't want you to do that," Beth stated emphatically.

"There's no way to avoid it," Alyson told her. "It's not as if I'm personally going to set fire to one of the apartments, but—"

"What are you talking about!"

"What do you think I'm talking about?" Alyson retorted. "I'm sorry, but I don't seem to be getting through. This isn't very nice, granted, but it's how business sometimes gets done."

"Not with me running things," Beth informed her.

"Well, what did you imagine I meant by not very nice tactics—yelling at the tenants?"

Beth shot her a hard, hot look that clearly telegraphed her displeasure at the lawyer's sarcasm.

"I'm sorry," Alyson said again, more calmly as she replaced the folder in the briefcase. "We're not getting anywhere. I don't blame you for not liking what has to be done, but Beth, it *has* to be this way. It has to be or everything your father worked for will be at risk."

"I know that, damn it!" Beth exploded, getting to her feet and crossing the vast expanse of living room to the French doors. Again, not even a whisper, "I know that." She turned to face the lawyer. "Alyson, I don't want you involved in anything illegal. You're an attorney and I don't care what we're paying you, it's not enough to risk a career for. And I don't want people hurt, so tell me, how do we protect the Methany Corporation without hurting you or those old people?" Her smile was rueful, the look in her brown eyes one of muddied intelligence, as if she had studied the definitive book on a subject only to learn that several key pages had been misprinted.

Alyson slowly rose, but did not approach Beth. "I think you have two choices: either you trust me and let me do what has to be done, or you take the chance that being ethical and honorable will get you what you want. You're the boss, Beth, you tell me which it'll be."

As acute as her disappointment was when Alyson Gentry confirmed her father's business practices, equally acute was her unexpected anger now. Beth was livid, rage dancing through her veins, behind her eyes, echoing in her ears. Damn him, she cried silently, cursing her father for making her good, but not tough; outraged with the suddenly irrefutable knowledge that one without the other doomed her to failure. He had, she now realized, assumed that just by being his offspring she would either inherit that trait as if it were a genetic factor like eye color or good teeth. Or not need it, her name and heritage enough to turn back potential adversaries. What hubris. And what stupidity. What she had was the one quality neither her father nor she had considered, a distinguishing characteristic that could destroy all he had left her, all he had taught her. She was left, alone, with a conscience.

"Do what has to be done," she finally instructed, "whatever has to be done." Her voice was steady; her eyes did not waver, but her heartbeat was beating double-time with the pain of her self-betrayal.

"You sure I can't convince you to stay?" Beth asked impulsively as she and Alyson strolled, barefoot, along the beach thirty minutes later. This time her invitation was sincere; she liked the other woman, and would not have felt her presence an intrusion but a pleasant change from her loneliness. "I have an extra toothbrush, nightgown, bathing suit, whatever you need."

"No, thank you anyway, Beth, that's very kind of you. I really should get back to the city and get some of these things in the works. Some other time."

"I hope so." Beth was silent a moment, then, impulsively: "You know, I've never had much time for friends. My father and the business always seemed to occupy me, at least to the extent that I didn't really know I was missing anything."

"You were married, though, weren't you? I haven't even given myself time for that—it's always been work, work, work."

"I was, but I never gave him or us a chance," Beth admitted. "I know that now, though at the time I thought he was demanding and selfish, wanting to do things with me when I had a *job* that required all my attention. And a father who was doing impossibly interesting things." Beth laughed self-deprecatingly at the not distant memory of her marriage, and how unfair she had been to her husband.

"David Methany had the capacity to eclipse all other men," Alyson said knowingly. "And the business . . ." She shrugged. "Well, it's like a living thing, isn't it? It demands love and attention and constant caretaking, but it's worth it."

Beth smiled with gratitude. "I knew you'd understand," she said, then, more shyly, added, "I don't know what it is, Alyson, but I feel so comfortable with you. I guess it's because you know the business and you knew my father and I don't have to explain things to you or convince you of what's important, because you already know."

"Oh, I do, Beth, I do."

Beth's expression turned thoughtful. "Sometimes, though, I question the sacrifice."

"You mean Ben Wyler?" Beth nodded. "Can't he get beyond his ambition, or at least separate it from his personal feelings?"

"He claims he can," Beth told her, "but I can't. I cannot feel close to him when he's bad-mouthing my father and when he's determined to hurt my business. Could you?"

Alyson was reflective. "No, I don't think I could separate the personal from the professional. For me, they're linked, soldered together." Before Beth could say anything further on the subject, Alyson turned away to face the various estates along Milton Point. "This is really extraordinary," she whispered. Then she looked hard at Beth. "You don't know how lucky you are."

Beth smiled. "Whenever I'm here I know it."

"Is that lighthouse still working?" the lawyer asked, pointing to an old white structure about half a mile up the Sound toward Connecticut.

"Yes. In fact, a few years ago some entrepreneurs from the city built a restaurant at the top that I hear is quite lovely."

"You haven't been?"

"No, and I don't intend to. I hate heights, I'm absolutely petrified of them."

"Really? How do you stand flying?"

"Fortunately, I don't do all that much of it, and when I do, I fortify myself beforehand with scotch."

"What about your office—you're on the forty-fourth floor— and your apartment?"

"I don't have time to look out the windows when I'm at the office," Beth said, laughing, "and the apartment is only on the seventh floor, with a view of trees, not treetops—very tolerable."

"I had no idea," Alyson muttered.

"Well, keep it a secret, please. I wouldn't want people to think the boss's daughter wasn't a force to be reckoned with," Beth joked.

"But she's more than that," Alyson reminded her. "She's the boss."

Beth laughed again. "That's right. Sometimes I really do forget."

"Your father would turn over in his grave if he ever heard that."

Beth stared consideringly at the other woman. "He would, wouldn't he? It's amazing how well you understand how his mind worked."

"Not so amazing. I did work with the man for several years."

"Yes, but I'm his daughter. You'd think—"

"You'd think it's really getting late," Alyson interrupted on a short laugh. "I'm sorry, but I've got to get back or before we know it it'll be Monday and we won't be prepared."

"You're right," Beth said, starting back to the house, but for the first time all afternoon there was something in the other woman's small smile, the steadiness of her hazel eyes, that unsettled Beth. And then, suddenly, she realized exactly what it was. Alyson Gentry's sense of purpose was so rigidly directed that she almost mistook it for rudeness. Ironic to recognize this so quickly in another, after her husband had accused her of being the same and she had denied it right through to the signing of the divorce papers. She wondered, for the first time, if her ex-husband had ever thought she was not only being rude but even calculating and devious—words that had leapt to mind at the sight of Alyson's impenetrable expression. How easy it was to misunderstand another, and how sad.

13

SOCIETY SWELL SUICIDE

METHANY MILLIONS ROLL OVER LAW

LITWIN NO MATCH FOR MASTER METHANY

A few more similar headlines, attached to articles that ran in
the *Herald Tribune, Journal-American, New York Daily News,* all
with datelines of 1956, tumbled out of the manila envelope. The
clippings, copies not originals, concerned Beth's father and his
problems with a Manhattan district attorney, Harry Litwin, who
thought David's business practices left a lot to be desired, legally
speaking. But then it seemed, according to the press, that he
didn't have sufficient evidence, and his wife, Lilly Jane, a society
princess, killed herself over the scandal to her illustrious name.
Her husband, this guy Harry Litwin, committed suicide himself
shortly after.

Beth looked in the manila envelope; nothing more. She
frowned, not understanding the purpose of those old articles
except to alert her to the fact that David Methany hadn't been
a particularly honorable businessman, at least according to one
Manhattan D.A. She accepted that as a truth now; she didn't
like it, but she accepted it. That didn't mean he had helped two
people kill themselves, if that was the purpose of sending her
these clips! Ridiculous. She turned over the envelope; not sur-

118

prisingly, there was no return address. Her name and home address had been typed; the postmark was New York.

The one curious aspect to these articles was the name of Lilly Jane Litwin, possibly the same woman Gene had heard had had an affair with her father. Even so, what difference could it make now?

With disgust, she tossed the clippings and the envelope into the wastebasket, then impulsively retrieved them and stuck them in her desk drawer.

Strange, she thought, that someone would send these old clips now, when the current Methany management was using similar tactics against the residents of Feldon Manor. The newspapers this week had been filled with old man Wilkes and the issue of the Central Park West building. In the papers early in the week, he had been all bluster; by today's articles, he admitted that he was not going to ask for landmark status for the building, the restraining order had been lifted already, and the mayor decided that there was nothing to be investigated. When asked why the bellicosity was followed swiftly by accommodation, Wilkes confessed that he had been acting like a foolish old man unwilling to accept positive, constructive change, and after having time to think about it, he knew that modernization was what revitalized a city and he had no doubt at all that the Methany Corporation would provide for the elderly residents as well as for the great city of New York. When asked by one reporter if he had been coerced in any way to change his position, Wilkes was quoted as saying that he was too ornery to do anything he didn't want to.

Beth knew otherwise. In only a few days, there had been a fire in one elevator at Feldon Manor, a snapped cable in another; roaches in Wilkes's kitchen, leaks in his air conditioners, and a flood from the bathroom of the upstairs apartment that dripped into his. Then there had been his neighbor, an old lady who used a walker to get around. She was threatened at knifepoint when she hobbled out to the incinerator, forced to return to her apartment and give the ski-masked mugger all her loose cash. There was the substitute doorman who was too drunk to get out of his chair. The washers and dryers in the laundry room seemed to spew out more lint than either water or hot air. The two mice on the fourth floor. And the letter to a member of the landmark committee revealing knowledge of the woman's lover, another married lady. All in only a week. Alyson had had no intention of telling Beth any of this, but Beth had pressed, and while she certainly didn't like what the lawyer had planned, she now would be able to go ahead with Methany Palace and that would help her with the banks as well as weaken Ben Wyler's position against Methany City North. Still, her conscience heaved with disgust at the immoral actions taken.

As she was thinking this, the telephone rang. She got up from behind the bedroom desk and picked up the extension by the bed. "Hello?"

No answer.

"Hello? Who is this?"

No answer. Not even heavy breathing. Beth took the receiver away from her ear, frowned at it as if it, personally, were responsible for the silence, put it back to her ear. "Hello? Hello?"

"Soon."

Beth blinked in surprise. She had been expecting an obscenity, perhaps an imprecation from a competitor or one of the hapless residents at Feldon Manor, but certainly not this one word in a voice she could not distinguish as male or female. There was no other sound, nothing to indicate who was speaking or from where.

"What? What did you say? Hello? Hello? Who is this? Talk to me. Say something, damn you!"

In response came the click of the receiver being replaced in its cradle, disconnecting from Beth.

Slowly, she hung up. She took several deep breaths, and then walked over to the window and pushed aside her gauze curtains, gazing out at the trees, their summer green leaves twinkling in the glare from the street lamps along Fifth Avenue. What was going on? she asked herself, willing herself to think rationally, stay calm. First the clippings, then this sexless voice and that one word: "Soon."

There are sickos out there, people who hated your father and who don't want you to succeed. Telling herself that helped. Instead of being frightened, she began to get angry; angry enough to pick up her phone and dial Ben Wyler's number, convinced without even considering it that he was behind these incidents to harass her. Disgruntled at his failure with Feldon Manor, and no doubt sensing similar failure with Methany City North, the ambitious politician was pulling out all the stops in one final effort to foil her. The bastard!

"Hello?" came his groggy voice sounding nothing at all like the genderless word of moments ago. It was then that Beth looked at her wristwatch and realized it was almost midnight. Now she was embarrassed by her rashness. Ben would never do this to her; regardless of how anti–Methany City North he might be, wasn't he the one who insisted he could care for her and not for what she did? Wasn't he the one who wanted them still to be together? What had she been thinking that he would ever scare her this way?

"Ben?"

"Beth? Is that you?"

"I'm sorry, I didn't realize how late it was."

"That's okay. I was only sleeping."

"Oh."

"Beth? What is it? What's wrong?"

"Nothing, I'm sorry, go back to sleep."

"Beth, we haven't spoken in weeks and then you call me at midnight on a Friday night and you're not going to tell me why? Come on, you owe me a little better treatment than that."

"You wouldn't understand," she whispered, feeling utterly miserable and ashamed.

"Try me," and she could tell from his voice that he was fully awake now. She envisioned him sitting up in his bed, resting against the teak headboard, his thick brown hair tousled, one hand groping for his glasses on the night table. How she missed him!

"Ben, I . . . I . . ."

"Beth, talk to me, damn it! Are you okay? What is it?"

"I don't know. I got this strange call and I thought . . . never mind."

There was a momentary silence on the other end, and when Ben again spoke, she could tell how hurt he was when he said, "And you thought it was me." Not a question; a statement of painful resignation.

"No, no, oh, Ben, I am sorry."

"You really don't get it, do you?" he said with some acerbity. "I am totally opposed to what your father had planned—your father, Beth—not you."

"We're one and the same," she muttered.

"No, damn it, you're not, although after what you pulled this week, I'm not so sure about that anymore."

"I didn't like it but it had to be done!" Beth exclaimed.

"Now you do sound like your father. First it's old people, then what, Beth, the disabled? Or will you oust the homeless from the streets if it's a street you need for a new co-op?"

"Damn you, Ben Wyler!"

"Shit."

Beth laughed softly. "That's more like it."

"Beth, you do know what happened this week was wrong." He paused. "Tell me that hasn't changed."

Beth shut her eyes briefly against the sweetness in his voice, more, against her own discomfort with the week's actions. "It hasn't changed," she whispered.

"Then maybe *we* still have a chance."

"Ben, don't—"

"Just know that I'd never hurt you, Beth, not even if it meant losing my fight against any Methany Corporation project. I'll be a loud and tough opponent against your business, but I'd never hurt you."

"I know that, Ben," she said slowly. "I don't know what I was thinking."

"Would you like me to come over?" he asked. "Just in case you get another call," he added, and she could hear the smile in his voice.

"I'd like that very much, but I don't think it would be a good idea."

"Beth—"

"Good night, Ben. I'm sorry." And she hung up before he could coax her into changing her mind.

Beth walked out of her room and into the informal sitting room where she poured herself a brandy from the bar in the entertainment unit. This was ridiculous, she told herself. A strange person named J. sending a postcard. Clippings thirty-four years old. A disembodied voice over a telephone. What the hell was going on? A man she cared about that she couldn't let herself be with. Horrendous acts against old, helpless people. For what? For the sake of business? Business! Something was wrong, off-balance. Nobody should get hurt on account of business.

And with another sip of brandy, Beth smiled ruefully at her own naïveté. What had her father always said to her? Whatever it takes, Bethie, whatever it takes, to get the job done the way *you* want it done. Sometimes, though, that was so damn hard to accept. Alyson Gentry understood it better than she did, Beth thought, stretching out on the blue velveteen love seat. But then, she told herself, it was far easier to perform *for* the boss than it was to perform *as* the boss. Beth had responsibility for so many; her employees had responsibility only for themselves.

As she lay there, letting the brandy soothe her, she began to wonder again about those old newspaper clippings. Too bad there had been no photographs of this Lilly Jane Litwin person; she would liked to have seen what the lover of her father had looked like back then, if indeed the gossip had been true. He would have been very young at the time, and not married long to her mother. Curious, very curious. If he had had an affair, then she couldn't have been the Lilly Jane mentioned in the twelve-year-long correspondence from J. She would have been dead all that time. It didn't make sense. None of it. And, she decided, putting down the snifter and heading back to her room, it didn't matter. What mattered was getting the business clearly on track. Put the Central Park West project back on ice until the tax abatement for Methany City North came through and she could renegotiate her arrangements with the banks. Then start building on Methany Palace when the banks saw that she, not her father, but his daughter, could be as tough and shrewd and as big a gambler as she had to be. Because it was a gamble to go against an apartment house full of geriatrics, and it was a gamble to play with banks' money, and maybe it was even a gamble to ignore strange postcards and letters and newspaper clips and telephone calls. But she'd be damned if anything or anybody was going to stop her father from being proud of her, no matter from where he was watching her . . . .

Rrr-i-i-ng.

Rrr-i-i-ng.

She jerked around, turning from her stomach to her back, caught in the vivid dream of being in Playland, in the bumper cars, and the place was alive with the ringing of cars hitting one another.

Rrr-i-i-ng.

She opened her eyes, and when the telephone rang for the fourth time, she finally understood that she had not been dreaming. She picked up the Tiffany table clock and saw from its luminous hands that it was 3:57 in the morning. What the hell—?

Rrr-i-i-ing.

"Hello?"

No answer.

No. *No.*

"Hello? Hello?"

No answer.

"Who is this, damn you? Answer me. Say something!"

"Soon."

This can't be happening. It can't! Beth's mind screamed at her. Who? Why?

"Please, who is this? Why are you doing this to me?"

Get the voice to talk again. Try to figure it out, male, female. Who? Why?

"Talk to me, damn you!"

But there was nothing further, only the black buzz of a disconnection.

Beth put back the receiver. She did not turn on her bedside lamp; neither did she try to go back to sleep. It would be useless. She lay there, the comforter drawn up to her chin, her arms rigid by her sides, her eyes wide open.

And for the first time in her entire life, Beth Methany knew fear.

The kind that made her heart pump hard.

The kind that made her eyes burn with tears.

The kind that made her fingers twitch on the comforter.

The kind that made her mind race.

Who? Why?

14

THEN

To my dearest child,

If all goes as I have wished, you are now a
young man or lady who has celebrated a twenty-
first birthday within the past month. In the
years that brought you to this age, I hope
with all my heart that you have known only
happiness, and most of all, the love of a
father and a mother who rejoice at every sight
of you.

How strange, you must be thinking. The letter
is addressed to my child, yet I do not know
if you are boy or girl and I speak of your
parents. I will try to explain so that you
need never wonder about your natural parents
or your bloodlines, but know that you are
unique, and this uniqueness should give you
pride and strength throughout your life.

I am currently in my seventh month of pregnancy—
with you. My wonderful, loving husband, a
generous and caring man named Harry, is not
your father. Foolishly, frivolously, and with
regrettable selfishness, in my life of too much
leisure, too much money, and too much self-

126

indulgence, an inconsequential life as a
society sweetheart except for the valuable
act of conceiving you, I took up with another
man. For the first time in my married life,
I was unfaithful to someone who deserved much
better. To make matters more shameful, my husband and your birth father were adversaries,
your natural father a far wilier, shrewder,
and more dangerous man than my husband could
ever be. Although your natural father wanted
me to abort you, my husband understood my
absolute refusal to do this, and if the father
were any but the individual he was, my husband
would have accepted you as his own, raised you
with all the love in his heart. But because my
husband, Harry Litwin, was a Manhattan district
attorney trying to form a case against your
natural father, a man by the name of David
Methany, with evidence that would prove him an unscrupulous and immoral real estate businessman who used
illegal means to achieve his desires, my husband
could not stand by and raise you. The thought of
being father to David Methany's child was, under-
standably, beyond even this good man's tolerance,
and so I was convinced to give you up for adoption.

In no way did I give you up out of lack of love. Even
now, twenty-one years later, know that your mother's
heart was broken the day I signed the adoption
agreement.

Edward Whittington is a lawyer Harry knew from law
school, in whose office you are now reading this
letter, given to him by me days after the adoption
agreement was signed. It was important to me that
someday you know the truth about who you are and
where you came from, and why you were adopted.

My dearest child, do not try to find me now.
Our lives are forever distinct and separate,
and to change that at this point would be
wrong, for you and your adoptive parents who
I pray have given you all the love I could not.
Know that you were cherished by me, and given
away with the conviction that you would be
equally cherished by *two* parents. May your
life be wiser than mine, and filled only with
love and joy and friends.

Your natural mother,

Lilly Jane Basille Litwin

The young woman of twenty-one looked up from the sheet of luxuriously thick blue stationery, blind-embossed with the initials LJBL, into the attentive eyes of Edward Whittington, a man she had never known existed until four days ago when her parents had explained to her that he had something for her from her natural mother, a letter he had been instructed to hold for her until her twenty-first birthday, also four days ago. Although she had known since she was six years old that she was adopted, she could not imagine parents more wonderful than the ones she had; she had never felt compelled, as were many adoptees, to learn more about her natural parents or why they had put her up for adoption.

Now she knew. More than she could ever have imagined. She studied the attorney, her light hazel eyes bright with surprise, her wide mouth set, her entire posture, face, hands rigid as if to move slightly would be to reveal the tumult of emotions racing through her. One of the things about her that had always astounded her adoptive parents had been her ability to exercise the most incredible restraint and self-control no matter the circumstances. Be it falling off her bicycle and requiring stitches in her knee after landing on a rocky outgrowth, or not getting 100 on a geography test, only a 98, she showed nothing of what she felt. She did not know how she came to believe that it was better to hide her emotions rather than reveal them for someone else's advantage, but so she believed. And that is how she conducted herself now in this lawyer's office. The difference this time was that she wondered if the trait of self-control came from her mother or her father. An adulteress would not be self-contained, she quickly decided. A successful and possibly unscrupulous businessman would be. So, this facet of her nature may have come from her father, some man named David Methany.

"Ms. Gentry, are you all right?" the attorney asked. "May I get you water, a brandy perhaps?"

"I'm fine, thank you," she replied softly. "Mr. Whittington, I do have some questions."

"Of course, I would assume as much, but perhaps it would be best to save them for another time after you've more fully assimilated the letter."

"I'd rather now." And there was a strength in her voice far older than her twenty-one years, the purposeful tone of one who has always known her own mind and been confident of its judgments.

"Well, then, I'll try to answer as best I can."

"First of all, do my adoptive parents know who my natural parents are?"

"No, although Lilly Jane and her husband, Harry, knew the backgrounds, but not the names of your adoptive parents. It was very important to Lilly Jane that you go to good people."

"The best," the young woman said, smiling warmly. "The very best." She turned pensive again. "Mr. Whittington, why you? Why wasn't a New York lawyer given this letter? Or did you arrange the adoption?"

"I did," he confirmed. "Harry persuaded Lilly Jane of the

wisdom in getting away from the eastern seaboard. My contacts even then were throughout the Midwest."

"A safety precaution for the sake of privacy, I understand." She glanced down at the letter, then up again, her look sharp and probing on the lawyer's face. "Why, Mr. Whittington? Can you tell me what the purpose of this letter is and why it was given to me now?"

Edward Whittington, a sophisticated attorney with one of the most respected firms in Chicago, found himself oddly nonplussed by this young woman's steely reserve. The question was chilling in its lack of emotion.

"Ms. Gentry," he began cautiously, "I think the answers to those questions are quite evident in the contents of the letter itself. Your mother wanted—"

"My mother is Francine Gentry, Mr. Whittington. This woman," she waved the letter, "this woman conceived me and carried me and gave birth to me. That does not make her my mother. So I'll ask again. What is the purpose of this letter?"

"To make you aware of your natural parents—who gave birth to you, under what circumstances, and why you were put up for adoption. Most adoptees want to know that sort of thing."

"But why now, when I turned twenty-one?"

"I really don't know. At the time I was given the letter, I was told that since you would be legally an adult at this age, it would be appropriate then. Now that I've met you," he nodded toward her, "I'm sure you could have handled it at a much younger age."

Janine Gentry smiled her appreciation of his compliment, then bent her head over the letter again. The almost-sixty-year-old attorney could not help but admire how her straight tawny brown hair shimmered in the late afternoon light streaking through the venetian blinds. She wore it long, to her shoulders and then softly turned under, an endearingly old-fashioned style that reminded him of his wife when they first met. A pretty girl, Ed Whittington decided, but not beautiful, at least not yet. He had met Lilly Jane in person a few times, and from what he could remember, this young girl had the almond shape of her eyes and the incipient sexuality in her slender body that Lilly Jane had carried with a sense of amusement but that Janine Gentry did not even seem to be aware she possessed. Her slightly too long, straight nose was David Methany's; her olive coloring, David Methany's; the planes of her jaw, the curve of her cheek-bones, David Methany's. Obviously, the lawyer thought wryly, the dominant genes were the dominant parent's. He wondered how the mighty David Methany would react if he knew he had an illegitimate daughter and one who bore so many of his char-acteristics, although from photos the lawyer had seen of the real estate mogul in newspapers and magazines, and on television newscasts, there was no way one could mistake this young lady in his office today as an offspring of his. Her natural mother's softness was very evident, and the full lips as well as that ex-traordinary hair were the girl's own. He had a feeling that her intelligence was singular as well, perhaps missing Lilly Jane's humor and David Methany's shrewdness, but acute nevertheless.

"Is there any money?" she suddenly asked.

"I beg your pardon?"

"Money. Is there any inheritance?"

"Why no, no, there isn't," the lawyer bumbled.

"Mr. Whittington," she leaned forward, earnest curiosity in her eyes, "I appreciate that my natural mother would want me to know about her and the circumstances of my adoption, but there has to be more."

Ed Whittington smiled gently. "There is no more, Ms. Gentry. All Lilly Jane wanted was for you to know about her and to let you know you were not given away for lack of love."

Janine Gentry shook her head, not quite understanding. "It

just seems like an awfully long time to wait to tell me, and then nothing again. Why do you think there was no financial arrangement?"

Ed Whittington shrugged, thoughtful. "I imagine that Lilly Jane, and Harry, too, no doubt, didn't want money to interfere with how the Gentrys raised you. And for you to have any now would be like buying someone's affections."

"But it's as if she's entered my life only to disappear again. I mean, of course it would be interesting to meet her now, but I would have thought that a financial legacy of some sort would be a way to establish a tie, too. I don't mean to sound mercenary, Mr. Whittington, but I just can't get past the feeling that there's a definite purpose to this letter. I suppose I'll have to wait to ask her in person. How do I go about doing that?"

"You don't. Or rather, you can't."

"I'm sorry, I don't understand. I'd like to arrange to—"

"Lilly Jane Litwin is dead, Ms. Gentry."

Janine sat back, as startled by this information as by the existence of Lilly Jane in the first place. She laughed uncertainly. "This is quite a day for surprises. First I find out about my natural mother, assume I'll be meeting her, and then learn she's not even alive."

"I'm sorry, my dear, I truly am," the lawyer offered.

"And David Methany?"

"Alive. Very much alive and well and prospering in New York City."

"Is this the same David Methany I've read about, the one with all those hotels and luxury co-ops?"

"The very same."

"I see."

"Your bloodlines, if I may use so old-fashioned a term, are exceptional."

Janine's eyebrows lifted with a humorless smile. "Are they?

A socialite mother who was an adulteress and a man who was being investigated for unscrupulous business practices. Frankly, Mr. Whittington, the parents I have—a high school English teacher for a mother and an electrical engineer for a father—strike me as much better."

"You have a point," the lawyer conceded.

"Does this David Methany know about me?"

"No."

"You mean he doesn't know who adopted me?"

"No, I mean he doesn't know you were adopted at all."

"How could my natural father not know about the disposition of his child?"

Ed Whittington did not answer immediately, but looked at the young woman across from him, wondering not if she could handle the truth—of that he had no doubt—but rather if it was at all necessary to reveal it. Yes, he decided. He owed the Litwins that much, their memory, their good name. Maybe his illegitimate child would get David Methany to finally bear the consequences of his acts.

"I think I'll have a brandy, Ms. Gentry. Will you join me?" She shook her head as he got up from behind his desk and walked over to a credenza. By opening one door and pressing a button, a shelf that served as a miniature bar slid out and rose to waist level. The lawyer poured himself a snifter of Courvoisier, then resumed his seat.

"Mr. Whittington?" Janine prompted.

"David Methany thought you had died when Lilly Jane died."

Janine frowned, absorbing the statement, trying to make sense of it. "Are you saying that Lilly Jane died twenty-one years ago?"

"She died in childbirth, but not while giving birth."

"I'm sorry, but now I'm utterly confused."

"Lilly Jane," the lawyer began, stopping to take a large gulp of his brandy to fortify him for what had to be said, "Lilly Jane was eight-and-a-half months pregnant when a night maid at the Rowland Court Hotel in Manhattan found her in a room there, still alive, though barely, from an overdose of liquid Valium."

Janine squeezed shut her eyes, breathed deeply, then opened them again. Her face was expressionless; only the unnatural brightness in her eyes revealed the pain of hearing this tale.

"It was pretty horrible from what Harry Litwin told me," the attorney continued. "She was rushed to a hospital and the doctor was able to save you, but not Lilly Jane."

"Why?"

"Why did she try to kill herself?" Janine nodded. "I'm not really sure to this day. Harry thought it wasn't because of you or the affair. He believed that he was responsible."

"Why, when he wasn't the father?"

"True, but he had been getting a lot of publicity for the case he was compiling against David Methany. When it became obvious that his case was actually more press than real solid evidence, he dropped it, and that was the kind of embarrassment and scandal Lilly Jane couldn't take. She came from an extremely old and respected family; not a breath of scandal had ever touched them. Even when Harry's publicity was positive, they probably cringed, and when it became negative," he shook his head, "as frivolous as Lilly Jane might have been on the surface, she was a very decent woman who never totally forgot her upbringing. Harry thought she killed herself because she was so humiliated by his failure."

"How horrible, how very, very horrible," Janine whispered. "Where is Harry Litwin now?"

"Dead. He killed himself, too, shortly afterward. He couldn't live with the guilt."

"This is all so grim." Suddenly, the sadness vanished from

her eyes and she became alert. "Didn't David Methany wonder what happened to his child? Didn't he try to find out—"

"David Methany didn't know you had lived."

"What! This isn't making any sense at all, Mr. Whittington."

"Harry and I discussed this the night Lilly Jane died, and we decided that since you were being adopted there was no legal reason for David to be told you had survived. There was nothing to be gained for you, since he had never acknowledged being the father. It was your mother's word against his, and he was already so powerful, even twenty-one years ago, that no one would go against him even if he were lying. Besides, he had wanted your mother to have an illegal abortion, so learning that you were alive would have been meaningless for him."

"But what about the people who knew of my existence? The doctors and nurses at the hospital? Didn't the press find out?"

Ed Whittington allowed himself a brief smile. "I suppose you could say we got lucky. Harry told me that it was about midnight when Lilly Jane was brought in and there was a skeletal staff— just the attending doctor and nurse on the maternity wing. There was never any real question of saving Lilly Jane; she was too far gone. The issue was always the baby. Harry told me that he made a simple request that the doctor and nurse not speak to the press, and given the tragedy of losing his wife, and she a woman known by anyone who read the society columns, they agreed. The press never went beyond the obvious—that Lilly Jane Litwin had died of a lethal overdose of liquid Valium, taking her own life and that of her unborn child. I flew in to New York two days later, got you, and brought you home to the Gentrys."

"And no one has ever revealed the truth about my existence to this day? Not the hotel people, the doctor or nurse or whoever signed hospital papers, no enterprising reporter, nobody?"

"Other emergencies, other news," Ed Whittington told her.

"And a sizable endowment to the small society hospital from Harry Litwin," he admitted with a knowing nod.

Janine ran her fingers through her hair, a gesture of frustration. "Mr. Whittington, I'm trying to understand, but it's so bizarre. I am born, there's a lucky convergence of elements so that few people know about this and those who do are persuaded to remain silent, and even my natural father is never told."

"Ms. Gentry, I know this seems terribly manipulative, but *you,* you as a human being, were of far less importance to people than Harry and Lilly Jane Litwin. The hospital people genuinely wanted to be of service to him, I am convinced of that. To safeguard their silence, he endowed the hospital. There's nothing wrong with buying a little security, Ms. Gentry, believe me. As for the press, you know yourself how short their attention span is. Lilly Jane's suicide was the news, not you."

"And as for David Methany," Janine continued for the attorney, "he wasn't told because he would have denied paternity."

"Exactly. He was, *is* not the kind of person to tolerate unwanted interference in his life, regardless of the circumstances. You did not exist for him; you were merely an unknown and unwanted nuisance. Don't blame David Methany for what is really not that unusual an attitude for a man."

"But isn't it possible that if he had known, he would have made some arrangements for me, financially perhaps, or adopted me himself? Was he married?"

"Yes, but there was no question of David Methany having anything to do with you. You see, the only one to whom he had acknowledged paternity was to Lilly Jane herself, and she shared that with me when she gave me the letter you're holding. As far as everyone else was concerned, you were Harry's child, which made Lilly Jane's suicide and your death—which is what the public assumed—so tragic that Harry had to take his own life."

"So David Methany walked away unscathed," she said slowly.

Ed Whittington did not reply, but took another sip of brandy, his eyes steady on her. What a remarkable young lady, he was thinking. Calmer than people twice her age would be after hearing of these tragedies. And he had only told her the public version, the accepted version.

"Mr. Whittington," Janine said, breaking into his thoughts, "you knew my mother."

"Only slightly."

"You knew her well enough to answer my questions, I think. Was she the type of woman to take her own life?"

"Ms. Gentry, I don't think I—"

"Was she the type of woman, Mr. Whittington, to take her own life and that of her unborn child—over a professional humiliation of her husband's? Surely you can answer me that."

Ed Whittington met the young woman's unwavering eyes, and had to look away at first. So she was more astute than the public had been at the time. Not surprising if she were David Methany's offspring, he thought bitterly.

"She took an overdose of liquid Valium, Ms. Gentry," he tried.

"You didn't answer my question."

He got up, poured himself another brandy, sat back down, took a swallow, and then slowly shook his head. "No, Lilly Jane Litwin was not the type of woman to take her own life regardless of what the circumstances might be, and she certainly would not have taken yours. She wanted desperately to have you and have Harry raise you. It was, as she wrote in the letter, Harry's pride that simply could not permit it because you were born of David Methany, his archenemy. And although you haven't asked, I'll also tell you that Harry Litwin was a helluva lawyer who would never, *never* manufacture evidence or gather evidence on a case that he wasn't damn sure would be airtight with a jury."

"Are you saying that David Methany had something to do with his dropping the case?"

"Who knows what to think, Ms. Gentry. It's history now, so it really doesn't matter."

Janine Gentry considered that, then said, simply, "Thank you, Mr. Whittington. I appreciate your honesty."

The lawyer got to his feet, a signal that their unusual meeting had come to an end. "I understand you're going to school in California, plan to join my profession," he remarked with an avuncular smile.

"Yes. Stanford Law."

"That's wonderful. Terrific school, terrific." He paused, his face resuming its mask of blandness. "I hope today hasn't upset you too much, Ms. Gentry. I imagine it's quite unsettling to learn about yourself in such a way, but at least now you have the comfort of knowing you come from extraordinary stock."

"It's a sad story, isn't it, Mr. Whittington?" she asked, also rising and moving toward the door. "A woman in the prime of life who had everything, the child who never got to know her, the man responsible for so much unhappiness able to avoid all responsibility. Sad."

"Yes, my dear, it is. But please try not to be distraught over knowing the truth."

She stopped at the door and turned to him, her eyes wide with surprise. "But that's the one thing I don't know, Mr. Whittington. The truth. Perhaps I can do justice to both my natural parents by finding out exactly that."

"Ms. Gentry, move on with your life, step forward, not back," the lawyer hastened to advise. "The letter was your mother's way of giving you a true sense of your identity. Don't sully her gift to you or her memory by dredging up the past."

"Sometimes, though, the only way to put the past to rest *is* by dredging it up."

He looked at her and knew that she was far stronger-willed than he could have imagined. "If I can be of any further assistance—"

After Janine Gentry left, Edward Whittington poured himself an unheard-of third brandy—and it was not yet four o'clock in the afternoon. He sat back down behind his desk and contemplated the events of the meeting, unsure whether he had handled any of it correctly.

He had known the contents of the letter for twenty-one years, because Lilly Jane had shown it to him, asking his advice long ago about bequeathing a financial legacy on the child. He had been against it then, as now, as a gesture unfair to the adoptive parents.

He had known that Lilly Jane had wanted to keep the child of David Methany; that Harry couldn't deal with that; that the real estate genius had been behind Harry's career disintegrating. Edward Whittington knew it all, except how he had gotten away with murder. Because whether Lilly Jane Litwin actually administered the liquid Valium to herself or not, David Methany was behind her premature death, of that he had no doubt, not a doubt in the world. He had no proof, of course, and certainly twenty-one years later no impetus to find out the truth, but wasn't that why, secretly, he felt gratified by Janine Gentry's remark about seeing justice done, despite his half-hearted attempt to dissuade her?

For all intents and purposes, to Edward Whittington's way of thinking David Methany had taken the lives of three people: Lilly Jane and Harry Litwin, and to the best of Methany's knowledge, the child she had been carrying that he had fathered. Edward Whittington hoped, therefore, that he would be around to enjoy the consequences of David Methany meeting the truth—tawny-haired and hazel-eyed and tall and lithe, and very, very intelligent as she had become.

15

That day a decision was made, arrived at with difficulty and pain, accepted with conviction of its rightness.

Janine Gentry left Edward Whittington's office feeling like a stranger to herself; even her skin itched as if it had been newly grafted. She took the el to her apartment in Lincoln Park, where she now sat among half-packed cartons and suitcases, holding Lilly Jane Litwin's letter in her lap, still in its envelope. Until this afternoon, she had given very little consideration to her future outside of planning it carefully and never doubting for an instant that it would not go according to this plan. Everything in her life had been so pleasantly ordinary—aside from learning that she was adopted—that it had never crossed her mind that things would not continue in similar fashion. She had been an honors undergraduate in history at the University of Chicago, and in three days she would be heading out to one of the most outstanding law schools in the country. She had always wanted to be a lawyer, liking the structure, the discipline of the law, the opportunity to administer justice. It was her ambition to become a public prosecutor and then a judge.

Janine had never questioned her goals or whether they were right for her; there had been no reason to until today. Now she did not know who she was or what was suitable for her. Intellectually, she knew that she had not changed, nor had her relationship with her loving and supportive adoptive parents. Yet, emotionally, she could not stop wondering how much of the self-absorbed society matron, the unethical businessman, was in her character?

Slowly, she removed the letter from its envelope and reread its contents, once, then again. As she did, a river of emotions overflowed within her: anger, confusion, curiosity; at no time, the pride and strength her natural mother had thought she would gain from knowing the truth. Gradually, anger at the frivolity and selfishness of these two people's lives turned to anger at Lilly Jane's need to unburden herself at the expense of her unknown child. Because wasn't it she, Janine Gentry, who now carried the weight of the truth after twenty-one years of ignorance? And what was she supposed to do with it? Start calling her parents by their first names, as if their love and support were abruptly erased by a letter locked away for years in a lawyer's safe? Run to New York City and look up relatives who would no doubt deny her existence, call the letter a fake, or dismiss it as the ravings of an unhappy woman? Announce herself to David Methany as his long-lost child? No, forget long-lost, she silently amended; how about his long-thought-dead child? At that, she grinned, a rictus of grimness.

Throughout Janine's years of growing up, people would invariably comment to her parents that she seemed older than her years, that there was a poise, a self-assurance about her that belied her age. Francine and Donald would repeat this to her with a sense of pride that they had given her the kind of happy home environment that led to peace of mind. She had never doubted that cause and effect, never wondered what part of her makeup was created by her adoptive parents, what part genetically handed down.

And so the anger became confusion. Who was she?

As she sat there, holding the letter loosely in her lap, staring across the room at the framed photograph of Francine and Donald Gentry on her dresser top, a sting of hot tears came to her eyes. Who was she? she repeated to herself. Was she her mother's child, silly, amusing, kind? No, she thought not. She had often been told, even by friends, that she was too intense, too single-minded in setting a goal and attaining it. Did that come from her father? It seemed reasonable. A successful businessman, shrewd enough to be unscrupulous, possibly even unlawful in his practices, and getting away with it would be a man both intense and single-minded.

And so the confusion became curiosity: who was David Methany? How much of her came from him?

It was then that she recalled what Edward Whittington had said about Lilly Jane not being the type to kill herself. About David Methany not knowing he had an illegitimate child. About him being powerful enough to deny paternity. And she remembered, too, her instinctive reaction, words that were spoken without thought or contemplation: that *she* would find out the truth and do justice to both of them.

Justice. It was a concept of the deepest importance to Janine. She could not abide wrongs to another in the name of a variety of weak excuses. To a large degree, Lilly Jane Litwin had committed an injustice against Francine and Donald Gentry by virtue of the existence of this letter. To a far greater degree, Janine realized, was the possible injustice done to her if suicide had not been the way she died.

Later, Janine would look back on this afternoon and wonder if her decision was made at that precise moment, when she understood what her instincts had been telling her earlier, when she consciously accepted that an injustice had been done to her natural mother's memory. And when she realized that, by extension, an injustice was being enacted against herself.

She considered, then dismissed, the notion of discussing the issue with her adoptive parents. They would not understand her need to act against the injustice rather than merely know and accept and regret it. No, something had to be done, and although it had not been her original intention, Lilly Jane's letter would inadvertently become the means to at long last get David Methany to take responsibility for his actions.

Janine did not know what she would do, but as the hours passed, and curiosity reverted back to anger—this time at lives wasted, lives hurt, lives led without accountability—she knew there was more, much more to the story of Lilly Jane Litwin and David Methany, more than the letter revealed, more than Edward Whittington knew. And so sometime in the middle of the night, when the anger had steamed in her slowly and steadily until it became a simmering rage, Janine decided that she would find out everything there was to know about her natural mother and the night she took the overdose of liquid Valium. She would find out everything about David Methany, then and now. She would be careful and patient and calm. If it took two months or two years or even twenty, she would wait until the right time to present herself, and then she would see that justice was served. There was no question, not one scintilla of doubt, even without factual evidence to back up her conviction, that David Methany *owed* Lilly Jane Litwin and Janine Gentry, and she was going to make sure he paid. Revenge and retribution. No. Justice.

Janine Gentry finished Stanford Law School at the top of her class, but instead of working in the D.A.'s office as she had originally intended, she began her career as a lawyer for one of San Francisco's most influential real estate firms. It was all part of her plan, a plan that had been simmering, like her rage, for quite some time. A plan that had, in the course of discovery, lost sight of its original target.

David Methany, a man of inestimable power and wealth, had a legal heir to his fortune. A daughter.

Except he already had a daughter, older by more than two years, first in line to inherit—if justice were correctly served.

16

"...your natural father a far wilier, shrewder, and more dangerous man..."

Regardless of how many times she had read the letter during the past almost fourteen years, Janine Gentry's eyes invariably returned to those same words, inspiration as she patiently plotted her revenge.

On this summer evening, she was still in her office, rereading the letter as she often did, more often since David Methany had died. The blue paper was now soft and worn, a favorite blanket whose nap had been eroded but whose warmth could still be felt. That's how Janine considered the letter; it provided her with a comfort that helped her get through the years. So many, many years, she thought, resting her head back against the ungiving leather of her desk chair. Years when she wondered if she would go mad with the need to act, the energy and discipline it took not to. Years of enterprise and discovery, when she had made it her business to learn everything there was to know about the night Lilly Jane Litwin had died, the people involved who had found her, operated on her, saved her baby's life. She had the names of the room-service waiter and the night maid, the ambulance driver, even the admitting nurse at Saint Cecilia's Hospital, a very private and exclusive and expensive

144

hospital for those who could afford to pay the most for exclusivity and privacy—and secrets kept buried for years to come. She never could find out the name of the doctor on duty that night or of the maternity nurse, Harry Litwin's endowment protecting them well. She had tracked down Lilly Jane's regular obstetrician, an old, old man who remembered her well and was aghast at the idea of prescribing liquid Valium to anyone. That had left little doubt in Janine's mind that David had doctored the champagne. What a typically Methany maneuver, the means of death colorless, odorless, virtually undetectable, and a plausible means of suicide for a scandalized society notable.

She could not quite remember now when the idea had first come to her; it seemed as if it had been there from the beginning, from that odd afternoon with the Chicago lawyer almost fourteen years ago. Of course, then she had had only an instinctive sense that he was not telling her all he knew, or, to give him the benefit of the doubt, could not tell her everything there was to be known about that night twenty-one years earlier at the Rowland Court Hotel because he himself did not know it. She had gone off to law school, only sporadically trying to uncover more of the past, her present life and the future she was building toward more important to her, despite the continuous, vague, gnawing sense that her future was intrinsically linked with the mysteries of the past. Then she came across an issue of *Business Week* with David Methany's photograph on the cover. Nothing had ever been the same since. The impact of that cover, the article, had never diminished over the years; they, like the letter on the faded blue stationery, had propelled her forward no matter how slowly the steps.

She sat up straighter in the chair, listening for sounds of activity in the office hallways, but at eight-thirty, only the cleaning crew remained, and they were used to seeing her here late. So she opened the bottom drawer of her desk where she kept her purse, reached in, and extracted a common brass ring on which she kept her apartment keys, mailbox key, and to minimize the file cabinet key from standing out, even several luggage keys, just in case the brass ring should ever fall into the wrong hands.

She got up and walked over to the metal file cabinet in which were kept all the cases she had worked on in her four years with the Methany Corporation, cases that ran the gamut from complicated transfers of property ownership to the initial problems with the Feldon Manor Hotel, to a burgeoning file on Ben Wyler and his interference in the future plans of the corporation. Dear little Beth would be shocked to the ends of her curly hair if she ever knew the amount of information amassed against her ambitious ex-lover. Like the fact that his driver's license had been revoked twice in college, twice since then for repeated excessive speeding. Like the fact that an uncle, brother to his father, had worked for the Methany Corporation for over fifteen years as a bookkeeper only to be fired unceremoniously, one of three scapegoats the year David had to pay close to $650,000 in back taxes, interest, and penalties to the IRS, a sum a team of accountants were responsible for, but who would go blameless because they knew not just where the bodies were buried, financially speaking, but how they had gotten into their graves. And like the fact that Ben's ex-wife had a serious cocaine addiction and her supplier was none other than the councilman's current press official. Yes, Janine thought, clenching her jaw, this was a file she particularly cherished. Not just for what it contained against a person Beth Methany cared about, but because it represented the fine art of David Methany's strategy for success.

Over the years, as she had delved deeper and learned more, Janine had read everything available in the libraries on Harry Litwin's case against David back in the 1950s. Then, when she had come to work here, observing David, being involved in actual cases with him, she had begun to respect and admire the very same methods that had caused Harry Litwin, and others over time, so much grief. The man had been a master manipulator, a brilliant opponent who believed in the basic weakness of man, and so knew that at any given time, the person who dared to defy him had something to hide, something that could be uncovered if one were patient, and used against him if one were ruthless enough in the desire to win, and paid enough to get the damaging information. Fair? Absolutely not. Ethical? An equally strong no. Professional? Not particularly. Successful? Yes, a powerfully resonant yes. For someone who had once considered the prosecutor's office and a judgeship the best ways to see that the ideal of justice was done, Janine had quickly come to appreciate how much more satisfying David Methany's approach could be to attaining success, and that, she had also learned, had turned out to be the sweetest kind of justice, if not the most ideal.

The key on the brass ring fitted the fourth and bottom drawer. There were no case files in here, only some medical insurance forms, an old pair of shoes in case she got caught unprotected in bad weather, an extra collapsible umbrella, and a rather large, unmarked manila envelope, closed, not sealed, by a flimsy metal clasp. It was this she now removed from the drawer.

Back behind her desk again, she carefully extracted from the envelope a selection of New York City newspaper articles from 1956 featuring Harry Litwin's reasons for going after David Methany. The copy machine had worked overtime to make decent facsimiles of the decrepit newsprint, but she had wanted them clearly legible so the effort was worth it. She also removed the twelve-and-a-half-year-old issue of *Business Week*, a clipping of a Walter Winchell column featuring a grainy photo of Lilly Jane Basille when she had been an eighteen-year-old debutante, a photo of her from *Vogue* magazine when she, as Lilly Jane Litwin, and three other New York society swells had done a fashion layout in 1954.

Janine studied the magazine cover of the man who was her father and had not known it; the man who had killed her mother and gotten away with it; the man who became her boss and her mentor and never knew it.

She studied the pictures of the woman who had loved her without knowing her; the woman whose selfishness had ultimately killed her. Not for the first time did Janine realize how that sentiment exemplified David Methany; anyone more human, less calculating, would say that when Lilly Jane went through with the pregnancy she had never acted more selflessly in her life. If she had aborted, though, she'd be alive still. Nobody was worth your own life, nobody, especially some *thing* without identity.

Janine had come to believe that her calculating nature, the emotional coldness that allowed her to view Lilly Jane's act so cynically, were only two facets of her father that she could claim as her own. Physically, there was no question who she more strongly resembled. She had his strong bone structure, his coloring. What was her mother's was the unique shape of her eyes. Her lips were fuller than either parent's, her hair her own. Her intelligence, she had no doubt, all his. Her sense of style, hers. Her patience and perseverence and tenacity and self-control and insistence on privacy, the pleasure she experienced in winning, the ease with which she could act ruthlessly, without conscience, without guilt, his, all his. Her rather weak, or perhaps merely sublimated libido? Given the history, that, too, must be her own.

How amazing that no one, not David Methany himself in the four years she had worked for him before his death, nor his daughter, nor anyone else who saw them together, had ever noticed the physical resemblance between Alyson Gentry and

David Methany. How could anyone miss it, unless, of course, they weren't looking for it.

As always, Janine concentrated on the magazine cover; not the fashion layout from *Vogue,* not the yellowed debutante photo, only the business magazine cover of the man bannered as "The Best" back in 1978. It was as if she were seeing it for the first time; in truth, every time was new again for her; every time re-created the entire process for her: the curiosity, the comparisons, the anger. Only when she opened the magazine, though, and looked at the photograph of Beth Methany standing alongside her father in his office, did the process reach completion— the hatred and resentment and envy bursting full-blown in her heart, an aneurysm of destruction poisoning her existence even as it gave it meaning and purpose.

Until that day when Janine had been twenty-two and had bought the issue of the magazine, she had no idea of how genuinely vast the Methany empire was; how powerful a man David Methany was; no idea that there existed an heir to all that wealth and power.

At first there had been no plan. She had come up with the idea of the cryptic correspondence merely as a form of nuisance. She enjoyed the image of David's uncertainty, maybe even discomfort at receiving cards and letters sent at random from around the globe, with references to Lilly Jane and signed by a mysterious J. This went on year after year, because she knew that she too had to be "wily" and "shrewd," and she had to be strong so that when the appropriate time showed itself, she would succeed. Patience made her strong. Self-control and discipline made her strong. And the years perfecting her abilities as an attorney honed her cleverness until finally a plan evolved.

She would step into his arena. She would *work* with him, learn from him, learn about him. And that was what had happened, but not without careful thinking beforehand. Her previous references, her entire professional history, was based on Janine Gentry, yet she knew she could not use that real first name with David; she had signed the initial J. so many times on the correspondence that she could not take the chance he wouldn't be clever enough to recognize it. She would use the references in her real name and claim that when she moved to New York she had the first name legally changed, a lie that no one would question, especially given her explanation, if pressed, that Janine had been the name of an aunt she particularly loathed, while Alyson had been her favorite grandmother's name. Lies, lies, a history of lies so like what her father had done. As it turned out, though, only Gene Cavelli looked over her references before hiring her on as one of Methany Corporation's counsel, and he had accepted her name change explanation readily. Since there was little occasion for her to appear in court, she avoided sitting for the New York State bar and the issue of her name that could arise with that. Careful thinking.

She believed her plan for vindication was worthy of David Methany himself, and in time, she would tell him the truth. He would admire her and welcome her, because she would be so far superior to the weak little idiot who was his legitimate heir. That was the plan, and the fantasy.

Always, from the beginning, it was Beth Methany who was her target, because it was Beth Methany who stood in the way of justice, that justice being that David Methany recognize *her,* Janine, as his firstborn, his legal heir. Beth Methany had no right to any of it; most certainly she had no right to be photographed standing in the large corner office of the Methany Corporation with her arm around the founder's shoulders!

If there was a certain warped reasoning to this attitude, it eluded Janine. To her way of thinking, David Methany was guilty of the crime of murder, absolutely, but committed to eliminate interference with the impeccably planned unfolding of his life. She understood and respected that desire to have one's life proceed in an orderly, systematic fashion, and the concomitant need to dispense with anything, anyone, that might endanger that. The unfairness was that since she did exist, she was *entitled*. If there had been no other daughter, she might have remained in the background, casually trying to learn the truth, never doing anything with the knowledge. But for Lilly Jane to have lost so much and then for someone undeserving to gain, that was not just, and that was what had to be redressed.

Even while working for him, she had continued to send David the occasional card or letter, still wanting him to dangle from a string of uncertainty. Of course he would never risk exposure, and of course she could never really threaten him in any significant way, but the cards and letters helped her feel, in a small measure, in control, as did the thirty typed pages she had in her apartment detailing the events from that night, events told to her and a private investigator she had used occasionally, by the people involved who fortunately were alive and appreciative of an extra dollar or two. They would never swear to these events in a court of law, but what they had remembered had made a convincing case for David's culpability.

If working with her did not prove her worth to him, and her worthiness as his successor, then telling him what she knew about him, the enterprise and single-mindedness of gaining all that information, would vanquish any lingering concerns about his so-called "legitimate" heir, and so the correspondence went on. As did her patience, because, in truth, she had never spent more productive years than those working for and learning from David. She had been willing, too, to tolerate Beth Methany, her ineptitude, her inferiority, because of her unshakable belief that the learning and the patience both would pay off someday. When she took her rightful place at the head of the Methany Corporation, recognized as much for her ability as for being the firstborn, Lilly Jane would be vindicated, the undeserving heir destroyed, and, at last, justice, *her* idea of justice, served.

And then he had died.

There had been no destruction. No righting of the will. No place for her at the top. No recognition.

No justice served.

She had been a fool. She had not been her father's daughter. David Methany never would have allowed fantasy to dim reality; David Methany never would have allowed emotion to obscure purpose. She had waited too long, because with the desire to destroy, the longing to see justice done, had also been an aching need to make him *proud* of her.

David Methany would have laughed at the weakness inherent in such sentiment. And used it against her.

What had she always heard him say? His formula for success was easy, he would tell her. "If I am here and I want something that's there, I will do anything to get from here to there. Simple, really."

It was the one lesson from him she had forgotten. She had complicated her purposes with need and feeling. It was not a mistake she would ever make again.

On this same evening, Ben Wyler was also in his office late, alone, his key staff members long gone while he polished a speech he had to give the next afternoon at New York University Law School.

He was exhausted, physically and mentally. Instead of being with the special woman who had once been so important in his life, he found himself resurrecting her memory whenever he needed to remember that warmth and caring and loving sensuality had once existed for him. Oh, sure, there were plenty of women out there eager to show the hotshot politico more than a little loving kindness, but Ben didn't want them, he wanted Beth, damn it. Typical male that he was, it had taken not being with her, the probability that they would never be together again, to show him how much she meant to him. But she was so damn stubborn! Why couldn't she get it through her head that what he said about her father had no bearing on how he felt about her? Okay, maybe he didn't have to be so heavy-handed about it; truth be told, he'd have reacted the same way if someone attacked *his* father, but still, she was an intelligent, usually logical woman. She should understand.

It had been two weeks since they had last spoken, and although the stink with Feldon Manor had gone away, it had gone away exactly as David Methany would have wanted, with the even worse stench of cruelty surrounding the superficial peace. At least Beth was not that different from the person he believed her to be. He did not for one single millisecond consider that any of the methods used had been her idea. She had someone, or several people, on staff who had learned well from the master and could implement his strategies with as little regard for human consequences as he had always shown. Lord, how he despised the man, and how he yearned for the daughter. Talk about ironies in life. And with the wonder that was autumn in New York just ahead, he had little scenarios dancing in his mind of him and Beth being together, driving out to the house in Rye and walking on the beach, or strolling through the here-today-gone-tomorrow shops of Soho and Tribeca. There was something so magical about the fall season in New York that it was a shame, he often thought, that it was the height of the political season as well. Something as cluttered with subterfuge as politics had no place in the pure air and sense of rebirth autumn invariably brought with it.

This was ridiculous, he suddenly decided. He wanted her, and she wanted him, he was sure of that. So why in the world couldn't they be together? Screw business. He would just keep his big mouth shut about her father and then they could be the way they were before he had died and before she had taken it upon herself to prove her worthiness. David Methany had never been worthy of one hair on his daughter's head, and here she was defending him and worrying about being good enough for him. Damn it!

He reached for the phone on his desk, and actually did a double take when it shrilled into the silence of the empty office before he had a chance to pick up the receiver.

"Hello?"

"Uncle Delbart."

"What? Hello? Hello?"

"Uncle Delbart."

"Who is this?" The thick brows on Ben's tired face creased with confusion. Uncle Delbart had been dead five years, so why was anybody calling now for him? And what kind of a voice was this? Strange, he couldn't figure out if it was male or female, almost as if the caller was using one of those high-tech voice scramblers or whatever they called them. Given that his chosen career was elected office, he could believe his two opponents capable of anything.

"Greg? Michael? What kind of sick joke is this?" he asked, putting a laugh into his voice as he invoked the names of his two rivals for the mayorship. "Come on, guys. What's going on?"

"Too bad David Methany had to sacrifice your Uncle Delbart, Ben Wyler. Too bad for you it provides such a perfect excuse to hurt the Methany Corporation and maybe even get some votes as well. Too bad for you, Ben Wyler."

The councilman was no longer looking confused nor was there the slightest element of humor in his attitude. "Who the hell is this?" his voice boomed, his hand gripping the black receiver with fingers turned sloppy wet with nervous perspiration. "Who are you and what do you want?"

"Did you really think you could get away with it? Beth is much smarter than you give her credit for, Ben Wyler, and not nearly as nice as you think. Your ex-wife, what is her name, wait a minute, let me check the papers here, okay, I've got it, Rachel, that's it. Rachel. Well, Ben Wyler, you really ought to do something about her before election time. That problem she has? The problem your press guy *deals* with? Don't make Beth unhappy again, Ben Wyler. There's no telling what she would do with information like that."

By now Ben's breath was coming in shallow gasps, and there was a burning sensation behind his eyes as if someone had popped off a hundred flashbulbs. His instinct was to take the telephone and slam it across the room, severing the connection in the most final way. But there was a horrified fascination to learn more, to listen and feel his insides crumble with disappointment at each new indictment against the purported decency of Beth Methany.

"Leave Rachel out of this," he finally scratched out.

"We will, Ben Wyler, we will. When you leave Methany City North alone, and everything else that has to do with the Methany Corporation. Stop pushing Beth, Ben Wyler. Or is exposing a corporation that most people believe profits at the same time it helps others, is exposing such an organization with suspected but unproven wrongs worth having your hopefully large electorate know about your ex-wife, or your own little problem, the one you've had since college, the one about speeding? And of course I don't think your constituents would believe you a man of the people as you so assiduously claim if they found out about your family connection to the Methany operation and how dear old Uncle Delbart took the fall after all those years of loyal service."

"Beth? Is this you? Is it?" Ben had to ask, the disguised voice one moment smooth as a woman's, then deeper, husky.

"What did you say?"

"Beth. Is this Beth Methany? If so, I can't believe you would—"

"Oh, nononono. But she will be enormously flattered you thought it was."

"Flattered?"

"Why, yes, of course. She's trying so hard to live in her father's image. She'll be very pleased you thought her capable of this much ... this much strength sounds appropriate." And there was the slightest echo of humor in the unnatural voice.

Not Beth then. Someone close to her, with access to confidential papers. Someone highly dangerous who had to have been given approval by Beth to act this way. No one would dare do something like this on his own, no one except David Methany himself.

And suddenly, Ben got angry, outraged that someone he had cared so much about, someone he had believed a little finer, a little more ethical than circumstances permitted her to be, was actually no better than she had been trained to be, no better than she had been bred to be. Damn David Methany and damn his daughter! They could both rot in hell!

"I don't know who you are," he bit off, his voice choking on his self-control, "or what you and your boss hope to accomplish with these assinine threats, but let me tell you what you can do with them. Go fuck yourself, you hear! Take your dumb disguised voice and your dumb information about me and my family and your dumb idea of scaring me off, and go fuck yourself with all of it! If you've done anything with this call it's to convince me even more that putting a stop to the Methany operation is of paramount importance. And one more thing. Make sure you tell your boss she'll be hearing from me about this. Now take your little voice scrambler and shove it!"

As he was about to replace the receiver, the jarring sound of muffled laughter assaulted him, a more biting insult than any of the threats. Even more infuriated, he did not bother to put down the receiver; he depressed the buttons to clear the line at his end and immediately punched in Beth's home number. He'd get her now. The nerve of her! The sick depths she would sink to—and for what? For what? More money. More power. Well, not at his expense, not if he—

"Hello?"

"Miranda? This is Ben Wyler. Is Beth home?"

"Oh, Mr. Wyler, how nice to hear from you. I'm sorry, but Miss Beth is out this evening. She's hosting a small dinner party for Lewis Wilkes, Jr., and the other residents of Feldon Manor."

"What!"

"Isn't that lovely of her? Such a generous—"

"Thank you, Miranda. No need to leave a message. I'll call her tomorrow."

"All right. Nice chatting with you, Mr. Wyler. Take care now and don't be such a stranger."

Ben hung up more enraged than before he had called. First the little bitch gets someone to threaten him, and then she has the audacity to do this while she takes his people, the men and women whose grievances he had championed, she takes these people out to a fancy dinner, buying off her conscience and their support. This bitch was more her father's daughter than even her father could have hoped for!

When Beth got home that night at ten-thirty, there was a note from Miranda on the hall table telling her that Ben had called, no message, not to call him back, he'd call tomorrow.

She considered calling him anyway, then thought better of it. She would undoubtedly blurt out where she had been this evening, and he'd get angry, considering it an act of treachery, and

then they'd go through the whole fandango again. But she had
had to do something. It had been killing her knowing that these
people had lost to the giant machinery of the Methany Corporation, and the wealth of strategic options available to it; they
had never stood a chance. She had needed to do something to
let these people know that they would be taken care of in the
future, and that they were not dealing with some kind of un-
feeling monster.

The dinner had been a success. Lewis Wilkes, Jr., and his
neighbors had gone from wary to warm over the course of the
evening and the expensive meal at Café des Artistes. But Ben
would think she had been up to something devious, something
to use against him, undermine him, so she would definitely wait
until tomorrow to call him, unless he called back first. She
wondered idly what he wanted, since they hadn't spoken, hadn't
even run into each other in over two weeks, ever since her
ridiculous accusatory call to him late that night. She still wished
things could be different between them, but there was too much
suspicion, too many ugly words already said to go back to what
they had been or to move forward beyond the negatives. The
sacrifice . . . the sacrifice. . . . She shook her head jerkily, an in-
voluntary motion that succeeded only in dismissing the thought
for the moment, not extinguishing it forever.

Janine Gentry waited in her office an additional thirty minutes
after making the telephone call to Ben Wyler. She was quite
pleased with herself and with how the conversation had gone.
She was waiting because she was hoping he might try to call
Beth or perhaps even show up in person, assuming she was still
in the office where she had coached some poor minion into
making those threats to him. But neither event occurred, which
was too bad since Janine would have enjoyed continuing the
performance.

She removed the voice scrambler she had purchased earlier in the summer at Spy, Inc., a silly little shop on First Avenue in the Fifties that sold every imaginable gadget and gizmo pertaining to spycraft, or at least spycraft for the amateur. She had bought the device for her calls to Beth, and she supposed she could have used her own voice with the councilman since he didn't know her, but why take unnecessary risks?

The call to Ben Wyler had served two excellent purposes for her: it would cause trouble for Beth since he would accuse her of being behind the call, and almost as importantly, he would now understand, in highly personal terms, the strength and the scope of the Methany Corporation machinery against an opponent. If he had thought their methods dirty and unethical, even illegal, before, he now had to contend with the reality that these same methods could be used against him and his precious career. That had to make him more cautious the next time he contemplated going up against a Methany project. And if there were a next time, Janine would do much more than threaten him with leaking damaging information. She would let nothing, no one, hurt anything that could be good for *her* corporation.

Smiling tightly with satisfaction, she allowed her mind to wander to the immediate future when she would make Beth Methany tremble with the terror of assault by a stranger, menace striking any time, relentlessly increasing the pitch of her fear. If anyone were in the office at this precise moment, they would have noticed, with an unsettling mixture of revulsion and trepidation, a plastic, doll-like opacity to her beautiful eyes; a disturbing flatness to those eyes as if they were looking inward, to a vision as secret and dark as her soul. And if anyone were in the office at this precise moment, they also would have observed an almost grotesque transformation to the young woman's entire face, the wide mouth spreading into an ugly slash of delight with her destructive thoughts, the pupils in the flat eyes dilating until they seemed to take over the eye itself, drugged with the venom of her hatred; her very coloring darkening, a flush of blackness mirroring the rot within. It was a face turned older by decades, a crooked crone whose youth and hope and innocence had been consumed from within. It was a pitiful sight to behold, were anyone unfortunate enough to behold it. But she was alone with her demons, as she had been for the past twelve years.

Ben Wyler had no patience left to go over his speech. He considered going to Beth's apartment and just waiting for her to come home so he could confront her, then thought better of it. He would acquit himself far more effectively in the morning, when his rage had subsided into a healthy, and manageable, anger.

But in the morning, he had one crisis after another so he never called her. And Beth didn't call him, because she figured he had nothing positive to say, so why go asking for trouble?

And in the morning, Janine Gentry again became Alyson Gentry, counsel for the Methany Corporation, watchdog for the president's plans not to go awry, and budding best friend of her self-avowed enemy.

17

"That's great news, Mr. Aurelio, just great . . . Well, thank you, I'd like to think he'd be proud, too." As Beth spoke on the phone, she gestured for Gene Cavelli, who had just appeared at her office doorway, to have a seat. "Fine, then, and thank you again. Bye now."

Gene looked questioningly at her. "Aurelio of First Manhattan?"

She nodded, her grin wide. "The same. He's the third to call this week. Looks like the banks are satisfied I'm not going to default. I guess the change at Feldon Manor convinced them I was another Methany worth backing."

"Have they renegotiated at a higher rate?" the attorney asked.

"Only Empire State Savings and Loan, another half a point, not too usurious. The other two gave me a six-month extension at the current interest rate. By then ground will be broken on Methany City North, and maybe even renovation for Methany Palace will have started. Plus the Japanese consortium have come through on that project in Rye. It looks like things are finally settling down for me." Her pleasure slipped away and her brown eyes turned serious. "I was worried," she stated simply.

"As well you should have been. But you didn't panic. And you won't the next time."

"The next time?" she repeated on a chilly laugh. "You mean there are more disasters to look forward to?"

"Of course," Gene answered cheerfully. "As you well know."

"I'm afraid I do." She picked up from her desk a glossy color postcard of the Empire State Building and handed it to Gene without a word.

He barely glanced at the photographed side before turning it over. The message was written in a peculiar type of backward scrawl, immediately suggesting to the clever attorney a deliberately disguised print. The message read: "Justice will be served. Soon." And then, in script, the initial J.

"Beth, what is this?"

"Exactly what *I* want to know," she said, her voice tight with frustration. "That's why I wanted to see you this morning. And this isn't the first piece of mail I've received. I've got more at home, letters and postcards. But this is the first with handwriting on it. The others either have no message, just the initial, or the message—and nothing really as ominous as this—has been typed." She frowned.

"You're thinking the sender is the same person who was behind that stuff your father kept around, aren't you?"

"I know it's the same," she told him. "I checked the initials on his letters and on mine. They're identical. And the funny thing is that that J. looks oddly familiar to me. Familiar beyond recognizing it from Daddy's file of letters."

The lawyer looked at the card again, studying it a moment. "The handwriting is familiar to me, too, Beth," he finally said.

"Is it really?"

He nodded. "I don't get it. I don't know anyone whose name begins with that letter, yet the handwriting on that initial *is* familiar." And had Janine Gentry overheard him, overheard the man say he knew no one with a name beginning with J, she would have appreciated, perhaps as never before, her natural father's instinctive contempt for other people's intelligence.

"This is ridiculous!" Beth exclaimed. "And the worst part is

I can't do a thing about it. I just hate that! All I can do is sit back and wait for the next installment."

"That's all part of the ploy to unnerve you, I'm sure, but why?"

"I'm not unnerved, dammit, I'm angry! What kind of sicko gets his jollies—or hers—from stupid cards with stupid messages? Probably the same kind of sicko who called me the other night," she grumbled.

"You've been getting strange calls, too?"

"Only one and it wasn't anything—"

"Tell me about it."

She did, leaving out only her suspicions about Ben. She needn't have bothered.

"I'm surprised you didn't immediately suspect Ben Wyler, given the trouble he's caused you lately. But you know he's too decent a guy to stoop that low no matter what." She looked away from him briefly, but he noticed the slight motion of avoidance. "Ah, so you did think he was behind it."

"But I was wrong," she hastened to assure him. She was thoughtful a moment, then looked the lawyer in the eye with her trademark unwavering gaze. "Gene, if this is the same person who had been writing to my father, what kind of justice had to wait twelve years, and why now? More curious, why me and not my father?"

Cavelli considered what Beth had said. "All good questions," he finally remarked. "And I'm afraid I don't have any answers."

"I think it's all related to that Lilly Jane person."

"Lilly Jane Litwin? What makes you think that?"

"It has to be. I've been giving this a lot of thought, Gene, and it makes sense. Hers is the only name ever mentioned in any of the letters or cards he got. Plus I also got an unmarked manila envelope with copies of old newspaper clippings about

her suicide and her husband's suicide, the man who was trying
to prosecute my father."

"You got an envelope of clippings about all that?" Gene asked,
surprised.

Beth nodded. "The manila envelope was in one of those
padded book bags. Postmark was Ronkonkoma out on Long
Island."

"And the other stuff you got? What about those postmarks?"

"I don't remember," she told him with an apologetic shrug.
"I do know there didn't seem to be any consistent pattern, like
only from the eastern seaboard or that kind of thing. But that
doesn't matter," she added impatiently. "What do you make of
my theory, Gene? That this is all connected somehow with that
woman who was supposed to have had an affair with my father?"

"But that was over thirty years ago. What could it matter
now?"

"Well, it obviously does to someone. What I find curious is
why my father kept the correspondence. It's almost as if," she
began to speak with more deliberation, the thoughts coming to
her as she said them, "as if he knew there'd be a day when the
sender would show himself. Herself. I really am convinced it's
a female. Someone who maybe was jealous of this Lilly Jane
person, who wanted my father for herself. Oh, I don't know. I
don't know what to make of any of this," she snapped irritably.

"But what would he hope to gain by keeping the correspondence?" Gene asked, ignoring Beth's outburst. "It doesn't make
sense. Your father wasn't afraid of anyone, and I can't think of
any other reason to keep those letters except fear that one day
the sender would appear, demanding money."

"So what kind of protection would the letters provide?"

"Not protection so much as proof to get the would-be blackmailer off his back." Gene's smile was thin. "Pretty absurd, I

admit it. The only other reason for holding on to that stuff was, as you said, because he expected the sender to show himself one day, and he wanted to go over all the cards, sort of review them with the sender. Your father would enjoy the irony of a sensible discussion with a potential threat, and then use his own superior intelligence to turn the threat against the opponent."

"Then why me?" Beth reminded him. "What have I ever done to anybody that they would want to threaten *me*?"

"Come on now, Beth. Nobody is threatening you."

"The message is pretty clear, Gene," she argued. " 'Justice will soon be served.' That's what the voice on the phone said, too. 'Soon.' Hardly what I call an invitation to friendship," she added acerbically.

Gene pulled his lanky frame up out of the chair and got to his Lincolnesque height. "You know what you need?"

A wry smile came to her face. "Do tell."

"You need to relax a little. Go out with Ben, have a wild time, forget who you are for a few hours. Be young and irresponsible for once." His eyes were warm with caring and his voice had deepened with his sincerity.

"You know I can't do that, Gene," she answered gently. "Forget who I am, I mean. And as for Ben, well, I'm afraid business took care of that, too."

"I'm sorry."

"I'm not," she said with more fever than she genuinely felt. "Hurt the business and you hurt me. Ben has never quite understood that. He's the one who should be sorry."

Gene Cavelli looked at the young president of the multi-million-dollar empire a long, thoughtful moment, and then spoke guardedly, watching her eyes for the truth. "You're not the company, Beth. You didn't build it so it's not your dream, only your responsibility. It's not who *you* are."

And as she had done when Gene had spoken of her suspecting

Ben of being the late-night caller, Beth now avoided the lawyer's intelligently probing eyes, thus silently telling him that she, too, knew how accurate his words were.

"If that's all—" he said softly.

She nodded distractedly, her mind still engaged in the ramifications of what he had said, and so she was not really aware when he left her office and Alyson Gentry took his place in the space of seconds.

"Beth? Beth? Hey, you okay?"

Beth smiled perfunctorily, then focused clearly, and her expression became warmer and more genuine. "Alyson, hi. Oh, I'm fine, just fine. Thinking about a couple of things, that's all."

"You had the most intense expression on your face. In fact, so did Gene when I just passed him. What's going on? Are you sure everything's okay?"

"Couldn't be better." She sat down, motioned for Alyson to do the same. "The banks are off my back, and the people at Feldon Manor don't think I'm the reincarnation of a Gestapo officer. That dinner was a brilliant idea if I do say so myself."

"Nicer and more generous than you needed to be. We had everything under control without your wasting your time on those old fools." Suddenly, Alyson's neck stiffened, and Beth found it rather amusing to observe how self-righteous the other woman's expression became, her eyes growing cold, her mouth feeding on itself until it became a thin, unforgiving line. All this for generosity, Beth wondered; one could only imagine how she would react if she were ever displeased about something important.

"You sound just like my father," Beth said, a smile in her voice.

"All lawyers are curmudgeons by training."

"And my father was one by nature," Beth supplied, now smiling openly.

Despite Beth's obvious mood of lightness, the lawyer was not about to accept her comment in the same cavalier spirit. "No one is mean-spirited by nature," Alyson said, her tone as unyielding as her posture. "Other people—their weaknesses and stupidity and jealousies—it's other people who make the strong and the smart, men like your father, make them protect themselves and what they accomplish by a veneer of coldness or meanness or even selfishness. It's their pride that makes them seem curmudgeons, not their nature, and it's a healthy pride, not a misplaced one."

Utterly taken aback by the vehemence with which the words were spoken, as well as the inappropriateness of them coming upon her seemingly innocent remark, Beth could only stare at her colleague and new friend, and wonder at her misplaced solemnity. There was a part of Beth that wanted to laugh aloud at Alyson's pomposity; another part of her that took umbrage at it, especially Alyson's talking about her father as if she had known him, the *real* him, better than his own daughter!

"Did you want to see me about something in particular this morning?" Beth asked in a pitch-perfect tone of superiority, letting there be no mistake as to how she had taken the other's words, nor as to who was in charge.

The response was so unexpected by Alyson that it took her a moment to remember her charade, a lapse she should have been able to control. *Don't underestimate her. She, too, is her father's daughter. And don't get sloppy. Not now when you're so close.*

"I have more good news for you."

"The tax abatement?" Beth asked, eyes alive with eager expectation.

"It just came through," Alyson confirmed. "It's not really official yet, but a very solid connection has assured me that the committee in Albany voted in your favor."

"Oh, Alyson, that is such great news!" Beth exclaimed. Her

vision turned inward, as if she were seeing her father now, seeing the expression of pride and pleasure this news would have brought him. For the first time since his death and her taking over the corporation, she felt as if she were worthy of being his daughter.

"We have to celebrate," she announced. "Just the two of us."

The lawyer immediately tried to demur. "Oh, no, that's not necessary. I don't—"

"No argument, this is an executive decision," Beth insisted, then, more seriously: "You really have been terrific, Alyson, and of course there'll be a generous bonus. But you've been here for me through some especially difficult times, and I'd like to say a small but more personal thank you."

"I've just been doing my job, Beth."

"And you do it extraordinarily well. If you hadn't alerted me to what was going on with Feldon Manor . . . if you hadn't taken care of that problem, the banks would have forced me to re-negotiate, and there is no doubt in my mind that the tax abatement decision would not have gone in my favor." She ran her fingers through her curly hair and grinned. "The Methany Corporation owes you, Alyson, and *I* owe you. Be selfish for once and let me do something for *you*."

If Beth were dismayed at the lack of enthusiasm in Alyson Gentry's face, the way her lovely hazel cat eyes remained unengaged, the way her mouth could not manage a small smile for Beth's contagious enthusiasm, she thought little of it. After all, she reasoned, Alyson had done all the dirty work, but it would be Beth who would determine the size of her bonus check. There was a certain measure of injustice in that, but there could be only one boss.

"Well?" she prompted.

"Thank you, Beth, I'd enjoy helping you celebrate. It's very generous of you to invite me."

"Oh, don't be so formal," Beth chided, laughing. "I want us to be friends."

"Friends. Yes, I'd like that, too," Alyson said softly, standing, unable to remain in the office, facing *her* behind that desk another moment.

"Tomorrow night?" Beth asked. "Or do you have plans?"

"Tomorrow will be fine. Where?"

"You pick it."

"How about my place?" Alyson suggested. "I'm sure you're as tired of eating out as I am." And suddenly, her face brightened, lost its tight, controlled expression of deliberate blandness, because the idea of having her in her apartment, learning more about her in an environment that was all her own, was enormously appealing.

"I *am* tired of restaurants," Beth was saying, "but why not go to my place instead? Miranda's a terrific cook, and I'd like to show you some of my father's things. I think you'd appreciate them."

"I'd like that very much."

Beth's eyes seemed lighted from within with the warmth of her sincerity. "I know this isn't a very presidential type of thing to say, but I just want you to know how much I appreciate you being here. And that," she smiled self-consciously, "is the woman talking, not the president. A woman who recently lost her father, a woman left with a huge responsibility to handle. You're helping to make a tough job a little easier, and I'm more grateful than you can imagine." Her smile grew wider and less embarrassed. "And now I promise—never another word on the subject!"

Alyson stared unblinkingly at her a long moment, offered a barely audible "thank you" through lips that seemed to her too dry to move, then abruptly left. Beth assumed she had flustered the usually poised lawyer. She had no way of knowing that Alyson had not trusted herself to speak; the taste of hate in her mouth was so rancid she might have spilled it out and then revealed too much. She was not yet ready to show her hand.

All the time she had worked for David she had devoted herself to him and to the job, with scant thought for Beth as a person, only as an impediment. But now she wanted to know everything about her, every weakness and fear, all her vulnerabilities. She wanted to use them against her and experience the pleasure of her torment, enjoy the power of making her suffer.

It would not be enough to merely depose her; she had to pay as well, pay for all her father's sins. Janine might never be able to forgive him for his selfish acts, but she accepted why he had done what he had, and more, respected what he had made of his life. There was no such esteem for Beth, only disdain; she had been given so much and deserved so little. Yes, disdain, and rage, too, at the unfairness of their situations. She owed it to both Lilly Jane and herself to stretch out Beth Methany's misery, and make her pay and pay and pay until her end would be a welcome relief. Justifiable suffering. She liked the sound of that.

The beauty of the deception, she thought as she returned to her office, was that she had to do so little in order to gain a great deal. Her victim was handing it all to her as if she, too, knew that justice finally had to be served.

"Ah, you must be Miss Beth's dinner guest. I'm Miranda. Come in, please," the housekeeper greeted Alyson the next evening. As she was taking her coat, Beth appeared, her hands covered with clay.

"Hi," she said, glancing down at the mess and laughing. "I was trying to get in an hour or so at my pottery wheel."

"I didn't know you were into that."

"Love it. If I weren't a high-powered business magnate," she joked, "I'd probably live in some little shack by the ocean and spin bowls and vases on my wheel all day. If you're interested, I'll show you the little studio Daddy had made for me. It's not like the old boat shed at Rye—I have a kiln there—but it's still pretty well-equipped. I should have showed it to you when you came up to the house. Next time."

"Come along, Miss Gentry," Miranda broke in. "I made some nice fresh vegetables and a healthy, nonfattening dip. If we let her, Miss Beth will talk clay and firings and glazes all night." She smiled affectionately at her employer. "What can I get you to drink, Miss Gentry?"

Before Alyson could answer, Beth spoke. "I think we'll have drinks in Daddy's study, Miranda. Alyson worked for him and I want to show her some of his things."

Beth went to clean up and was not gone long enough for Alyson to do a thorough examination of the wood-paneled study. When she had first entered, she immediately walked over to the model rendering of Methany Place, the flagship of the company, but as soon as Miranda left, all her attention was focused on the photograph of Beth and David Methany on his desk.

"A wonderful picture, isn't it?"

Alyson swung around, her thoughts so deep and roiling that she had not heard the housekeeper reenter.

"Yes, lovely," she managed, her eyes again on the photograph she now held in her hands.

"You're just like Miss Beth. Her idea of a cocktail is diet soda and yours is fancy water. Whatever happened to old-fashioned drinks like martinis?"

"They're not good for you," Alyson said, forcing herself to be polite when every fiber in her body was aching to be left alone, in this room, with this photograph, with her hate.

"Now you even sound like Miss Beth," Miranda laughed. "Well, here's some of those veggies and dip. Dinner'll be ready in about thirty minutes. Fresh fish—nice and healthy."

"Sounds great. And Miranda? Thank you." She was using the tone of voice that always made older people melt with admiration for her. "It's very kind of you to do all this for me."

"Kind has nothing to do with it," the housekeeper assured her. "It's a pleasure to have my girl at home one night without her head buried in a pile of papers. Just like her daddy, Miss Beth can't bear to be doing nothin'. It's good to see her relaxing with a friend."

"Well, thank you anyway," Alyson said with that same oleaginous graciousness.

Miranda smiled, then left. When Beth came in a short while later, Alyson's position had not altered. She was still holding the photograph, staring at it, one finger gently outlining the contours of David Methany's face.

"He was very handsome, wasn't he?" Beth asked gently, coming up to her.

"Yes, he was," Alyson replied, tearing her eyes from the picture. "When I knew him, he was old, but you could still tell he had been good-looking. This photo of the two of you is wonderful. A lot of love," she managed, swallowing to moisten her throat as resentment sucked the very breath from her.

She turned to replace the photo. "You must miss him a lot," she remarked, not looking at Beth.

"I miss him as a father and of course as the genius behind the company. But to tell you the truth, sometimes lately I wonder if what he left me is all that fabulous."

At that, Alyson faced her. "I don't understand."

"I mentioned this to you that day in Rye. The sacrifice just seems so enormous. You wouldn't understand, I guess, because you can have a personal life, but everything I do, everyone I see seems connected to the business. Occasionally it gets to be a little claustrophobic," she admitted with a small, rueful laugh.

"Maybe you're not cut out for it. Maybe you should live in that little house by the ocean and make vases and bowls." There was nothing in Alyson's tone of voice, no indication in posture or expression, of the animosity drumming in her ears, pounding so loudly in her chest that her knees felt weak with the exertion of staying on her feet, as if she were running a marathon, and the self-control it took to act normally was the effort it took to reach the finish tape those last twenty, ten, two yards.

"My father would haunt me from the grave if I ever did that," Beth said. "Ever since I was a little girl it was taken for granted that I would follow in his footsteps. I can't begin to count how many times he told me that everything he had ever done was to make sure that his only child never wanted for anything."

Alyson, needing to put physical distance between them, went over to the large leather easy chair and sat down. By it, on a leather-topped table, rested the vegetables and drinks. "Do you think he ever missed not having a son?" she asked.

Beth took her soda but remained standing near the model of Methany Place. "No, well, maybe, but he never really showed me that he did. No, I think he was pleased with me. That's why it's so important that I do well. He gave me everything. I owe it to his memory to be worthy of inheriting what he built, except there are those times when I—"

Suddenly, there was a dull *thwack*. "Alyson, are you all right? What happened? Oh my gosh, you're bleeding!"

Beth ran over to the other woman, who remained sitting in the leather chair even as the designer water ran over her cut fingers onto her skirt. Shards of glass lay in her lap; a few pieces had fallen to the carpet. The wedge of lime lay obscenely on one thigh.

"I'm sorry," Alyson muttered. "I don't know what happened." But she did; of course she did. She was only human. How long could she have sat there listening to her, word after word an insult, a travesty. She couldn't take any more, she just couldn't. The discipline, the patience, were wearing thin. She had no business putting herself in this kind of situation, confronting the enemy, surrounded by all that should be hers. No one could withstand such punishment. But she needed to learn, and the most effective way was to get close to her, lull her into admissions of weakness that could be used against her. The price was so high, though. She had to be more careful, control herself even more rigorously. There must never be a moment of suspicion, or everything would be for naught.

For months now, ever since David Methany had died and reality had smacked her in the face, she had known what she had to do. But that was the finale, and she still had to act out each important scene before that last moment of deliverance. That was why it was so vital she not give herself away with any more inexcusable blunders like the one that had just occurred. It was only for a little while longer. She had waited for over twelve years; surely time was irrelevant when an issue as vital as justice was at stake.

"Come on, let's get you fixed up," Beth said.

Moments later they were in Beth's bathroom, where Alyson was washing off the superficial cuts.

"I think you'll survive," Beth remarked.

"I'm glad to hear that. I have a very important job and I'd hate to miss a day of work. My boss is a real tyrant."

Beth grinned appreciatively. "I really am sorry for causing you all this trouble," Alyson went on.

"Forget it. I'm just glad it wasn't more serious. Now I think we'd better head for the dining room or Miranda will be insulted."

Over their first course of melon and blueberries, Alyson commented on the apartment. "It's a beautiful home, but don't you find it awfully large for just one person, or rather, two, you and Miranda?"

"I'm planning on selling it," Beth told her, "but not until I feel more in control of things at the office. One headache at a time."

"I love all the flowers you have. I always mean to keep fresh flowers in my apartment, but somehow I forget to buy them, or when I do, I forget to water them and then they just dry out."

"My mother loved flowers, so it's just one of those habits I took up, too."

"Any favorites?"

"Mmm, not really. Although there's one kind I *won't* have around me. I'm sure you've heard about this. There was a big stink in the office about two, three months ago over it."

"No, I don't think I know. What happened?"

Beth then told her about the incident in late spring when a bouquet of white tulips had arrived for her at the office, a gift from a wealthy Belgian industrialist who was trying to seduce her into reducing the cost to buy two floors of apartments at Methany Place. The night before they had gone out to a very pleasant dinner, but it hadn't been pleasant enough to get her to forget one of her father's primary rules of business: name your price and always stick to it; to reduce it for any reason is to signal weakness that can be used against you at a later time.

The next day the flowers had arrived and Beth had sat there in her office quietly and uncontrollably sobbing for more than fifteen minutes before taking the box of flowers and tossing it across the room so that the velvety white petals fell like fat snow drops. With uncharacteristic temper, she had stormed out of her office and announced to anyone within earshot that never, under any circumstances, were flowers to be accepted for her before someone checked out whether one single white flower of any kind was included, and if so, the entire bouquet was to be returned.

"But why?" Alyson asked. "Usually white flowers are the rarest and most expensive."

"I know, but that doesn't matter. You see, when my mother died, the apartment, the funeral parlor, my father's office were blanketed with white flowers, and they sickened me, the sight of them, the scent. I knew they were beautiful, special, but they struck me as being too beautiful, as if a gift to my father in celebration of my mother's death." She shrugged. "I know it doesn't make much sense, especially since my mother died twelve years ago, but I really can't bear to have those things around me to this day. I guess they'll always be a reminder to me of how little my mother was mourned."

"I'm sorry, I had no idea you were so close with her."

"I wasn't, I didn't even like her all that much," Beth admitted. "She had her own problems to contend with, though, which I'm beginning to appreciate as I learn how difficult my father could be. Anyway, the point is that irrational as my aversion is, that's how I feel. Long story for a short point, and here's Miranda with our fish."

"This is delicious," Alyson soon complimented. "What is it?"

"Baked sole," Miranda told her.

"It's not like any sole I've ever had before."

"Miranda's secret sauce. I think she puts it on everything from chicken to tuna fish," Beth teased.

"I most certainly do not," Miranda huffed. "It's a shallot-and-wine sauce with lots and lots of garlic. Anything to cover up the blandness of those fish Miss Beth eats."

"I'm allergic to all forms of shellfish," Beth explained. "Miranda thinks there are only shrimp and lobster and an occasional crab in the fish world; anything else constitutes bland so she creates these sauces to make *her* feel better."

"I'm like that about champagne," Alyson offered. "I get horrendous headaches from it. From all kinds of wine."

"That's too bad—you're missing out on one of the true joys in life."

The meal continued pleasantly, Alyson eating and chatting as if her mind were not otherwise engaged in a series of scenarios that warmed her with their diabolical cleverness. Allergic to shellfish. A neurotic reaction to white flowers. Vertigo. With thought, perhaps even her pottery could be used against her. Justifiable suffering. It really was quite the most delicious way to describe what Beth Methany would soon be enduring, the perpetration of which was a fitting reward for her own years of herculean patience.

After Alyson had gone, Beth turned to her housekeeper with an expectant smile on her face. "Isn't she great?"

Miranda did not answer immediately. "She's a pretty thing," she allowed. "Unusual eyes."

"You don't like her," Beth stated, understanding the signals and subtleties of the other woman. "Why not? What's wrong with her?"

"Did I say anything about not liking her? I have to clean up now, Miss Beth. Is there anything more you need?" She started to clear away the coffee cups.

"Miranda."

The housekeeper hesitated, then put down the cups and looked at her employer. "Just something funny about her. That business with the glass, for instance."

"What about it? It was just an accident."

"The only way I've ever heard of a glass breaking while a person was holding it was if that person was so angry they gripped the glass hard enough to make it break. Angry, Miss

Beth. That friend of yours is walking around with a lot of very unhealthy anger in her."

Beth's laugh was weak, a flutter of sound without feeling. "That's ridiculous. What would make her so angry she would—"

"You don't know her, Miss Beth," Miranda told her, the license to speak this freely coming from her many years of service in the Methany household. "You work with her; she's helped you out. I know you've been lonely lately, but—"

"I'm not lonely."

"Fine, you're not lonely. But if my social life were spent with people who wanted nothing more than business with me, I'd call myself lonely. Not to mention a few other things," she chuckled.

"Miranda!" But Beth was smiling.

"Just be careful, Miss Beth," the housekeeper went on, serious again. "I'm glad you've found someone you like, but be careful. Your daddy was a very powerful man with a lot of enemies. There's no telling who might be out there waiting to get at you."

"Me? But that's—"

"Miss Beth, listen to me, just listen. Your daddy hurt some people along the way. You know that, I know that, a lot of folks know that. But he was so damn powerful that nobody could get at him. You're different. You're female for one thing. You're young for another. And you're not mean and selfish, David Methany's child or not."

"Miranda!"

"It's true so don't go Miranda-ing me like you never knew that about him. All I'm saying is that the sins of the father could be visited upon the child. Be careful, Miss Beth. That's all, just be careful."

"But Alyson Gentry is only a few years older than me," Beth

argued, "and she's not even from around here. She has absolutely no connection with Daddy."

"Don't act stupid, Miss Beth. That's undignified for you and insulting to me."

Beth was silent a moment, then she went and put an arm around Miranda's shoulders. "You may be right," she conceded. "I agree Daddy made a lot of enemies, and one of them might want to get revenge by hurting me. But not Alyson Gentry. You know why she's okay, Miranda?" The housekeeper glanced at her dubiously. "Because she's too ambitious. She'd never do anything to upset the boss, and that's me!" Beth was now grinning merrily, and she planted a loud kiss on Miranda's cheek.

The housekeeper said nothing, knowing that whatever she might say would be meaningless to Beth. The trouble with innocence, she had long ago realized, was that the one who possessed it never could believe someone else might act with deliberate malice in mind.

18

The next few weeks shimmied with the frantic pace Beth maintained, which included flying up to Albany for the final, and favorable, determination of the tax abatement, and driving out to Essex, Connecticut, where her team of property scouts had found a superb waterfront parcel along the Connecticut River. These had been twenty-six-hour days when she felt she barely had time to shower and change clothes, let alone catch a few hours' sleep. She had lost six pounds, which was fine, but she was exhausted through and through, as if the very movement of blood in her system had slowed down from fatigue. There were constant meetings, with groups and individuals; an endless mountain of papers and prospectuses to get through; and decisions, always the decisions she and she alone could make.

While she could not deny that it was exhilarating to be in charge of such a powerful conglomerate, that gnawing feeling of the position not quite being worth the sacrifices not only persisted, but had grown stronger. Especially during the past three days, the time that had elapsed since seeing Ben with his current "special woman friend," a newscaster being touted as the next Diane Sawyer. Beth was not distressed over her feelings for Ben so much as for the loss of anyone like him in her life. She had gone to the dinner-dance at the Waldorf-Astoria, a fund-raiser for AIDS research, with Fred Lincoln's nephew, an architect with the Methany Corporation and proudly homosexual. Ben and she had seen each other, exchanged a cordial nod

and nothing more. To be fair, she conceded, there had been no
opportunity to speak with each other privately. Nevertheless,
the entire evening had left her even more aware of her responsibilities and their toll.

On this particular afternoon, a summer storm thrashed outside
her office window, and as she was thinking, with amusement,
that the thunder seemed to crack only when she signed another
check, like applause, her intercom buzzed.

"Yes, Karen?"

"I have someone on the phone who is insisting on speaking
with you, but won't give a name, and Alyson Gentry wonders
if you have a few minutes."

"I'll take the call," Beth said, waving Alyson in. She pressed
the lighted button on her phone. "Hello? This is Beth Methany."

"Justice will soon be served."

"What! Who is this? Damn you, who are you and what do
you want?" Beth could not control the outburst, ignoring Alyson
as she concentrated on the telephone, willing her mind's eye to
see the person attached to the threat, to make some sort of link
that would help her understand why this was happening to her.

"You don't deserve any of it. Justice. Soon."

"Who are you? Why are you doing this? What do you want
from me? Answer me, damn you, answer me!" But the line
was already dead.

Slowly, Beth replaced the receiver, eyes vacant as she silently
replayed the ominous message.

"Beth . . . ? Beth?"

"Sorry." The smile was plastic. "Is there something you
wanted, Alyson? I'm a little preoccupied at the moment."

"Never mind about me, who was that on the phone? You're
white as a ghost." Caring was etched on the lawyer's lovely face,
the mask of sincerity as deceptive as the mask of sanity worn
by the sociopath.

"I don't know who was on the phone."

"You don't know who you were talking to?" Beth nodded. "Didn't Karen get a name?"

"No name, not even the gender."

"What? Look, why don't you tell me exactly what's going on."

"There's nothing much to tell." But Beth proceeded to unburden herself, sharing with Alyson everything that had occurred over the past several months, starting with the correspondence, through the call at home and her foolish suspicion of Ben, to today's threat.

"And I really can't tell whether the voice is male or female," Beth concluded. "The voice now was bubbly, garbled as if submerged under water. If it didn't sound so damn paranoid, I'd say the caller used one of those voice scrambler devices."

Alyson was thoughtful a moment. "Have you considered going to the police?"

"And tell them what? Some person whose gender I can't determine is sending me weird letters and making strange calls saying justice will soon be served? Given the number and types of crimes in this city, I hardly think the police would attach much importance to any of that." She looked at the lawyer a few minutes, but was seeing past her, trying to think logically.

"I'm sure it has something to do with my father," Beth said. "He had a drawer full of similar cards and letters, some of them dating back twelve years."

"He kept correspondence that long?" Alyson asked, surprised.

Beth nodded. "It was signed by J. too. And a few of them made reference to someone named Lilly Jane."

"But why keep it so long?"

"I don't know, but there had to be a reason for doing so. Daddy never did anything without a purpose, and I'm sure whatever that reason was has something to do with me now." She frowned slightly with recollection. "Miranda said something

funny the evening you came over for dinner. About the sins of
the father being visited upon the child. I thought she was just
being a worrying old fool, but maybe she's right. Maybe my
father has an enemy out there who isn't satisfied with just his
death, but wants to see me hurt as well." She ran a hand through
her curly hair, then grinned with embarrassment. "Listen to
me, will you. And I'm calling Miranda a worrying old fool."

"Don't dismiss this so quickly, Beth," Alyson advised her.
"There are loony-tune types out there by the droves, and you
know it. I think you should get a professional involved, someone
to tape your calls or something."

"Don't be ridiculous. Whoever this is will show himself, or
herself, eventually. I've got a definite feeling that there's a plan
involved and that its execution is just a matter of time."

"What makes you think that?"

"I don't know. I guess because I want it to be that way," Beth
admitted. "Whoever is behind this I wish would just come out
and do whatever it is he wants to do to teach me my lesson. At
least I assume that's what this is all about. Punish me for whatever my father did to him, or her, years ago."

"If your father kept letters from twelve years ago," Alyson
said slowly, "then whoever is behind this has patience, a lot of
patience. I wouldn't count on there being any quick resolution."

"Then why keep telling me justice will be served *soon?*" Beth
countered. "No, I think the person is finally getting restless.
Maybe my father's death was premature in terms of his scheme,
and he doesn't want to take a chance that something will happen
to me before he gets that damn justice he's seeking." Beth's eyes
then took on that familiar steady gaze that both revealed and
demanded the truth; a look of such open, implacable, fearless
honesty that only a fool or someone mad with desperation would
dare discount its strength.

"I don't like being threatened. And I don't like being blamed for anything I didn't do. Most of all, I don't like the role of victim." Her voice was suddenly hard and uncompromising, the voice of one drilled with the lesson "to do whatever it takes to get the job done the way *you* want it done." There was nothing, that voice was saying now, she would not do to make sure justice was indeed served, her way and in her favor.

Alyson's voice was equally unusual for her. It was tinged with admiration, as distinct as a color-tinted black-and-white film, and similarly disconcerting. "You sound just like your father now."

Beth leaned forward across her desk, every muscle in her body taut with confidence. "I *am* my father's daughter, Alyson. I may not approve of all his methods, and I may be reluctant to use the same, but I would have been a poor student indeed if I had not learned the first lesson he taught me, and learned it well."

"And that is?"

Beth sat back again, her smile uncharacteristically crafty. "Why, to win at any price, of course. I was sure that you, in particular, had learned that lesson, too. You seem to practice the philosophy so adeptly."

Alyson laughed out loud. "Well, well. Here's a side of you I've never seen before, and I must confess to being impressed."

Whether it was the lawyer's amusement or her words, Beth was suddenly self-conscious about her display of bravado. "Did you want to see me about something, Alyson?" she asked with deliberate distance in an effort to get the situation back under her control.

Alyson quickly understood. "Actually, I wanted to invite you to dinner, this time at my place. These past few weeks have been brutal for you—me, too—and I thought we could both do with a little R and R."

"Cooking isn't exactly my idea of relaxing, but I'd love to have dinner at your place. When?"

Alyson named a date the following week, then got up to leave. At the door, she turned back. "Beth, your father would no doubt approve of your spirit, but not if it put you in danger. Be careful, okay?"

"Yes, madame counsel, I'll be careful," Beth teased.

"Mademoiselle counsel, if you please. Oh, before I forget, one small piece of business. Gene and I figure the ink should be dry on the contract with the Japanese consortium for the Rye project by next week, the latest. A ceremony with full press coverage might not be a bad idea, just to put paid to any lingering bad feelings about the Feldon Manor incident."

"Good idea, consider it done. See you later."

For Beth, later was merely another paper to sign, another dilemma to weight. But later for Alyson meant having the opportunity to close her office door and rewind the tape that Beth had heard. The exquisite duplicity of perpetrating the danger yet being the one to advise Beth to be careful was nothing compared to the pleasure of sitting in the bitch's office while the tape she had prepared earlier played, turning Beth white with fear. But then that show of strength, what a surprise! Damn her to hell! Calling herself her father's daughter as if she had any claim to that title, that privilege, that position. She was second-rate, only second-rate, and second-born with no right whatsoever to the keys of the kingdom.

As Janine Gentry sat there in her office that afternoon, considering her future, she found herself wishing, for the first time, that the end she had conceived of might not be necessary, that the reins of command would be turned over graciously, perhaps even gladly, obviating the need for more . . . forceful action. While she certainly did not like Beth Methany, she had to admit, now that she had gotten to know her a bit better, that her hatred was more for what she had been given unjustly than for her as an individual. This was a feeling not dissimilar to what she had come to experience for her father. There was a grudging respect for Beth's acuity in discerning that the person behind the cards and calls was getting restless, speeding up the campaign of harassment. There was a grudging respect, too, for her honesty and innocence, and the power both gave her. Under other circumstances, she conceded it not unlikely that the two might have been friends in the way Beth now foolishly believed they actually were; maybe even closer, the closeness that came from being related. But it was too late to wonder what might have been or to permit any weakness of emotion from altering her plans. She had made that mistake once before. Still, perhaps the very end might not be necessary . . . might not have to be quite so . . . so final.

First, though, the dinner. Oh, what a surprise she had planned for her dear half-sister. And before then, who knew? She was sure to come up with a few disturbing incidents to leave Beth atremble. With the image of herself as the one responsible for Beth's suffering, all traces, ephemeral as they were, of regret for what had to be done were effectively killed and buried within her. In fact, that image so intensified her absolute belief in what she was doing, and why, that she immediately decided not to wait until next week's dinner to take further action.

19

One of the privileges of position that her father had used and that Beth had immediately given up was a car and driver to take her the forty-odd blocks to their midtown offices. Most days, she enjoyed the walk to work; it served as exercise and gave her thirty minutes or so to review the day ahead. Since her evenings often took her directly from the office to some function, tonight's walk home in the brisk autumn air was a rare indulgence, as was the empty evening looming ahead. Perhaps an hour or two in the studio, a light salad and soup for dinner, and the latest issue of *Vogue* instead of *Real Estate Weekly.*

"Soon. Soon, little lady. Justice will soon be served."

Beth spun about. She couldn't believe it. Had she been imagining those words or had someone actually spoken them?

She was on the eastern side of Fifth Avenue at Fifty-ninth Street. There were three other people stopped at the traffic light with her: a man, a teenage girl of about fourteen, a bag lady. Beth looked from one to the other, and each of them looked right back, directly into her eyes. She approached the bag lady.

"What did you say?"

"Hey, get lost. Leave me alone."

The voice was a croak, scratched with the abrasive effects of too many years drinking too much rotgut whiskey. It was not the garbled voice on the phone; it was not the muddy, back-in-the-throat kind of voice that had just spoken in her ear.

Quickly, before the light changed, she moved over to the teenage girl. "What do you want? Why did you talk to me?"

The girl edged away, muttering, "I'm sorry, miss, I never spoke to you." No, not her. This voice was soft, young.

She glanced up at the man. He was tall, slender, well-groomed. The voice that had spoken to her had been deep but definitely not masculine. No, not him.

Unless she had made it all up. Thought it, but never heard it. Ridiculous. And certifiably mad.

She continued to walk home, her pace less leisurely, her senses alerted to every movement around her. She was aware when the bag lady crossed the street at Sixty-third and went into Central Park. She noticed when the teenage girl entered a doctor's office on the ground floor of a doorman building at Fifth and Seventieth, the man taking a right going east on Seventy-second. By the time she got home fifteen minutes later, she had almost convinced herself that she had made up the entire incident. The only thing that stopped her from completely believing that was her even stronger belief in herself and her sanity.

Someone *had* spoken to her at that corner. Someone had said the words that were guaranteed to frighten her. And she was furious, angrier than she had ever been in her life. She felt like a programmed robot, conditioned to react on cue. Even more infuriating was her lack of control over the situation. Cards and letters. Calls. And now strangers coming up to her on street corners with the same damn threat. She hated it, hated not knowing, not fighting back, hated the overwhelming sensation of being a victim, the target of an enemy who could strike out at her at any time. She only hoped the anger would fuel her, enable her to strike back should she ever have the opportunity to come face to face with this clever adversary.

"You all right, Miss Methany?"

She smiled up at the doorman as she entered her building. "Fine, Leo. Just thinking."

"Beautiful flowers that came for you."

"Oh? Someone sent me flowers? How nice."

The doorman nodded, puffed up with self-importance, pleased with his scant seconds of superiority over his wealthy tenant: he had knowledge she had not yet learned. "Beautiful white ones, they are. Don't know what kind, never know that stuff, though the wife, she can name every kind of——"

"White ones you say?" Beth's throat constricted.

"With petals like velvet, Miss Methany, I swear. Never seen such thick white petals. My wife says that that's a——"

"Thank you, Leo. Good night." She hurried to the elevator bank.

"Nice flowers came for you today, Miss Methany," the elevator man said when she got in.

"Yes, Leo told me," she managed, her attention on the inside of her purse, where her keys seemed to have intentionally become elusive. She did not think she could wait the breath of time it would take for Miranda to answer the doorbell; she had to see them now, see the card, find out who would do this. Don't be silly, she scolded herself. Lots of people don't know about this aversion of yours to white flowers. Get real, Beth. But she could not calm down, and she could not think clearly. Her gut was telling her that the white flowers were a deliberate act of viciousness. The same way the bodiless voice at the street corner had been deliberately engineered to frighten her.

Finally, the elevator opened on to her private landing. "Thank you, Ellis. Have a good evening." She was acidly amused by her politeness. Even panic did not override proper breeding.

She found her keys at exactly the same moment Miranda opened the door. Ellis and his elevator lingered until a brisk wave from Miranda shooed him on his way.

"Miranda, where are—"

"I threw them out, Miss Beth. I threw them out immediately."

"But I want to know who sent them. Who would do this to me?"

"Come now, Miss Beth. It could be anybody. Don't do any good thinking it came from someone who knows how you feel about white flowers. That's just foolishness."

Beth stopped her forward progress into the apartment, turned, and observed the worried expression on her housekeeper's face. "It may be foolishness," she said in a voice a tremor above a whisper, "but the flowers were definitely from somebody who wants to hurt me. Someone who hates me very much. I know it, I just know it."

Miranda immediately objected. "But who could hate you, Miss Beth? You're the most honest and kind and—"

"Someone who hated my father."

Miranda stutter-stepped to a stop, drew a deep breath, marshaling her strength. "So it's happened at last," she muttered. "I can't say I'm surprised, you know that. He made lots of enemies, that man did. Well, you come on now and let me get you a drink, and not that fizzy water stuff." Then, with more authority in her voice, she said, "There's nothing to worry about, Miss Beth, nothing at all."

In spite of the situation, Beth smiled. "I suppose you'll protect me, you old goose."

"Yup, me and some of my uptown friends from my favorite precinct."

"I didn't know you were still seeing Sergeant Rico."

"My relationship with any man is of no-never-mind," she stated huffily. "The point is that if anyone dares to hurt you, we've got special friends who can help."

Beth looked at Miranda a heartbeat, put down her briefcase and purse, and hugged her hard, words unnecessary between them. With the warmth and love she felt from that hug, Beth shook free of the tension that had accompanied her since Fifty-ninth Street.

"I did save the card," Miranda told her as they walked into the kitchen where she poured Beth a brandy. "Drink this. Now." She reached into the pocket of her sweater and put the white card on the little round French bistro table.

" 'Know how much you love white flowers. Enjoy. Justice. Soon. J.,' " Beth read aloud, then sank into a chair. "Oh, Miranda. What's going on?"

"I was hoping you'd be able to tell me that," the housekeeper said, joining her at the table.

"Someone really is out to get me, Miranda. Someone who thinks that the way to exact vengeance against my father is to hurt me. Whatever my father did to this person must really have been awful for him to be willing to wait twelve years to strike back."

"What do you mean? And who's J.?"

"I don't know, but let me show you what else we have from this person."

Beth took Miranda into her father's study, opened the desk drawer, pulled out the file of cards and letters. While Miranda read, Beth retrieved the correspondence she herself had received, bringing them from her bedroom to the study. "There've been calls, too," she told Miranda, "here and at the office. And then today someone at Fifth and Fifty-ninth spoke to me about justice, just like on the card. It makes no sense, but I don't know what to do about it. I can't stand sitting by helpless, but I can't very well fight back against a phantom. I don't even know if I'm dealing with a man or a woman!" All the frustration and exasperation of recent events filled her voice, reverberating back at her in silent mockery.

Slowly, methodically, Miranda assembled David Methany's

correspondence and put it back in the folder, then the drawer. She took Beth's letters and placed them in a neat pile on the desk top. All this while she did not look at Beth, who did not take her eyes from the housekeeper's face.

"You know something," she stated. "Tell me, Miranda. You have to tell me so I understand and then maybe I can fight back."

"It was such a long time ago."

"What was? Please, Miranda," Beth implored, "tell me whatever you know."

"Lilly Jane was Lilly Jane Litwin, a very wealthy society lady."

"I know that," Beth told her with some impatience. "Gene Cavelli, one of the lawyers in the office, explained something about a scandal with her and my father back in the fifties. You were with him then, weren't you?"

"With your mother," Miranda corrected. "Your grandmother, your mother's mother, sort of made me a wedding present to your mother. My mother worked for her family and had always taken a special liking to Isabel—who was a different person before your father got to her." She glanced briefly away from Beth. "Sorry, but that's the truth."

"Go on," Beth urged, nodding her acceptance of the housekeeper's disrespect toward David.

"Anyway, this Lilly Jane killed herself and then her husband, a big-shot lawyer type, killed himself."

"I know about all that. I still don't understand what any of that would have to do with me, thirty-odd years later."

Miranda took her time answering. "I'm not sure, Miss Beth, but I do remember that at the time there were whispers about Lilly Jane being pregnant by your father."

"What!"

"No one could ever confirm it, of course, and then she died."

"But how could such a rumor have started?"

Miranda shrugged. "Who knows how these things get started? The only reason I know about it is because one morning I heard your mother asking your father about it. He denied it, no, actually he didn't. I remember distinctly because he wouldn't confirm or deny it, and I was so angry at his treatment of your mother." She shook her head in grave recollection of that morning. "Sometimes he could be just plain mean. I remember thinking at the time—and we were all so young then, but still, I knew even then—that your father was a powerful man, a mighty powerful force to be reckoned with, and thinking, too, that to every rumor there's a grain of truth. If Lilly Jane were pregnant by your daddy, there's no question he would have made her get rid of it."

"But that's horrible!"

Again Miranda shrugged. "What choice would they have had? Each married to another the way they were? That's probably why she killed herself."

"Was there ever any further mention of a child?"

"Not that I know of. Certainly not at the time of her death."

"I still don't see what all that has to do with me, now. It's not as if I had anything to do with those people."

"Miss Beth, for all we know it could be some crazy relative of Lilly Jane Litwin's, deciding to take out vengeance on you. Innocence has no bearing when you're dealing with the kind of rage that makes one mad."

"Why do you think Daddy kept the correspondence, Miranda? That's odd, isn't it?"

"I suppose, but knowing your daddy, I imagine he had a real good reason for keeping it. Maybe figured the sender would show himself one day and this was some kind of protection against the sender, to prove he was dealing with a madman or something, I don't know."

"Me either." Beth grew thoughtful. "Miranda, whoever sent

the flowers knew about my aversion to white flowers. Whoever
sent them wanted me to be upset."

"I'll agree with that now, and that's why I'm telling you we
might want to get a little extra help. This person won't stop
until he gets satisfaction. Sergeant Rico could—"

"No. Not yet."

"He could at least put some men around the building
so—"

"No. Besides, I haven't really been threatened in any way,
not physically at least. So whoever is behind this is playing some
weird kind of psychological game with me, big deal. Nothing
dangerous about that. I *am* David Methany's daughter, after all,"
she said, grinning.

"Oh, honey," Miranda said on a laugh, "you may be David
Methany's daughter all right, but you'll never understand what
cunning and ruthlessness really mean. You're strong, but few
people are *that* strong, believe me."

Beth said nothing, then reached for the telephone. "Who you
calling?" Miranda was impertinent enough to ask.

"Alyson Gentry. She's smart. Maybe she can tap one of her
sources and find out who's behind all this."

"Now there's someone strong enough," Miranda stated, not
disguising her distaste for the woman in question. "She's cold
enough to do whatever is necessary to get what she wants, just
like your daddy used to be."

"You really do dislike her, don't you?"

"I've liked others better," was all Miranda would say. "I'm
going to fix you an omelet and some soup, okay?"

"Lots of onions in the omelet."

Alyson answered on the second ring. "Alyson, it's Beth. I
hope I haven't disturbed you."

"Not at all. I was just going over the press release on the tax
abatement. What's up?"

"There's been another incident, Alyson, and if possible, I'd like you to call on those sources you have, those nameless ones you don't want me to know about."

"You mean the ones who got me the information on the residents of Feldon Manor?"

"The same. Can they do a little personal investigative work?"

"Tell me what you need done."

Beth then explained about the flowers and read her the message on the card.

"I don't suppose your housekeeper remembers the address on the delivery slip?" Alyson asked.

"Hold on and I'll check." Beth put down the receiver, ran out to the kitchen, and was back in seconds. "Winthrop Florists on Ninety-second, that's all she remembers."

"That's good enough. Although don't be too hopeful. I'm sure the order was placed by phone."

"Then how would it have been paid for, credit card? I doubt it."

"Good point. Okay, I'll see what I can find out. But Beth, what will you do with the information?"

"It's knowledge, Alyson. That's about as good a weapon as I can get my hands on right now. But at least I'll feel as if I'm doing something, fighting back a little."

"Maybe you shouldn't, fight back that is. It could be dangerous."

"Alyson, this is the first time in months I'm taking a step forward against this person. Even if it turns out to be nothing, I want to try to find out whatever I can."

"You can check out the florist yourself, Beth. You don't need my special resources for that."

"Of course I can, but I've become a pretty recognizable face lately," she reminded her colleague, "and I can do without additional press coverage of any kind. For all I know the florist could see this as a great way to pick up a quick dollar or two from one of the tabloids—you know, 'Heiress Questions Florist About Mysterious Bouquet Sender.' Besides, I really don't have the time, and you did once tell me this is easy for you to do." There was that telltale edge in Beth's voice now, a certain impatience she had developed since her father's death that was a clear signal she considered herself the boss whose requests were orders to be obeyed.

"Will you do it?"

"Yes, of course. Is that all?"

Alyson's coldness was as unmistakable a signal as Beth's imperiousness, but the latter had no tolerance for niceties now. "That's all, Alyson, and thank you. I hope you can get back to me soon on this."

"I'll try."

"Alyson?"

"Yes?"

"Do better than try." Then, more gently: "Please."

"Good night, Beth. See you in the morning."

" 'Do better than try.' "

The bitch! The fucking little bitch! How dare she! How *dare* she!

Janine's rage choked her as if a wad of cotton had gotten caught at the back of her throat, stifling her, blocking off air and rational thought. Tonight was supposed to have been a celebration of her cleverness. For a mere five dollars, she had gotten that old bag lady on Madison and Fifty-seventh to do exactly what she wanted. Janine had then crossed over to Central Park at Sixty-third where the old lady had found her, as instructed; the five dollars had been exchanged, and Janine had gone home, thrilled with herself. It had been a totally spontaneous action. She had been coming out of the hairdressers on Madison and Fifty-sixth when she had spotted Beth turning left on Fifty-seventh toward Fifth Avenue. The bag lady had been poor but not stupid; two blocks later the ominous words had been delivered perfectly. The little scare had been irresistible.

The white flowers were something else again, orchestrated to perfection with a telephone order and messenger-delivered cash as payment. The unexpected bonus was Beth calling on *her* to track down the sender; the irony was delectable, almost as fulfilling as Beth confiding in her in the first place. She should be feeling great, but instead, a vapor of defeat surrounded her, making her limp with its weight.

Suddenly, without warning, the force of her rage dissipated and she sank to her living room rug, her head bowed as her body shook with sobs. Her hands formed two fists and she began to pound lightly against the sides of her head—to remind her of her purpose? To remind her to be patient? To deaden the pulsating force of her needs? Hate took so much energy, retribution even more. She felt herself weakening, her strength ebbing like the flickering light of a dying candle. Perhaps because the end was near, or perhaps because she had accelerated the action, whatever the cause, she was unutterably exhausted from the effort it took to hate. It had been so long that that emotion had sustained her, she wondered if, when it was all over, she would be capable of the opposite feeling, if she had the capacity to love with equal fervor and commitment. Was that what was saddening her right now? Was it the dawning realization that she had given so much to hate there might be nothing left over for love? Lilly Jane would not have wanted that, no; Janine was sure her natural mother had been a caring and generous-hearted woman, a woman who knew how to love and be loved, perhaps unwisely, but at least not stingily.

Janine slowly got back on her feet, brushed the hair away

from her face, and walked toward her bedroom with new purpose. Wasn't it for love, in whatever odd manifestation it had taken, that her mother had lost her life? Wasn't it for love that Lilly Jane's husband had killed himself? Perhaps she was better off, after all, with her hatred.

She would know soon enough.

20

"Were you able to find out anything?"

"I'm sorry, Beth, I haven't had a chance to breathe these past few days."

"Oh, Alyson." The tone was one of complete disappointment.

Alyson smiled complacently at her end of the telephone. "I really am sorry, but Gene's had me working around the clock on a nuisance suit from one of the porters' locals."

So absorbed was Beth in the issue of the mysterious menace that she did not have any interest in the business problem Alyson mentioned. Her attitude these past few days was to leave business to the professionals she employed; she had her sanity, maybe even her life, to worry about.

"Look, Alyson, I'm going out to Rye for the weekend. I'd like to hear back from you with some kind of information before Friday, okay?"

"I'll do my best, I promise."

When Beth hung up, she began to go perfunctorily through her mail, and she did not need to turn over the postcard of Rockefeller Center to know that J. had struck again. Dread and disgust mingled within her, rising like bile to the back of her throat. She placed the card message-side-down on the desk, folded her hands in front of her schoolgirl-fashion, and began to breathe deeply. She closed her eyes, inhaled, exhaled, slowly, but not even a breeze of calm fluttered through her. Her heart was racing, the pounding echoing in her ears in a noisy rush of panic.

She separated her sweat-damp palms and reached gingerly for the postcard. "Soon it will all be mine. As it should be. Lilly Jane would approve. Feel the fear. J."

Beth stared at the message, drowning in agitation, then, abruptly, she held the card in one clenched fist and squeezed with all her might, crunching the malevolent life out of the laminated paper, and smiled tightly, sadly, at the absurd sense of accomplishment this small feat gave her.

She straightened out the card, tossed it into her bottom drawer. Without realizing she had made the decision, she picked up the telephone and called her home.

"Methany residence."

"Miranda, it's me."

"Are you all right, Miss Beth?" the housekeeper asked with immediate concern, knowing Beth never called her in the middle of the day.

"I'm fine. I just wanted you to know that I'm taking off for Rye earlier than I had planned. Please have the garage get the car ready in an hour."

"But Miss Beth, it's the middle of the week. Are you sure you're—"

"I'm fine, really. I just need to get away for a few days. You should take some time off, too. See your friend Sergeant Rico. I won't need you again until Sunday evening."

"It's this business with the letters, isn't it?" Miranda guessed. "And the flowers. Well, I am not leaving you alone. I'm going with you and that's that."

"No."

"Miss Beth, I can't let—"

"I'll see you Sunday, Miranda. Don't forget to call the garage."

She then left instructions with Karen that she was going to

spend the rest of the week and weekend at her house in Rye, and only in case of the direst emergency was she to be disturbed. She allowed that Karen would have to determine—with great care—what constituted direst.

A few hours later Beth was bundled up against the autumn wind coming off Long Island Sound as she walked on the beach in Rye. With her brown curls flying, and the tip of her nose and her cheeks bitten by the brisk air, she felt cleansed, the recent incidents becoming harmless and insignificant. It was the pressure of the business that was making her see danger where none existed. And even if she did not quite believe that, the fresh air and her wonderful house helped give her back a sense of order that had been missing.

That same evening, Janine/Alyson paced her apartment, twitchy with frustration. She had not counted on her opponent having the guts to just up and leave. She had underestimated Beth's strength, her ability to disregard her duty to her father. Somehow, she had to turn this situation to her own advantage, find opportunities to bring Beth closer to the edge. What was it the bitch had said . . . about wishing the person would just show himself. Well, Miss Rich Bitch, remember the old saying: Be careful about what you wish for—you just might get it!

But not yet. No, she was not ready to show herself quite yet. First there should be a little more torment to be enjoyed, a few more incidents to display the superior intelligence she had inherited from her father. She wanted Beth Methany fearful, helpless, out of control . . . as Lilly Jane must have been that night.

It did not take Janine long to devise several new scenarios with which to plague her nemesis. She was even able, while doing so, to admit to herself that she, too, was getting closer to the edge, the one that separated desire from obsession—but she could not stop herself, nor did she want to.

And so she rented a car.

And bought some very basic tools.

And after learning from Karen that Beth had given Miranda the time off, calling to make sure, she had gained access to the Fifth Avenue apartment. The doorman on duty was, fortunately, a substitute. But if he hadn't been, she would have figured out another way . . . she always did.

With the sweet sound of David Sanborn's saxophone coming from her portable double-cassette player, and the light from Long Island Sound a crystal blue as luminous and pure as innocence, Beth could not imagine any place on earth where she would rather be this October morning than here in her pottery studio in Rye. A restful night's sleep, a walk along the shore earlier, a breakfast for once consisting of more than a cup of coffee, and now, the music, the light, that special sensation of moist clay being shaped by her hands against the unique rhythm of the wheel, all contributed to a sense of well-being that confirmed she had made the right decision by coming out here for a few days.

Despite its proximity to the Sound, the air in the converted boat shed was not overly damp, and usually she was able to glaze and fire her pieces the day after throwing them. She finished the fruit bowl she was working on and put it on the drying shelf with a slightly moist rag over it, then began to glaze a few dried pieces she had brought with her from the city. After that, she painted designs on pieces that had been left here, glazed but not decorated. The day sped by, and it was well after three when she realized that she had not eaten and that the cassette player had automatically shut off.

Before leaving, she checked the electrical switch and the temperature control gauge on the kiln, and opened the door to the kiln; everything was in order for firing tomorrow. Maybe she would doodle a few new designs tonight, or drive in to Port Chester and rent a few videos....

It was seven o'clock when she awakened from an unexpected nap that had lasted hours instead of the fifteen minutes she had intended when she closed the issue of *Vogue* on her lap and put her head back against the sofa cushion. The sybaritic luxury of a day without meetings, people, decisions seemed to be more exhausting than she could have imagined—or was it simply the release from stress that was freeing her body to refresh itself with much-needed rest?

Feeling more lethargic than before her nap, she wandered into the kitchen and rummaged about for something to eat that would not require cooking. Miranda had, of course, alerted the caretakers, so the cupboards were well-stocked. While the soup was heating, she went upstairs and changed from jeans and sweatshirt to nightgown and robe, all thoughts of driving over to the video store tabled until the next day. It was too late to check in with Karen at the office, she realized, a pleased smile on her face. This kind of irresponsible behavior would doom her to failure, she warned herself with that same sunbeam of a grin.

She fell asleep with the television on. She was sure it was the sound of the rebroadcast news at one o'clock in the morning with that supercilious sportscaster again giving the day's scores that had awakened her now, but she saw by her bedside clock that it was almost two-thirty, well past the hour for the rebroadcast. She used the remote control to switch off the television, but there it was again, that peculiar scratchy sound.

Her room was above the three-car garage at the south side of the house. She got out of bed and pulled back the curtain to the window that overlooked the asphalt driveway. There was her Honda exactly where she had left it yesterday. In fact, she must remember to put it in the garage tomorrow night; it was getting too cold to leave it out in the open.

She walked over to another window and looked out to the front of the house; nothing but the black expanse of lawn and night. Where in the world was that odd metallic scraping coming from? As if someone were dragging a tailpipe. And then she made a wry grimace. Of course. That's exactly what it was, someone who had driven by with his tailpipe dragging. Probably got lost, drove back in the opposite direction. That's why she had heard it twice. Satisfied with her explanation, Beth went back to bed and was immediately asleep.

The next morning was overcast, but that didn't stop her from feeling the same exhilaration as the day before. She put Aretha Franklin tapes into the cassette player, appropriate music for firing, she decided, and set the temperature control. While waiting for the kiln to heat up, she checked over the various pieces she had prepared for firing, and was perplexed by what seemed to be two, no, three fewer pieces than she was sure she had worked on yesterday. There were supposed to be three mugs and matching sandwich plates, a pitcher, vase, and candy dish. The vase and two of the plates were missing. Loss of the vase was particularly disappointing because she had earmarked it as a gift for Alyson.

She looked around the studio, lifted the lids off the already opened two-gallon drums of clay just in case she had put some of the pieces there by mistake; unlikely, but given how preoccupied she was lately, not impossible. The only thing in the clay drums was clay. And then she spotted it—shards of royal blue pottery with rounded edges, the sandwich plates. What in the world . . . ? She was losing her mind, that had to be it. Obviously, she had dropped a plate and simply forgotten. But then, what about the other plate and the vase? Oh well, maybe she had brought them up to the house; she'd check later.

But Beth Methany was not absent-minded or stupid or given

to reaching for straws when a straw was more palatable than
the truth. She knew that she had not dropped one of the plates
just as she knew that she had not brought the other pieces into
the house. But because she was enjoying her respite from the
office, and because her pottery work so gratified her, she decided
to ignore the doubt that rang alarmingly in her mind, telling
her that something was wrong, very wrong. She ignored it by
utilizing that remarkable capacity intelligent people have for
self-denial.

She checked the thermometer, opened the latch of the kiln
door, reached over to get the firing mitts, her goggles. Her
goggles . . . they were missing, too. No, here they were. How
odd, she always put them and the mitts together on the shelf
beneath the pieces scheduled for firing. This morning the goggles
were over by the door. If it weren't so paranoid-sounding, she'd
swear someone had been in the shed, messed around with her
stuff, and forgotten to put the goggles back in their correct place.
Obviously broke a few of her pieces, too. But who would do
such a thing, and why? Her phantom J. didn't know about the
house here in Rye, or her workshop, so it couldn't be him . . . her.

She put on the goggles and mitts and took one of the mugs
to be fired. Soon she had all three mugs lined up with a comfortable amount of space separating them, which was necessary
for the circulation of the heat. It was not a professional-size kiln
so its capacity was modest, as well as the degree of heat it
generated. She always had to temper her eagerness to get her
pieces done, knowing that the kiln was slower because of its
size.

She turned up the control to firing heat, slightly over 925
degrees, took off the mitts and goggles, and sat back at her work
table, thumbing through a catalogue of potters' tools and equipment. There was a new kind of clay she had heard about,
supposedly less porous than the standard and it might be—

Thwack.

The crack bounced off the walls of the kiln, dulling the sound but making it no less recognizable to Beth. She immediately turned off her tape player.

Another crackle.

"Shit!" she exclaimed.

Another pop, another, another, the sound of exploding ceramic thudding throughout the small shed. Beth jumped off the stool and lowered the temperature control. She impatiently counted to 100 to make sure the immediate heat died down, and then she unlocked the door. All her pieces lay in shards. More upsetting, though, was the incredible heat wafting from the walls of the kiln, far hotter than it should be with the gauge lowered.

She looked at the control; the black metal needle was still at the high end when it should have been stationary in the OFF position. She stuck her hand back into the kiln, quickly withdrew it at the feel of the high heat. Something was seriously wrong; she pulled the plug from the wall socket. Only then did the needle settle into the OFF position.

When she was convinced that the kiln was no longer operational, Beth sat down and succumbed to nerves, her breathing shallow, her hands shaking visibly.

The potential danger in what had just occurred was too horrendous to contemplate. Were she not so indoctrinated with the safe ways to work with a kiln, there was no telling what might have happened when she opened the door. She had heard awful tales of potters checking their work and getting burns and blisters on their faces. She would take the temperature gauge into White Plains and her friend at the art supply store, but she did not really need him to tell her it had been tampered with somehow. She wondered if whoever had done that had also deliberately broken her plates and the vase, or had that been just a sloppy accident? No, the only accident, Beth suddenly felt sure, was her own cautiousness.

When she backed the car out of the driveway, she noticed a dark puddle on the asphalt. Water from the radiator, she determined, knowing this happened whenever she used the heater. Since the art store was near her favorite garage mechanic, she'd have him check it out.

Although it would have been quicker to take the Thruway into White Plains, Beth preferred the more scenic route of the Boston Post Road. Where strip malls and traffic lights did not interrupt the surroundings, the landscape was almost rural, and lush with fall foliage.

Maybe it was the stop-and-start flow of traffic that caused it, but midway to White Plains she was amazed to see her gas gauge needle hovering near EMPTY. She shook her head, confused. She definitely had filled up in Rye, right before arriving at the house, so she wouldn't have to bother for the rest of the week. What in the world was going on? she wondered with only slight concern.

Which grew deeper as she heard the chuck-chucking of a motor without fuel for energy. She was rapidly running out of gas, no question about it. There was a station up ahead and she pulled in; no time to wait for her favorite mechanic. She'd have this guy fill her up and check the radiator at the same time.

"You made it just in time, Miss. Had maybe another quarter of a mile in the tank, if that. Traveling far?"

"What? What did you say?"

"I was asking if you'd been traveling far?" the young man repeated. "Tank's empty."

"But that's impossible," she objected.

"Sorry, Miss, no question about it."

"But—" She caught herself. There was no point arguing with the guy; he knew an empty tank from a full one, and although she had a sinking suspicion that the puddle in her driveway was not from water, she asked him to check out the radiator and water level anyway.

"Radiator's fine. Water level okay, too. Might want to consider adding some more antifreeze soon what with the weather changing."

"Thanks, I will," she said, handing him cash for the gas.

She drove into White Plains, her mind awhirl. A broken temperature gauge on her kiln. Shards of her ceramic work lying about. Goggles not in their usual place. A gas leak. Somehow J. had found out about the house in Rye, about the studio. Somehow J.—had that been the sound that had awakened her last night?—had come up here or arranged for someone to come up and do these things, things meant not so much to seriously hurt her—surface burns from the kiln, perhaps; running out of gas on an isolated road, the worst that could have happened; it would have been far more dangerous if the brake fluid had been leaked. No, these were acts meant to frighten her, unnerve her, get her off-balance and jittery, but not to actually harm her.

Beth had no doubt that J. was behind all of it, and she experienced a perverse sense of satisfaction by understanding that the more physical the threats, the more desperate the mind behind them. Beth believed, therefore, that it would all be over soon, but first there would be other, perhaps far more vicious attacks. She was positive of this. After someone harbored a hunger for justice for years and years, the taste of retribution would be too sweet to experience only once or twice.

And meanwhile, all she could do was continue to wait, the inactivity as much a part of her punishment as the fear. How cunning, and how dangerous an enemy she had somehow made.

Brig Lewis, the owner of the art supply store, greeted Beth warmly. "Beth, how good to see you again. It's been a while."

"Yes, it has been. How are you, Brig?"

"Good, thanks. What can I do for you? I got a shipment in of some special Chinese glazes. Would you—"

"Not this time," she cut him off, then reached into her jacket pocket. "Take a look at this, would you, Brig? I was working earlier when the needle just went berserk and the stuff I was firing cracked; everything was ruined. The heat in the kiln must have been fifty, sixty degrees over what I thought I had set it at."

"Which was?"

"A little above 900. The oven can only take 1250. When I turned off the kiln, the needle remained at the hottest. Only when I unplugged it from the socket did everything start to cool down."

"Not good," he agreed. "Let me take a look."

He disappeared into a back room, returning in less than ten minutes with his palm outstretched. "Look here."

"What is that?" Beth asked, taking the little copper-colored ball from his palm and studying it.

"A magnet. An electromagnet to be precise."

"An electromagnet." She repeated the word, a sour pill she had no choice but to swallow. She did not have to ask what it meant.

"Easy enough to get in there," Brig went on, indicating the little screw he was holding that attached the top and bottom of the gauge. "Held in place by a small strip of Velcro, see," and she did. "Guaranteed to drive the metal needle crazy. Strange."

"Yes, it is, isn't it?" she muttered.

"Wait a sec and I'll screw the gauge back together for you."

"No, Brig, let me keep it this way, but I could use another one."

Once back in the car, all the terror she had convinced herself she did not really feel washed over her in a tumbling cascade until she tasted the salty sting of her tears. She wasn't sure how long she sat there in the car like that, her hands on either side of the steering wheel, eyes staring unseeing straight ahead as she cried and as her stomach twisted into a hard knot of nerves.

Somehow she eventually managed to start the car and drive back to the house, locking the car in the garage, locking the boat shed, checking every door and window.

There was no rest for her tonight, only long, endless hours spent alternating between agitation at what was being done to her and anger that J. had dared to invade her most cherished sanctuary. Early the next morning, without any plan but with a strong need not to be alone, she drove back to New York. If Miranda had taken these days off, she could call Alyson, or go into the office where there were sure to be a few people, even on a Saturday.

Once home, she took a leisurely bath to soak away the mood of despair that had traveled with her from Rye, then she made herself a cup of coffee, deciding to wait until eleven o'clock to call Alyson. Miranda had left her a note telling her she had gone off to Atlantic City and where she could be reached, if needed, and when she'd be back, but Beth had no intention of disturbing her. It was better to discuss what had happened with Alyson anyway; she would have a less personal, more clear-headed reaction than Miranda.

She headed for her father's study, a refuge for her with everything in it so masculine and larger than life, as he had been.

"I need you, Daddy," she whispered. "You'd know what to do to stop this madness." She walked over to the desk, put down her mug of coffee, and picked up the suede-framed photograph, the picture of her and her father always a source of comfort and reassurance to her. She turned it over, needing the sight of his warm brown eyes, his loving smile to—

"Oh God no! NO!"

She shoved the framed photo from her, dropping it back on the desk, face-side down, the shattered glass burning her hands, scorching the very blood in her veins into a fever of terror. The beating of her heart was so loud, so fast that she was convinced she would faint from the sheer effort of breathing. Tears streamed down her cheeks as she forced herself to again look at the obscene picture, try to make some sort of sense of this latest violation.

With shock strumming in her head, she saw that the glass over her face had been hit hard, that particular area obviously the prime target. The spiderwebs of line fractures splintered down from her face over the rest of the photograph except for one area where care was taken to keep it untouched: David Methany's face. There were those brown eyes, reflecting the affection and caring few people had ever actually witnessed. But for the first time, Beth looked at this photograph and was not reassured or comforted. Instead, a wave of resentment soared and crested within her as she saw not affection and caring, but posture and hypocrisy.

Stop it! Stop it! she cried in silent self-disgust. But the bitterness would not be checked as she blamed him for everything that was happening to her and everything that was missing in her life and everything she was forced to do because *she was his daughter.*

As suddenly and unexpectedly as the storm raged so did it die, leaving only the detritus of shame. It didn't matter. It didn't matter that he had been mean sometimes, or demanding, or even ruthless. It didn't matter that perhaps her mother suffered not because of her shallowness but because that shallowness was her only protection against his cruelty, his callousness. It didn't matter that he had had other women, or an army of men to do his dirty work, or an attitude of expendability toward anyone who got in his way. None of that mattered because he had loved *her* and he had left her the great gift of his empire. Her ingratitude was a nervous reaction, nothing more, nothing heartfelt.

Cradling the damaged photograph against her chest, she moved around the side of the desk and sat down in her father's chair, picked up the telephone, dialed information, then the number.

"Alyson? It's me, Beth."

"Beth, hello. How's Rye? Karen told me you went out there early."

"I'm back in New York."

"That was fast. Anything wrong? Beth, are you okay?"

Beth shut her eyes briefly at the wonderful sound of concern in her friend's voice. "Actually, Alyson, I'm not too okay. I could really use a friend right now."

"I'll be over within the hour."

"Thanks, Alyson. You have no idea how much this means to me."

"An hour, Beth," and the line went dead, although the unseen smile was very much alive.

21

"I can't tell you how much I've been looking forward to tonight," Beth said as she glanced around at Alyson's spacious apartment. "Did you do all this yourself or did a decorator help?" She gestured at the lovely oriental rugs, the abundance of thick-cushioned chairs and sofas, the collection of gilt-framed mirrors of varying sizes and shapes. "It's so old-fashioned," she remarked, "and I mean that as a compliment. I would have expected a much more modern style."

"I wanted something as different from where I work as I could get, and something that would be sybaritically comfortable. Probably if a professional had helped it would have turned out better."

"Oh, no, it's great." Beth handed Alyson a gift-wrapped bottle. "Better keep it chilled," she advised, following her to the larger-than-standard New York kitchen, with its glass-fronted cabinets, stainless-steel appliances, and gray granite countertops.

"Any kitchen this modern is a cook's kitchen," Beth enthused.

"I really do enjoy cooking. It's such a change from briefs and depositions," Alyson said as she unwrapped the paper to the bottle of Piper-Heidsieck. "Beth, this wasn't at all necessary."

"I love champagne, and you deserve it after all—"

"But I'm allergic to champagne, I thought I told you that."

Beth's face fell. "Oh, Alyson, I completely forgot, I'm sorry. I've been so out of it lately I just wasn't thinking. Here, let me take it home with me."

"No, don't be silly. I can always use a bottle of vintage champagne for a special friend," she said, her smile so painful that
she had to turn her back. *The bitch didn't forget! She knew;
she just wanted it for herself. Selfish bitch!* And it was because
Janine/Alyson had stepped further into the abyss of obsession
that she could not imagine her enemy capable of any act not
deliberate and premeditated, and harmful—as were her own.

"Mmm," Beth sniffed, "something smells fantastic. Lots of
garlic if I'm not mistaken."

Alyson faced her again. "Angel hair pasta primavera, but
done with olive oil and garlic instead of cream; salad of mush-
rooms, radicchio and curly endive; tomatoes baked with bread
crumbs; and garlic bread. Very simple and very garlicky. Good
thing neither of us has a date tonight," she joked.

"Can I help with anything?"

"Absolutely not. In fact, there's little to do, so how about a
drink? Liquor, wine, your champagne?"

"A glass of white wine would be great."

Alyson poured a glass, then shooed her out of the kitchen.
"Give me a few minutes. You go relax but talk loudly while
I'm in here."

Beth went into the comfortably sized dining alcove, the space
taken up primarily by a large, round mahogany table, heavy
and old and beautifully laid out with what she immediately
recognized were Battenberg lace placemats, Lalique crystal, and
Rosenthal china. "Your table is lovely," she called out. "A family
heirloom?"

"No."

"What about the crystal and china—from your mother?"
This time, no answer. All that could be heard was the rapid
chopping of knife against wooden board. "Alyson?"

*My mother gave me nothing as insignificant as lace and crystal,
bitch, just a reason to live.* "Sorry. No, I picked everything out."

When Alyson had not responded, Beth had walked, quietly, back to the kitchen doorway. "You have wonderful taste."

The lawyer, startled by the proximity of the voice, twisted about, knife in one hand, the fingers of the other quickly curling into a fist. "I didn't hear you."

"Didn't mean to surprise you. I wanted to watch you work."

Alyson forced a smile. "There's nothing very exciting to see, just me chopping vegetables and stuff. I'll be done in a couple of minutes. Besides, it makes me nervous to have someone watching me while I cook."

"Okay, okay."

As soon as she was gone, Alyson turned her back to the doorway, quickly gauged if Beth could have seen anything and was confident she had not; the pieces were small, the chopping rapid, and the way she was standing over the cutting board would have blocked her vision. Satisfied, she placed the shrimp she had been clenching back on the board, carefully slicing the shellfish into thread-thin slivers, without taste or texture, invisible to all the senses. In her salad. In the breadcrumb topping on her tomato. Mixed artfully with the broccoli and carrots and cauliflower and zucchini of her pasta primavera. Artfully, and in just the right amount to cause a violent, painful but not quite deadly allergic reaction in Beth.

"Delicious," Beth commented later as she ate. "This is exactly what the doctor ordered, Alyson. Thanks a lot. And thanks again for coming over on Saturday. That business with the glass on the photo of my father and me really had me going. Especially coming on top of what happened in Rye." She shook her head, remembering. "What a nightmare. I don't know how I would have gotten through any of it without you."

"You just needed someone logical and unemotionally involved to help you make sense of what happened, see that everything had a very reasonable explanation. And I know you told me

Miranda insists she didn't drop the picture, but Beth," and here Alyson smiled with warm conspiracy, "it is possible, isn't it, that she's too embarrassed to admit the truth to you, knowing how you felt about that picture?"

Beth nodded. "It's possible. And you're right, it's also possible I screwed up the kiln gauge, or maybe it got damaged from the summer heat and humidity. It never happened before, but it's not impossible that that would explain it. And your reasoning for the gas leak could, I suppose, be that the guy who filled me up when I got to Rye monkeyed around with something. All these things are plausible. The trouble is I don't buy any of it, not any of it. That damn sinister J. is behind it, and I can't do a thing about it. Yet. But I will, you can bet on it! Until then," she said, grinning, "I'm just grateful to have a friend like you to help me through the rough times."

Alyson looked at Beth with a new seriousness in her expression. "There's something that's been on my mind, but I've hesitated to talk to you about it, especially with the strain you've been under. I'm still not sure I'm doing the right thing, but I'd never forgive myself if anything happened to you or the company and I hadn't helped as much as I could have."

Beth put down her fork. "What is it, Alyson? From your tone of voice, this is obviously pretty bad."

"Well, it could be, I guess. I shouldn't have mentioned it now, I knew it. See, you've stopped eating."

Beth took a bite of her garlic bread. "Okay, I'm eating again. Now tell me what's wrong."

"It's Ben Wyler again, I'm afraid."

"Oh no. What's he up to this time?"

"Beth, did you know his uncle was fired years ago from the Methany Corporation?"

"No, I had no idea. Are you sure?"

"Positive. I was going over the papers for the porters' case when I came across the name of Delbart Wyler in connection with a similar incident years ago. He was an accountant who had to sign an affidavit about overtime pay regarding another union. Anyway, it seems that your father, or someone else, no doubt, fired him for not reporting income correctly to the IRS. It's not impossible that your friend Ben Wyler—"

"Former friend."

"Former friend has a real grudge against us." Alyson spoke slowly, her attention caught by the pop of perspiration on Beth's brow, the sickly gray in her cheeks. "You okay?"

"I don't know," Beth answered on a short, nervous laugh. "All of a sudden I feel kind of queasy. Maybe it's because you're about to tell me something sickeningly unpleasant."

"It can wait. I'm sorry I brought it up in the first place. Sometimes I forget that it's possible to have a conversation not centered around business."

"I need to know when anything's wrong, minor or major, and usually there's no appropriate time for passing on that kind of information. So out with it—what has Ben done?"

"Well, when you were up at Rye last week, he appeared on a televised debate with his two political opponents, and he made a rather pointed statement about cracking down on the corrupt real estate business as practiced by some of the giants. When pushed, he named names, and Methany was at the top of the list. In fact, it was a list of one. Beth, he really has to be stopped."

"Oh, it doesn't mean anything, Alyson. If it helps him get elected, I don't care. I think he'll make a great mayor, and we can deal with him when he goes on the attack."

"You can't be serious."

Beth smiled at her colleague's shocked expression. "I know Ben. He wouldn't do anything he didn't believe in, not even for votes, and he wouldn't go after us to retaliate for something done to a relative of his. He's bigger and smarter than that. We beat him when he went after us with Feldon Manor and Methany City North, and we can do it again. You overestimate his ability to hurt us."

"Did you know his wife is a cocaine addict?"

"No! Really? Ex-wife, though. I wonder if he—" Suddenly, she frowned and a hand flew to her mouth. "This is really embarrassing, Alyson," she faltered, getting to her feet, "but I think I'm going to be sick. Your bathroom?"

Alyson pointed and Beth ran from the table. To the unmistakable sounds of someone retching, a toilet flushing, Alyson, for the first time that evening, ate her food with genuine appetite.

A few minutes later Beth emerged, ashen, and sheepish. "Sorry. I can't imagine what happened, but you didn't put any kind of shellfish in the food tonight, did you?"

"Of course not. I know you're allergic."

"Strange. This is exactly the kind of reaction I get to shellfish."

Alyson rose and walked to the wall of glass at the far end of the living room. "Come here, Beth. A little fresh air will make you feel better."

Beth made it to the sliding-glass door, but wouldn't step out on the terrace. "This is as far as I go."

"Come on, Beth," Alyson urged.

"The view is great and I can breathe the fresh air from here, safely inside. Forty floors up is thirty-nine floors too high."

Alyson grabbed her by the forearm. "You're being ridiculous. Now come on out here. There's absolutely nothing to be afraid of."

"NO! I hate heights, hate them!"

"Please, trust me, Beth. Step out here a minute and breathe deeply. You'll feel better, I know it, and I'll hold on to you the whole time."

Even as she shook her head in mute refusal, she took one tentative step, then another, finally another, and then she was on the terrace. Immediately, she began to hyperventilate.

"Don't think about the height, Beth," Alyson encouraged, still holding on to her upper arm. "Look straight out. See how clear and beautiful the sky is."

"Beautiful," Beth parroted. "Let's go in now."

In response, Alyson placed her free hand at Beth's back, edging her forward to the terrace railing.

"Stop it, this is far enough." Beth was too frightened to even blink, lest somehow her eyes glance downward. She reached behind to push away Alyson's guiding hand.

"But isn't your nausea gone?"

"No. In fact, it's gotten worse." Mustering her strength through the battle anger was having with panic, she shook free of Alyson's grip and stalked back into the apartment, breathing shallowly before rushing into the bathroom where the sound of vomiting again could be heard.

"I'm sorry, Beth," Alyson called out, smirking to herself. "I thought it would help."

"I think I'll be going now," Beth stated when she came out.

"Will you be all right? You're awfully pale. Maybe we should call a doctor?"

"No, I just want to go home."

Alyson retrieved Beth's coat from the hall closet. "Want me to go down with you for a cab?"

Beth shook her head. "Sorry I spoiled your dinner," she offered on a weak smile. "Must be a new strain of flu starting. I'm sorry about that little scene on your terrace, too."

"Oh no, I apologize for that."

"You were just trying to be helpful." Impulsively, she leaned over and kissed Alyson lightly on the cheek. "Good night."

As soon as the door was locked, Alyson/Janine went into the kitchen and took from the refrigerator the half-dozen jumbo shrimp and the cocktail sauce she had prepared as her own special treat. What a wonderful, wonderful night! Everything done to perfection, she rejoiced, the satisfaction of her success tastier than any delicacy of food. It really was a shame she couldn't tolerate champagne; it would have been the perfect drink with which to toast her triumph.

Tonight there had been no glitches; not one thing had gone wrong. Unlike what had occurred up in Rye, when the battery in that damn penlight had died and she had dropped the wrench right there in the driveway. She had had to grope around, her fingers so cold she couldn't grasp the icy metal without having it slip out of her reach, twice making what seemed a deafeningly loud scraping sound on the black asphalt. She had held her breath, fully expecting Beth to come to the door, but nothing had happened, and she had been able to finish what she had gone up there to do. She had parked the rented car in the street, three houses away, and that had been a cause for concern, too. In such a residential neighborhood, any strange car parked in the street, not a driveway, would be considered unusual, possibly even alarming. But the late hour had helped; everyone was asleep. Tonight had been so different, everything totally under her control, no surprises. She knew she would sleep peacefully, whereas Beth, well, if the nausea didn't get her, the new seed of doubt about Ben Wyler should just about guarantee a troubled night.

And Beth did suffer throughout that night. Miranda wanted to call the family doctor when, at three, Beth vomited for the fifth time, nothing now but watery bile. Beth resisted medical attention. She obviously had eaten something that disagreed with her. Probably from that chicken salad she had at lunch. The mayonnaise, she explained to Miranda, must have been rancid. The housekeeper asked her repeatedly if she was sure, absolutely positive, that her friend Alyson had not served shellfish. Since she was a little girl the only thing that ever caused Beth to get sick to her stomach was shellfish. Beth itemized the menu for Miranda, dish by dish. No shellfish. It had to have been the mayonnaise, or the chicken itself.

Finally, at five o'clock in the morning, her body had nothing left to give up, and Beth was able to escape into sleep.

She awoke early the next afternoon with a raw emptiness in her stomach, and the stubborn memory of her terror as she stood on that terrace, forty stories in the air. Miranda was able to remedy the former with a bowl of homemade consommé; the latter, Beth knew, would vanish as soon as she busied herself with other things, and heading the list was to again apologize, maybe send flowers, to Alyson, and to have it out with Ben once and for all.

But she never got to speak with either of them, because that day's mail at home brought a typewritten letter from J.: "How does it feel to be at the receiving end of someone's power? Are you ready to pay the price? The cost of justice is high. Be careful, Beth. And be afraid. J."

After she read the letter a second time, she vomited again, this time sick, to her soul, with fear.

22

Two days later Beth had regained her strength, emotionally and physically, and the first item on her agenda was Ben Wyler. The time she had spent recuperating had also been spent thinking, and she had come to the realization that she had treated Alyson's concern about Ben's motives too cavalierly. His uncle's dismissal from the Methany Corporation definitely needed further investigation.

At lunchtime, she took a cab down to Irving Place where Ben had his campaign headquarters. With only a few weeks left until the election, and with the polls showing Ben running slightly behind the incumbent and far ahead of his third opponent, Beth believed he was pulling out all the stops, and with the Methany Corporation always fodder for the press, he was using the company the way Rudolph Giuliani had used organized crime, as a political whipping boy. That tactic had backfired, as Beth was sure this one would for Ben.

She was entering the main room as he was leaving his private office, and they saw each other immediately. It was the first time they had been in the same place since the AIDS fundraiser.

"Beth, what are you doing here?" His smile was instant and warm as he approached her with a quickened step and outstretched hands. Then he slowed, and lowered his arms, and the smile faded; he was replaying that sinister call.

"Hello, Ben. Do you have a few minutes? I'm sorry I didn't call first . . ."

"Come on in, but we'll have to make it kind of fast. I have a rubber-chicken lunch with the police commissioner and some of his politically influential cronies."

Once in his office, with the door closed, he behind his desk, Beth in a mercilessly hard chair, seconds of silence ticked by as they stared at one another, remembering better times, each aware of the hurt they had caused the other.

"Beth—?"

"It's about your Uncle Delbart," she began.

"Oh shit, not this again."

"I'm sorry about what happened to him," she continued, jolted by the unexpected remark, choosing to ignore it. "But really, Ben, to attack me because of something that happened to a relative of yours years ago—" She pursed her lips with disappointment. "It's beneath you, Ben."

"Dammit, Beth, stop this once and for all!" He slammed his palm down on the desk, a sound almost as unpleasantly loud as his voice. "You tried this shit with me about Uncle Delbart before, and I told you then and I'll tell you again that I won't—"

"What do you mean you told me before?" she broke in. "I just found out two days ago that you had an Uncle Delbart who worked for Methany. What are you talking about?" she demanded, hot with indignation.

"Oh, excuse me," he said with exaggerated sarcasm, "I forgot. Just like your daddy, you had someone else do your dirty work. Very modern, Beth, using a voice scrambler of all things. I'm impressed. Have you thought of going into politics? The way you operate would fit right in."

"Ben, has the pressure of the election gotten to you? You're talking madness."

"*I'm* talking madness?" he repeated on a hollow crack of laughter. "It was one of your minions who threatened me about Delbart and Rachel's drug habit and my speeding record. It was your minion who thought he, she, whatever the hell it was, would get a big fat raise for being so clever and tough, just like a real Methany. So don't sit there playing the innocent babe and pretend you don't know about this, Beth, when you've made it very clear you'll do anything to silence me and keep me from exposing your father and his company."

Ben went on a while, steaming with outrage, but Beth was staring at him, through him, only one thing he said of any consequence to her.

"Someone called you using a voice scrambler?" she asked, her rancor replaced by a whisper of incredulity.

"Oh, come off it, Beth. You know damn well—" and he stopped, not doubting for a minute the fear and confusion and complete lack of knowledge making her eyes glassy and round, her cheeks white, her posture stiff. "You too?" he barely muttered.

She nodded jerkily. "I'm sorry, Ben, I thought it was you behind... Never mind, I've got to go. I've got to figure out what's going on. I really am sorry, about so many things. I wish it could be different between us, you know."

"Me, too. At least let me try to help you. You're obviously in some kind of trouble. Talk to me, Beth. Let me help."

She smiled sadly. "That's what I thought you'd be able to do when I decided to come here today and confront you—get you to stop harassing me. Unfortunately, I was wrong about you, which I should have realized from the beginning. You're just too decent a person to stoop—" She shook her head and looked away from him.

"To stoop as low as your father, is that what you were going to say?" he prodded softly.

She met his eyes. "Yes, it was," she admitted, again smiling sadly, again shaking her head with disbelief at the treachery of her thought. "But I won't condemn him, Ben," she quickly added. "I might not approve, but I won't condemn, and I won't let you do it either."

"Let's leave your father out of this for once. It's you I'm concerned about. But I can't help you unless you tell me what's going on."

"It wouldn't make any difference if I told you because I don't know what I'm fighting or why." She got up and went to the door. "Good luck in the election, Ben. Believe it or not, I'm going to vote for you."

"Just for that I may leave your company alone for a while," he teased, going over to her. This time he did not stop himself from embracing her. "If there's anything..."

She said nothing, just lightly caressed his cheek, and left, strangely relieved that even though she was no better off than before she came to see him, at least now she knew that Alyson had been wrong about Ben and she was glad for that. She must remember to ask her who else knew about Delbart Wyler.

The rest of the week flew by without Beth having a minute to herself; she even had to go into the office on Saturday to sign some papers for Gene and Alyson that they needed early Monday morning for that porters' nuisance suit.

"You two should spend the rest of the day the way other young women spend their Saturdays—go shopping," Gene advised after the papers were signed. "The work's finished here, and I'm heading off to Litchfield for what's left of the weekend."

"A little shopping sounds good," Beth said. "Alyson?"

"Why not? Gene, are you sure there's nothing more that has to be done?"

"Positive. With these affidavits from other building owners, I can prove those porters are treated better in a Methany building than anywhere else. Now, out, both of you, and enjoy. I'll lock up here."

After Beth and Alyson had walked along Madison Avenue in comfortable silence a while, Alyson suggested stopping in at a jewelry shop on Sixty-fourth Street that had a pair of earrings in the window "with my name on them," she told her.

"What kind?" Beth asked.

Alyson described the amethyst and citron drop earrings, how unusual buying good jewelry was for her, and Beth forgot to mention about talking to Ben; Alyson almost, but only almost, forgot that she was with her enemy. The autumn afternoon was nippy, with the sun peeking in and out of roving clouds, and the fashionable avenue was lined with well-dressed browsers and buyers. For just the briefest while, each woman enjoyed a respite from her individual concerns.

It was not to last.

"Here we are," Alyson said, stopping in front of the display window for Kronna Jewelers. "See, over there in that corner. Aren't they gorgeous?"

"Oh, they are. Come on, let's go in and get them."

Alyson laughed. "What's this 'we' business? I'm the one who has to pay for them."

A short while later Alyson had the earrings on. "What do you think?"

"The colors are beautiful on you," Beth complimented. "You have to have them, Alyson. They'll make anything you wear special."

The lawyer took another look at herself in the mirror, another glance at the price tag, then nodded and smiled at the salesman. She removed the earrings before getting out her credit card.

"I'm sorry," the salesman said. "No credit cards. Only cash or personal check."

"No problem," Alyson said easily, taking out her checkbook. "I should make it out to ... ?"

"K-r-o-n-n-a Jewelers," the salesman spelled out, and then tallied up the amount with the tax.

Beth stood to Alyson's right, leaning slightly against the counter, her eyes wandering appreciatively over the various displays of jewelry. She was smiling, pleased with her friend's indulgent purchase, when she glanced down to see if Alyson was almost finished writing out the check. She could do with a stop for some food; she was starving and had a craving for ...

At first it didn't register. At first, all that registered was that she was putting her signature to the check so they'd be leaving soon and she could eat. But then, as if in delayed replay, Beth absorbed what she was seeing. Kronna Jewelers. *J*—ewelers. She would always, anywhere, for all time know that *J*. She had seen it on years and years' worth of letters and postcards to her father. She had learned to dread the sight of it on letters and postcards to herself.

The smile faded slowly from her mouth. There was a gray mist of disbelief in front of her eyes, and a wave of dizziness made her totter backward, away from the counter, away from the truth that had finally showed itself to her.

"No. No. It can't be. No." The denial, the refusal, were breathed, not spoken. Her eyes were unblinking with horrified shock, disbelief.

Alyson frowned at her curiously, looked down to tear the check from the checkbook. And then dawning understanding appeared, first in the widening of her eyes, then in a slow, thin smile.

"So now you know."

"Who are you?" Beth managed, her mind spinning as it rapidly made all the grotesque connections, came to all the irrefutable conclusions. "Who are you?"

"The name on my birth certificate is Janine Gentry." The

words were unadorned by emotion; instead, they were spoken with chilling deadness, now mirrored in her eyes as well. All that planning and patience, the pride she took in her intelligence—not intelligent enough or she would have realized the mistake the minute she wrote out the check. Again the slow, thin, empty smile as she decided that perhaps this one little lapse was not such a bad thing after all, forcing the issue at long last.

"Janine." Beth repeated it, tasting the letter *J*, its bitterness, its poison.

"But I'm really Janine Methany. David Methany was—"

"NO!"

"Miss, the check, please," the salesman spoke, hand out expectantly.

With the practiced poise of frequent deceit, Janine put away her pen and checkbook, plastered a regretful smile on her face. "I'm sorry, but I'll have to get the earrings another time. My friend here isn't feeling too well, and I think I'd better get her out into the fresh air before she messes up your lovely shop. She's got a real history of not being able to control it when her stomach starts acting up."

The words had the desired effect as the salesman immediately backed away, his attention riveted on the extraordinary sight of these two well-dressed, attractive women, one edging away from the other, the taller one, the one who was going to buy the earrings, reaching out and grabbing the other, pushing her toward the door, while that one kept shaking her head and trying to pull away, unsuccessfully.

"You. All the time it's been you." Beth spoke as if to herself, while she was being led up the street with all the freedom of a dog on a leash. The air around her suddenly crackled with one, two notes of hysterical laughter, a sound like a slap, stinging her for her stupidity, her blindness, her neediness.

"I told you everything. Each time something happened I turned to you and all the time ..."

"Yes, Beth, you did. Beautiful, isn't it? You trusted me, handing me everything I needed. But of course, that's as it should have been, because I deserve what I'm going to get, and it's only right and fair and just that you, you who don't deserve one damn thing you've ever gotten, should be so instrumental in helping me."

"You're insane."

"No, Beth, David Methany's firstborn child is what I am, and that entitles me to a whole lot. I'm angry at the injustice, but insane? No, not at all."

"I don't believe you. My father had only one child and that's me."

"No, you fool, no."

Beth stared at hard hazel cat-eyes, at a nose familiarly long, aquiline, a strong jaw, prominent cheekbones; the mouth was not his, too wide, too generous, even now with meanness narrowing its lips. It was possible, but then, who—?

"Lilly Jane Litwin," she guessed.

Janine nodded. "My natural mother. David and she were having an affair when she got pregnant."

"How do you know it was David who was the father?"

"Because her husband couldn't have children."

"You're making this all up," Beth stated, heart hammering with the fear that she was hearing the truth.

"I have proof, Beth, which I'll share with you at the proper time. The important thing for you to realize and accept is that your days as the head of the Methany Corporation are over. I was born before you, which makes *me* the legitimate heir to David Methany's empire, *me!*"

"Justice," Beth uttered with dawning comprehension, revulsion choking her. "That's what this has all been about, your perverted, sick idea of justice."

"The only perversion," Alyson cut her off sharply, "is in sitting by watching you gain what should be mine. But that'll change

now. I admit I wasn't planning on the end coming quite yet—
I made a foolish mistake back there in the jewelry shop, just
not thinking. But everything can be ready quickly, I've seen to
that, so you—"

"Alyson—"

"My name is Janine. Janine Methany." The fingers bit into
Beth's arm, the lips narrowed further with spite.

"Janine, then," Beth allowed, shutting her eyes briefly against
the pain, the threat of tears, the ugliness. "Why don't we go see
Fred Lincoln, Janine. He's my family's lawyer. If you really have
proof that you are who you say you are, I'm sure we can work
something out, make an arrangement you would find fair."

"You still don't get it, do you?" Janine hissed. "I am about
to pay you and your father back for what you took from my
mother and me. I am about to get everything we were meant
to have, and you're going to lose it all. Work something out?
Make an arrangement I'll find fair?" Her laugh scissored Beth's
nerves. "Oh yes, there'll be an arrangement, all right, I'm seeing
to that."

"Aly . . . Janine—"

"Shut up!" Janine began to walk faster, dragging her victim
alongside her, flicking away at Beth's hands whenever they tried
to loosen her iron grip. Suddenly, she made a sharp left, and
Beth almost tripped as they went up a short flight of marble
steps. To the right of the double teak doors was a polished brass
plaque with the Rowland Court Hotel discreetly etched in script.

"Janine? What are we doing here?" Her voice throbbed with
anxiety. "What's going on? Janine? Damn you, talk to me!"
And the spasm of anger warmed Beth, and reassured her that
she could, and would, put an end to this madness.

The moment of confidence was short-lived.

Janine looked over at her with a smile of indescribably ma-
lignant serenity. "Why, I'm going to kill you, of course."

23

"Ms. Adamson, how nice to see you," the reservation clerk greeted as Janine and Beth approached the front desk. "And this must be the cousin you told us would be visiting some day."

"Adamson? Cousin?"

"Shut up and don't even think of trying to get away. This clerk knows me. The hotel manager knows me. No matter what you claim, they'll never believe you."

Beth shrank back into silence, and her captor lowered her grip to her forearm, a less obtrusive place for the tight manacle of her pinching fingers.

She could not believe this was happening, that she was actually a prisoner in a maniacal nightmare of distorted values and twisted desires. Beth could feel the rage flowing from the vise of flesh into her own skin. It was all too grotesque. This hotel. The pretense of being this woman's cousin. This woman. She had considered her a friend, an invaluable colleague. But the person behind the helpful advice and caring smiles had been scheming with Machiavellian shrewdness, and mutilating the confidences of fear and confusion with butcherlike precision; each secret shared being a blue ribbon of excellence awarded for her clever and perfect portrayal of "friend." The evil was inconceivable to Beth. There was no other word to describe what could sustain an anger or hurt or need through so many years. Patience alone could not do it. Or conviction. Not even madness. No, to be able to live so effectively, perhaps even happily at times, *as a lie*—only evil could nourish a soul capable of that.

"Your suite is available, Ms. Adamson. I do wish I had had some advance notice," the clerk said with that twitch of his lips that was the supercilious form of reprimand adopted by those used to taking orders rather than giving them.

"My cousin just decided to come down to New York—a very last-minute decision." Janine held out her hand for the key.

"Room service at the instructed interval, Ms. Adamson?"

Beth immediately turned her wary attention from the clerk to Janine, who merely nodded her response and tightened her grip as a warning for silence.

"The champ—"

"Let's keep it a surprise, shall we," Janine immediately broke in, halting the reservation clerk's streak of familiarity. "This is my cousin's first trip to New York so I want everything to be extra-special. You understand."

"Of course," and now the mouth was plumped up into a smile of patronizing superiority for the country bumpkin.

"Her luggage will be arriving later," Janine went on, and then with a perfunctory "Thank you for everything" for the clerk, she was dragging Beth off in the direction of the elevator bank.

"You've had this planned for some time, haven't you?" Beth asked. "Arranged all the details beforehand for this little play of yours."

"One, sarcasm doesn't become you, Beth, it's not your style, and two, your timing for it is way off. I can smell the stink of your fear as if I were knee-high in a sewer."

Beth looked away in disgust, but the nip of fingernails through her clothing to her skin demanded her attention again. "I didn't know when I would bring you here," Janine went on, "but yes,

I've had it planned for some time. This hotel and Suite 23 in particular had to be the scene of our confrontation, yours and mine. It was all so beautifully, irresistibly ironic and appropriate. The attorney in me admires symmetry."

"Full circle?"

"See, you can be bright when you put your mind to it."

Beth tugged hard then, but the grip remained a pincer of pain. She mentally willed herself not to show her fear. Nothing would frustrate and unnerve this evil creature more than a victim who refused to be victimized. But the soft edge of panic was creeping closer, a snail's pace toward loss of control. She didn't know how much longer until the words and voice and attitude of brave strength trembled into plastic pretense. She pulled hard again for release, but the clasp remained like iron.

Janine shook her head. "You're being a fool again, Beth. You can't win this one, you can't, because you don't deserve to. You see, that's the whole point, the reason for every little thing I've done. You don't deserve what you have so I must take it away from you. Had our father known, he would have wanted it this way. It's really just a matter of *right*. Right and honor and justice. I told you once I enjoyed the interpretation of the law, as did our father. What I'm going to do to you is merely an interpretation of justice. You must understand. It makes so much sense."

"You're mad," Beth breathed, eyes locked on Janine's composed face. Suddenly, she shook her head, once, again; shut, opened her eyes. For just the briefest, impossibly wild second there, she had seen her father. Seen the selfish pleasure in his eyes when he had abused her mother with a particularly effective insult or remarkably cruel slight. Seen the satisfaction in his smile when he had vanquished a competitor. Seen the ferocious strength in his self-importance that replaced pride with arrogance, need with entitlement.

"If I am mad, then it's the same kind of insanity our father suffered from," Janine stated as if reading Beth's epiphany. Her voice was smooth as a bolt of velvet, her eyes stone, and the easy ability to manufacture both filled Beth with genuine dread.

The elevator doors opened onto a wide, carpeted hallway. At midafternoon on a Saturday, most guests at any New York City hotel were at the theater or a museum, or more than likely, shopping. There was only silence, stillness. For Beth, the quiet struck her as an army of allies for her enemy.

"You weren't expecting to come here today," she remarked. "How did you arrange to have a room ready?"

"Ah, money—the great persuader. A little spread to this palm, that hand, and a promise of a major corporate function one of these days."

"If you told them you were with Methany, why the false name?"

"But I didn't tell them I was with Methany," Janine corrected. "I told them I was a lawyer, yes, because that word contains an implied threat I've always found useful—but a lawyer with a Wall Street firm. I explained I needed a suite available at a moment's notice, preferably Suite 23. People in the firm were forever having overnight visitors who needed just the right environment for their hotel," she added, allowing a wispy smirk of pleasure for her cleverness.

"The desk clerk knew you would want champagne," Beth said, tripping to keep up with the accelerated pace of her captor as she strode down the corridor.

Janine's smile was as cold and fast as the dart of a snake's tongue. "Oh yes, there are very clear instructions on what time it is to be brought to the suite, and what kind of champagne, too."

"Didn't the management here ever wonder why there were no visitors?" Beth asked.

"I told you," Janine answered with harsh irritation. "I've been paying them handsomely not to ask questions, not to wonder about anything except what I want them to do for me. Besides, it hasn't been that long—just since David died."

"Since my father died? Why then?"

"The only thing you need to know is that you're going to die!" Janine shot back, yanking Beth to a stop in front of the door to Suite 23.

With her hold on Beth never loosening, Janine entered the suite of rooms that had become as familar to her as her own apartment. There was the champagne-colored brocade sofa, nine feet long, sensuously comfortable. She had always wondered if *he* had sat there, calmly drinking his undoctored wine while her mother had cramped with lethal pain in the next room. It was entirely feasible. To be capable of conceiving such a plan and then to act upon it were indisputable indications of a character committed to self, regardless of consequence, moral or legal. If he were troubled by the suffering in the next room, expediency would have eradicated that concern, just as sitting on this sofa in another room would have placed him at pitiless remove from reality.

Ah, there was the writing table, Queen Anne, of course, that had served so handily as the resting place for the silverplate tray of raspberries, Roederer Cristal champagne, and the two Waterford flutes. Designer poison. Designer crystal. Fitting.

The drapes. How many times had she pulled away the damask and green velvet drapes to look out on the well-tended garden and courtyard where no one ever strolled. In the beginning, when she had first determined to act, she had stayed here in Suite 23 on several occasions, ordering the champagne and fruit, gazing out the windows, sitting on the sofa. She had tried to imagine Lilly Jane as she must have been that night, perhaps self-conscious over her ungainly bigness, yet no doubt pleased to see her lover. She would have pulled back the drapes and looked down at the courtyard, her hand to her belly, a smile on her face.

There was one of the two television sets, the remote control device on a lamp table between the sofa and an easy chair that was covered in a hideous green floral chintz. Janine disliked yet appreciated the decor; it was so tawdrily refined and suitably shabby as to please both the arriviste who did not know better and the old money for whom this was all familiar.

Without needing to look, Janine knew that only steps down a short hall was the bathroom, with its heated towel rack and wicker basket of miniature grooming aids, modern concessions no hotel could do without today. To the right, the bedroom.

"So what do you think?" she asked expansively, finally releasing her prisoner, but only to a larger dungeon.

"What do I think?" Beth repeated incredulously, rubbing at her forearm. "I think you're crazy, and I'm getting out of here." She started for the door, but Janine's obsession gave her the confidence to discount failure, and so she was almost leisurely in walking to the door, reaching it before Beth, as she had known she would. The justification for what she was doing gave her power, strength. She stood with her back against the wood, and as Beth tried to get at the knob, she poked her finger at the tender spot below Beth's throat, flaying hands pathetic against that one targeted finger. Beth stumbled backward, eyes round and shiny with stupefaction and, Janine felt sure, fear.

"You are not going anywhere," she snapped. "Don't you get it? Don't you understand that this is it, the end, finito? Now get away from this door and accept your future." Her eyes simmered with hate. "What little of it is left."

Beth stepped haltingly back into the living room, sat down in the club chair.

"No, not there. In the bedroom," Janine instructed, pointing.

"The bedroom?"

"Move. Now."

"You can't really hope to get away with whatever it is you're planning," Beth said as she got up and walked into the bedroom, Janine close behind her. "No one will accept you as a Methany, you've got to realize that. No one. You'll be challenged in everything you try to do, you'll have to go to court to prove—"

"Prove! PROVE!" Janine shouted, shoving Beth aside so she could get into the bedroom, into a position where she was facing her nemesis. "I don't have to prove a damn thing, you little idiot! I have the letter from my mother stating that David was my natural father. That's all the proof I need. That and the date on my birth certificate."

There was a tufted boudoir chair and Beth started toward it, glancing at her keeper for approval.

Janine nodded. "And take off your jacket. It's hot in here." A grin twitched. "I wouldn't want you to think I was inconsiderate."

Beth removed her jacket, folded it across her lap, placed her shoulder bag on top of it, her actions smooth, mindless, as if she were not in this hotel bedroom with an artfully devious woman determined to kill her for the sin of being David Methany's legitimate heir.

Even now, as she sat there trying to make sense of this bizarre situation, considering her options, her chances for escape, survival, even as she reluctantly accepted the possibility that she might soon die, an odd sense of relief surged through her, purging her of any straggling remnants of loyalty to her father, shreds she had been holding on to as justification for her own existence. Whatever Janine Gentry might have discovered about David and Lilly Jane Litwin, Beth needed no convincing that it was true. How she had warped truth to the point that she craved such a final vindication was not the result only of a disturbed mind, an anger swollen to rage, an intelligence poisoned by hurt. No, Beth too readily recognized the awesome ability to selfishly corrupt reality regardless of cost to another as an inimitable Methany quality. But a David Methany trait, unmitigated by the humanity—sometimes weak, sometimes foolish—of a mother like Isabel. Whatever goodness Lilly Jane Litwin had possessed, she never had the opportunity to pass it on, to provide her child with the strength—Beth's own, misplaced for decades—that would one day allow her to part the curtain of power and influence, money and success, that draped David Methany's windows to the world, and see the desert landscape of loneliness that curtain was used to hide.

Perhaps it was not too late to share that strength now.

24

"Tell me about the letter. If what you say is true, then you're absolutely right, a terrible injustice has been committed as you claim. And I'll see that it's rectified, but without going to this kind of extreme. It's not necessary."

Beth hoped her voice was projecting the right note of reasonableness. The only way to get through this ordeal was with calm reason. And should she get through it, what then? She instinctively doubted she could ever go back to the company, not if she were to use this experience as the eye-opener it could be. And what of this poor delusionary woman? What would her future be—psychiatrists' offices? Prison? No, not that. Not if there were any other way.

"Janine?" Gentle, coaxing: "Talk to me. Please."

Janine gauged Beth's sincerity, accepted it. "It's too late to stop me. I've waited long enough to get what I deserve."

"That's what you keep saying, so help me believe you. Tell me about the letter."

Another measuring stare, an abbreviated nod, then: "When I turned twenty-one, a lawyer out in Chicago gave me a letter he had been safekeeping for Lilly Jane Litwin—he had been part of the adoption process. No, I don't have the letter with me," she quickly anticipated Beth's question. Her lips pursed. "As we both know, I wasn't exactly expecting today to turn out this way. But it's in my office, locked in a file, very easy to get to for the proof you think is so important."

"You obviously think it's important, too, or you wouldn't have kidnapped me and threatened to kill me on account of it," Beth flung out, momentarily losing her composure. "About the letter—"

She saw Janine hesitate, probably making up her mind whether to go on or punish Beth somehow for her sharp retort, she thought. But surprisingly, she began to talk, describing the contents of the letter, the conversation with the lawyer, her confusion, questions, shock.

"I believe you," Beth eventually said, slowly, considering, absorbing, and then accepting what was being related. "But why didn't you come forward, speak with David directly, tell him that you knew, tell him—"

Janine's laugh sliced the air, tattering the decorated gentility of the room into a rag of ridicule. "Tell him! Tell the man who wanted me aborted, who tried to *kill* me, who succeeded in murdering my mother, the mother of his first child! Tell him that 'Hey, Daddy, you missed!' Are you mad? Or just as stupid as I've always thought!"

Beth gripped the edges of the boudoir chair, trying not to cringe from the fierce rage on fire in front of her. Reason, she reminded herself. She remained silent, sure that more poison would spew forth without provocation. Janine Gentry needed to explain as much as she herself needed to understand.

"At first I wasn't going to do anything," Janine resumed more conversationally, walking over to a padded luggage bench at the foot of the bed and sitting down. "I was curious, of course, who wouldn't be? But I didn't have this need, this obsession I suppose you'd have to call what it's become, for justice. I never really blamed him, odd as that sounds."

"Why not? If he actually did what you allege, then—"

"In a certain way, I understood. He was on his way up. An

illegitimate baby by a married woman, married to a man out to get him, well, this wasn't part of his life's agenda, was it? And you know how I feel about eliminating opposition."

"Oh, I know all right," Beth commented acidly.

"It was you who changed everything."

"Me? How? Why?"

" 'Why?' 'How?' " Janine mimicked, getting up, too tense and eager to sit still for long. Beth edged further back in the little chair, feeling the weight of Janine's resentment as if it were a pillow held over her face, smothering her.

"I read about you," Janine continued, looking out the bedroom window, a view of nothing but brick wall. "When I learned that you existed, and that the vast empire, the incredible power created by David Methany, *my* father, belonged to someone else, well," and suddenly she turned, her lips thin and vicious in a smile of such loathing Beth felt her stomach lurch, "that's when I knew justice had to be exacted. No one is allowed to get away with murder, you know. Sooner or later, somewhere along the way, someone has to pay. In the case of David Methany, payment falls upon *you,* the second-born, the undeserving."

Beth swallowed to bring moisture to her throat, the horror of what she was hearing, the madness, sucking her dry. "Janine," she tried, "why can't we share? Why can't we work out—"

Another snigger of laughter, stingingly derisive. "Share? You mean, *you* would give *me?* No, no, I don't think so."

"Why not?"

"Because sharing the wealth is not justice. Death is. As David tried with me. Death." She tasted the word again, cat-eyes glinting from the flavor.

"But he didn't know you," Beth objected. "He didn't have any—"

"Lilly Jane was eight-and-a-half months pregnant! Eight-and-a-half months!" Janine cried. And because there was nothing to be said against such testimony to her father's selfishness, Beth could only look away.

There was a knock on the door, and Janine grinned. "The champagne. Right on time. You see, I told you. Money is magic, absolute magic."

As soon as Janine was out of the bedroom, Beth was on her feet, scanning the small room for a means of escape. None. The room was on the sixth floor, with that one window leading nowhere. She had no choice: the living room and then the door. Heart racing, she gulped in air and forced herself to walk steadily down the short hall when every cell in her body was screaming at her to run. But that would only give her captor an excuse to enlist the aid of the unsuspecting room-service waiter. No, the only way out was to act as if nothing were wrong.

Janine's back was to her as she entered the living room; she was signing the room-service chit for the waiter, who spotted Beth, causing Janine to look around.

"I have to go now," Beth said, tacking on a smile as she glided past Janine. "Thanks for everything, but I've—"

The hand whipped out before Beth could take another step. "Oh no, not yet, *cousin,* certainly not yet. We've hardly begun to catch up with each other's lives." The hand was a lead clamp, the voice as grating as a metal key in a prison cell lock. Beth pulled, hard, again, maintaining the pose of a smile for the waiter while she tried to wrest free. But a marathon runner has strength; a singularly focused one, superhuman strength. Beth was hopelessly locked in Janine's grip.

"I really must be going."

"Not. Yet."

The waiter glanced from one woman to the other. One had signed a considerable tip on the bill, the other seemed to be upsetting her. "You can't leave before having some champagne, Miss. It's Roederer Cristal, our finest. And the raspberries are a specialty of the hotel."

"See that, Cousin. You just have to stay for a glass or two of the hotel's finest."

The waiter beamed at Janine, who nodded her dismissal of him. As soon as he was gone, she walked over and double-bolted the door, maintaining her hold on Beth. Satisfied that both bolts were securely fastened, she released her, only to slap her hard across one cheek.

Beth's hand flew to her face, shock biting worse than the slap. Her brown eyes became large and round, then, surprisingly, hard and cold and flat with fury. Her expression turned imperious, dismissive. It was a look she had seen her father use to aggravate her mother, especially when she requested his attendance at some social function. It was a look she had seen him use to twist the knife in deeper with a recalcitrant union official, or to signal his disgust with an unctuous French waiter. It was a look designed to convey contempt; she used it now, in the hope it would accomplish for her what it had for her father: sniveling retreat.

She took her time walking over to the sofa, sat down, arms outstretched behind her, legs crossed. With her heart knocking and nausea threatening to erupt, Beth Methany summoned every ounce of self-control, every measure of inner strength, to keep this other woman from seeing how deeply petrified she was. If calm reason would not work, arrogance must. If only for the few seconds it would take to reach that door . . . .

"Get back into the bedroom," Janine instructed.

"No."

"Don't be stupid. The end is here. There's nothing you can do about it."

"You're wrong. I'm getting out of here and you're going to be put away in some madhouse where you belong. I am Beth Methany, and I don't care what kind of scheme you've concocted in that sick mind of yours, you can't beat me. You can't and you won't."

At first Janine looked at her with the shadow of a smile nipping at her mouth, a tentative mark of approval for the bravado. But then the sight of the unflinching flatness in Beth's eyes, the absolute fearlessness that flatness represented, turned Janine's amusement first to disbelief, then to confusion.

"Get back inside," she tried again.

Beth's camouflage of confidence was such that she did not even deign to answer.

"Very well. I don't suppose it matters that much." Janine then uncorked the champagne bottle and poured into one flute. She reached into her shoulder bag, took out her makeup case, extracted a brown-tinted glass bottle, and unscrewed the eyedropper top. One bead. Two. Another.

"What are you doing?" Beth asked, hands now down on the cushions as she leaned forward, unable to keep the alarm from her voice, her posture, her eyes.

"What am I doing? Why, exactly what was done to Lilly Jane." She glanced over her shoulder. "You still don't get it, do you? This is a re-creation, Beth. An ironic salute to our father's canniness, and my own desire for the long-eluded justice. Same room. Same champagne. Same fruit. Most important, same method of death."

"What are you talking about?" Beth demanded.

"Oh, I must have forgotten to mention how David killed her that night here in Suite 23 at the Rowland Court Hotel. It was with liquid Valium, Beth." Another drop into the flute. Still another. "Clear. Odorless. A not unusual way for a society belle drenched in scandal to take her own life. Liquid Valium. Painless but deadly, I'm told."

"And you just happen to carry a bottle of it around with you at all times?" Beth shot back, clammering to her feet, stalking over to grab the bottle, but Janine just laughed at her, palming the bottle.

"Actually, I do keep it handy," she admitted. "I wouldn't want it to fall into the wrong hands."

"Convenient."

"No, just careful. The way our father was. The dosage he gave my mother was enough, he no doubt thought, to kill her and their unborn child. You won't require quite that much, I don't think."

"You're making this up, all of it! There's no letter and David Methany was nothing to you. You're a sick woman with some kind of warped delusion about—"

"Shut up and drink." Janine held out the glass. Beth's hand soared and sent it flying across the room. Before Janine could recover, Beth raced to the door, hand shaking as she sought the safety bolt.

Again, too slow. No, she realized with a sinking sensation of defeat as fingers circled the back of her neck, squeezing her into obedience. No, not too slow. Just not fortified with the strength of madness.

The fingers held on as she was led back to the lamp table where Janine poured again, using the eyedropper three, four times.

"Now drink," she ordered, not letting go. She lifted the glass to Beth's mouth. Beth shook her head, back and forth, lips sealed, eyes enormous, but there was the glass, pressing, pushing, until she felt it against her teeth, and with the claw around her neck, and the stink of hate in her nose, she could do nothing but open her mouth and feel the deadly bubbles moisten her tongue and her throat as she swallowed. The five-fingered noose came off. Another glass was at her lips. This time she did not resist. She took the flute in her hand and sipped.

"Drink. You're not at a deb party."

Beth took a mouthful of the lethal liquid. "It was you who tinkered with my kiln up at Rye, wasn't it?" she abruptly asked, desiring complete knowledge before she died, and she knew that was happening. She could feel it in the new, almost pleasant heaviness in her limbs, and in the cotton batting filling her mind, and the little silk strings pulling her eyelids shut. She tottered over to the sofa, sat. She wanted, well, probably more than even her freedom right now, she wanted to put her head back against the plump sofa cushion, close her eyes, sleep. Just sleep. But there was more she needed to know ... if she were to rest in peace.

"And the car? Was that you too? What about dinner at your place, when I got sick? You did put shellfish in the pasta, didn't you?"

Janine's laugh this time was a tinkle of charmed delight. She leaned against the writing table, the lines of hate and bitterness vanishing from her face, leaving smooth planes of contentment, and a bright gleam of happiness in her eyes. "So many questions. And the answer is yes to all of them. I sent the white flowers, too, and got a very stupid and helpful substitute doorman to let me into your apartment while your housekeeper was away and you were in Rye. That's how I was able to smash that photo of you and your ... our father. I also threatened your precious Ben, assuming he would blame you, but that never got as far as I would have liked. But yes, I did it all."

"The calls? They were you, too, I presume?"

"Of course. With a scrambler. And the newspaper clippings—part of a very nice collection I've amassed over the years."

Beth nodded, almost impressed with the mind at work here, a mind her father would have approved of heartily. "Why the cards and letters to my fa—to David? If I was the one you were after, why bother with him? And why did you wait so long? You had many opportunities to eliminate me, why go to all this trouble?"

"So many questions, but you're entitled to answers, that's the least I can do for you." Beth was continuously blinking her eyes, jerking her head back from resting forward on her chest. Janine could see that it would all be over soon; there was no risk in revealing everything.

"I sent the cards and letters to David just as a way for him to be off-guard, knowing that someone was out there aware of his relationship with Lilly Jane, maybe aware of much more. If I am to be any judge of why he kept them, I imagine it was out of concern that someone knew the truth and would someday show himself. So maybe he kept it all as a reminder to always be careful. When I went to work for him, I honestly came to respect and like him, and I also really believed that my superiority would win him over, that he would give the reins of command willingly to me as the better child, the more deserving as well as the older, who had a rightful claim to those reins. But then he died."

"Selfish to the end," Beth garbled.

"At first I just wanted to frighten you. I had the whole scenario planned just to scare you into relinquishing control over the company, but then . . . I don't know, one day that stopped being enough. I knew I wanted you out of the way. Permanently. You're right, I could have done it sooner, but I was enjoying myself. I liked playing with you, tormenting you. It made us more like the sisters we are."

"What!"

"Sharing pain. Mine for all those years of injustice. Yours as the price for that injustice."

"You could be wrong. You could be." There was nothing for it. She had to put her head back, close her eyes. Just a second, maybe two. All right, one more, that's it, though. Stay alert. Get to your feet. Walk around. That'll help.

"Sit down."

Beth blinked, ran a hand through her hair. Had she risen?

From the glorious muffling in her brain, in her ears, behind her eyelids, on the roof of her mouth, in her fingertips, the backs of her knees, beyond this really quite delicious layering removing her from the immediate assault of reality, a layering just waiting for her to snuggle under, into, came words, a voice.

" . . . found the ambulance driver, the admitting nurse at Saint Cecilia's. Lilly Jane's husband paid for the doctor's silence, but the driver and nurse remembered her, remembered the surprising strength of the fetal heartbeat . . . took a while . . . found the night maid who discovered her and the bottle of liquid Valium in her hand . . ."

With a flash of lucidity stabbing her waning consciousness, Beth jerked forward from her narcosis. "No proof it wasn't suicide," she declared, twitching her nose at the thickness clogging her ability to articulate. "No evidence my father was involved."

Before answering, Janine poured another glass of champagne, put more Valium in it.

"No. Enough," Beth resisted, a rag doll shaking her head in protest.

"Don't give me a hard time," Janine crackled. "You're just prolonging the inevitable this way."

"All right, I'll drink it, but first tell me why you think my father was involved with your mother's death."

"Our father." Janine placed the glass on the lamp table.

"Okay, okay, our father."

"The room-service waiter was the key. He was fortuitously easy to find because he's now the manager here." Her grin was pornographic in its pleasure. "His memory is a lawyer's dream, or nightmare, I suppose, depending. Anyway, he recalled David being in the room, signing for the champagne and fruit. He recognized David from other visits, with Lilly Jane, as well as other women. Suite 23 at the Rowland Court Hotel turned out to be David Methany's favorite trysting place, and Nico was David's favorite room-service waiter. Nico, now known as Nicholas, even remembered David saying good-bye to him in the hallway, and commenting that his guest would be staying a while longer because she wanted to rest before attending some fancy function later that night. All very neat and tidy and logical. With not one fragment of physical evidence to link David to any of it. Incredibly clever. Makes me proud to be his daughter." Her face unexpectedly altered again, once more hard with hate. "Now drink."

"That's still not real proof. Coincidence. Conjecture. Not proof."

"It's good enough for me. Now drink!"

"My death won't bring you what you want," Beth managed, taking her time in getting hold of the champagne glass, both because she wanted to and because her body could move only one way, slowly. "You need me to turn everything over to you, nice and legal."

"The letter is my proof, as legal as your death warrant will be! The satisfaction of having you out of the way will be worth any kind of legal difficulties I may have, and I won't have any, believe me. I learned very, very well from our father. There isn't anybody who will dare to stand in my way who I won't be able to stop."

"Janine . . . Janine." Unconsciousness buzzed close by, blurring the vision of the tall young woman looming over her, placing a little brown glass bottle in her hand, closing her fingers over it. "We could have been . . . friends . . . like sisters . . . we are sisters . . ." Her voice, so weak, so distant. "I liked you . . . I'm sorry . . . He didn't deserve us, either of us . . . didn't deserve our respect, our love . . . You're punishing the . . . wrong . . . Methany . . . ."

And then she could resist no longer.

Epilogue

"You sure about this, Miss Beth? There's still time to cancel with the movers, change your mind."

"What about the new owners of the apartment? They've put down considerable money, Miranda, plus signed all the appropriate papers."

"You can get Mr. Cavelli or Mr. Lincoln to help—they'd figure something out."

Beth smiled softly at her housekeeper. "This is what I want to do, really. Of course," she said on a more teasing note, "if you think you'll find that country air hard to take, I'll understand. I've told you you didn't have to go with me."

"And leave you alone with no telling who you'll become friends with?" Miranda sniffed, eyeing her employer with defensible smugness. "No, I'll just come into New York every now and then for a pollution fix," she joked.

They were in Beth's bedroom, putting the last of her clothes in trunks, suitcases, and movers' wardrobe cartons for tomorrow's departure from the Fifth Avenue apartment. Beth had sold it last month, three days after the anniversary of her father's death, yet another touch of bitter irony to this whole extraordinary year.

"You okay, Miss Beth?" Miranda asked, spotting the film of sadness come over Beth's eyes.

"I'm fine, just fine. And I'm going to be even better once we're settled up in Rye."

The housekeeper eyed her dubiously while continuing to fold sweaters. "I don't know," she mumbled, "I just don't know."

"This is as it should be, Miranda," Beth assured her. "I'm finally going to be doing exactly what *I* want to do. Not what I think my father would expect of me or what would please him, but only what I want to do." She stopped packing shoes and looked at the caring face of the woman who had sensed an enemy so quickly that Beth had pridefully believed she had no alternative but to reject her warnings. "I want to live out in Rye, Miranda. And I want to work on my pottery. I may not want to do this forever, maybe not even for a month, but it's what I want right now, I know that, just as I know that I will never go back to the company. Never. It took far more from Daddy than it ever gave him back, and it was doing the same to me."

"Almost took your life, it did," Miranda remarked.

Beth nodded, and then her eyes again took on that dull coating of sadness that recollection of recent events invariably brought. She took a deep breath, turned away from the diligently observant Miranda.

"I could do with a cup of hot soup," she suddenly requested, needing to be alone, needing not to hide the wash of pain.

The housekeeper regarded her closely a moment, understood, and left without further word, closing the door softly behind her. Beth sat down at the foot of her bed, squeezing shut her eyes against an onslaught of images that refused to be ignored. It happened like this every now and then, less frequently lately than in the beginning, first in the hospital, then in the rest home in Madison, Connecticut. She had wanted to go immediately to the house in Rye, once the doctor in Manhattan had released her from the hospital, but he had insisted on further recuperation in a rest home where there was medical attention, should it be needed, and an excellent psychologist on staff.

She had made use of neither, the winter cold coming off the

cherished Long Island Sound on Madison's shore, the opiated sleep, the idle hours providing rest, and with the rest came strength to think and understand . . . and forgive. She expiated her guilt during the month in Connecticut, the months back in New York, here under Miranda's care. Guilt over her lifelong treatment of her mother as a greedy, mindless, insignificant appendage to her father's greatness. Guilt for the mockery she had made of her marriage. Guilt for Ben Wyler and others like him whom she had hurt on behalf of her father. She was starting, but had not yet succeeded, in forgiving herself for the weakness that had not only blinded her to the truth, but that had compelled her to ignore it even after recognizing and admitting it.

There was, she knew, still a part of her that could look at the restored photograph of herself and her father, and experience the sensation of a heart filling with love, remembering his patience, his generosity, his affection. There had to have been, once, goodness in the man. Isabel had loved him. Someone very special named Lilly Jane Litwin might have, must have, loved him. The daughter he believed he had killed had, in her strange way, loved him. And the daughter he had nurtured, albeit in his own image, had loved him. There had to have been goodness for there to have been this much love. But it got lost in the greed and the power, and it got corroded, rusty with lack of use, then dead from lack of need.

She had returned to the office right after the first of the year, meeting with lawyers, advisers, resisting all entreaties to change her mind as she signed the necessary papers. The Methany Corporation was no longer a privately held company. It was now traded on the New York Stock Exchange; it had a board of directors, and Gene Cavelli was its chief executive officer, with a man seduced away from the Trump Organization as its new president. Beth maintained her position as a major stockholder with 40 percent and a seat on the board of directors because, regardless of all else, she *was* a Methany, and to abandon the company entirely would be an additional insult to her mother who had made her own kinds of sacrifices.

In addition to taking the company public, she had made another major change. Janine Gentry now also owned 40 percent of the corporation as well as a special trust fund, set up by Beth against Fred Lincoln's vigorous objections. This fund contained exactly half of what had been in Beth's trust fund and would be administered in the future with the same diligence and by the same bankers as Beth's. Both women were financially set for life. When asked, Beth had offered no substantive explanation for her actions other than that Janine had contributed greatly to the success of the company. Isabel, Beth had decided, would have approved.

At Christmas, she had received a letter, postmark Chicago, no return address. Beth smiled now in wry recollection of the thumping heart and glacial palms when she had slit open the envelope. She had destroyed all the correspondence from J., both to herself and to her father, and though she now knew who J. was, the envelope with its Chicago postmark, where she knew no one, and the lack of return address, triggered an immediate fear.

Beth was not as surprised as might have been expected to get the letter from Janine. She had known instinctively she would be hearing from her again someday. She was writing to tell her that she had decided to live in Chicago, near her "parents," and work for the prosecutor's office with an eye toward a judgeship eventually, as she had once planned. There had been no words of apology or regret—but Beth hadn't needed any to make the changes in the company, the special arrangements for Janine.

Beth had survived because Janine had saved her. She had called for emergency help before the liquid Valium could take its full and final effect. The doctor had explained it to her when she regained consciousness, impressing her with the need to be grateful to her cousin, who had prevented the attempted suicide just in time.

Afterward, during the period of introspection and forgiveness, she came to believe that Janine had not been able to go through with the murder because a flicker of rational thinking had somehow ignited, burning out the madness. Certainly, the obsession was over, as indicated by the letter at Christmas. It was as if she were telling Beth that she had reclaimed her *self,* exactly as Beth had. And because she understood too well the hold their father had had on both of them, the price each had paid, Beth gave to her half-sister what was her inherited due.

"Soup's ready, Miss Beth." Miranda's voice from the other side of the large apartment jolted her out of her memories. She got to her feet, tugged down her sweatshirt, ran a hand through those unruly curls.

Maybe someday, she mused, leaving her room, maybe someday they'd be able to see each other again, when the inheritance from their father dwindled merely to money.

Janine Gentry endorsed the dividend check from the Methany Corporation, made a notation in a notebook, did a quick calculation.

It was good, very good. Certainly more than she had ever dreamed would be hers when she had lost her mind for the last time and called 911 for Beth Methany. She would never fully understand what had made her do that. She had thought of little else these past months, and she had to admit that it had been a lapse, a moment of weakness that she had thought long conquered by hate. It could have been use of the word "friend" or "sister" or when she had said "the wrong Methany"—something had punctured her with doubt. Suddenly, what she was doing struck her as obscene, and the consequences should she not get away with it as easily as had her father . . . that did not bear thinking about. So she had called 911, and now she was wealthy, thanks to the one she had set out to destroy.

And she still would someday. Why should Beth Methany have 40 percent of the company? Why should she have any share of David's inheritance? She had had it all for far too long. Justice could never be served endorsing dividend checks. No, true justice could only happen when she, Janine, and only she was the sole Methany in existence.

Next time would be different. Next time she would not allow the trap of conscience to ensnare her. Next time the deception would be family, not friend. Much more clever. Much more deadly.

Only there would be no next time.

What remained in her mind now was a fantasy of power fading with acceptance of the truth: Much as she might be her father's daughter, she was also her mother's. His evil had inspired destruction, but her decency had proven stronger, strong enough to rescue a life.

How much better could true justice be served than that?